Sleeping Beauty
and the
DEMON

Books by Marina Myles

Beauty and the Wolf

Snow White and the Vampire

A Warlock's Dance
(novella)

Sleeping Beauty and the Demon

Cinderella and the Ghost
(coming February 2015)

Sleeping Beauty
and the
DEMON

MARINA MYLES

KENSINGTON BOOKS

KENSINGTON PUBLISHING CORP.

www.kensingtonbooks.com

KENSINGTON BOOKS are published by

Kensington Publishing Corp.
119 West 40th Street
New York, NY 10018

All Kensington titles, imprints, and distributed lines are available at special quantity discounts for bulk purchases for sales promotion, premi-
ums, fund-raising, educational, or institutional use.

Special book excerpts or customized printings can also be created to fit
specific needs. For details, write or phone the office of the Kensington
Special Sales Manager: Kensington Publishing Corp., 119 West 40th
Street, New York, NY 10018. Attn. Special Sales Department. Phone:
1-800-221-2647.

Kensington and the K logo Reg. U.S. Pat. & TM Off.

First Electronic Edition: August 2014
eISBN-13: 978-1-60183-281-8
eISBN-10: 1-60183-281-1

First Print Edition: August 2014
ISBN-13: 978-1-60183-282-5
ISBN-10: 1-60183-282-6

Printed in the United States of America

For Mum and Dad
With love and gratitude

ACKNOWLEDGMENTS

Seeing this story come to publication is a dream come true. Heartfelt thanks go to my extraordinary editor, **Peter Senftleben**, who is always on the same page with my writing and who helped greatly with setting ideas for this book, and to my marvelous agent, **Louise Fury**, who manages so much and does such a fabulous job at it. I'd also like to thank the amazing team at **Kensington** that exudes patience and professionalism!

To fellow authors **Cathy McDavid**, **Pamela Tracy**, **Libby Banks**, **Connie Flynn**, **Terri Molina** and **Helen King**—you ladies make critique meetings a hoot. I'm truly honored to be part of your group. Thanks also to the knowledgeable librarians at the **Scottsdale Public Library**.

Finally, I want to tip my (imaginary) hat to magicians everywhere. You confound us and astound us—and make the wonderment so much fun.

The most beautiful thing we can experience is the mysterious.

—Albert Einstein

When stars align at the hand of the Underworld God, a chosen few are but puppets on strings.

—Ancient Egyptian proverb

PART 1

CHAPTER 1

New York City
1912

A torrential downpour bounced off the sloping roof of the Sunshine Theater. Inside the auditorium, an eager audience sat riveted by Dragomir Starkov's onstage presence.

Dressed in black, he moved with confidence. With his hair slicked back from a widow's peak and his eyes drawing the crowd into his mirage, he spoke in a heavy, Romanian accent. "Ladies and gentlemen, I will now attempt something few magicians dare. I will bring a creature back to life."

Turning to the rear of the stage, he hid his hands from view. When he faced the audience again, he presented the body of what appeared to be a dead kitten. The small animal hung limply across his open palm. Murmuring a low chant, he waved it from one side of the stage to the other. Then, with a flick of his white-gloved fingers, he urged the kitten back to life.

The small cat sat up erect and blinked in astonishment. As it let out a satisfied "meow," it sprang to the floor.

The audience clapped wildly. In turn, Drago stepped forward.

That's when he spotted the woman he had willed to come to tonight's show.

With an abundance of flaxen hair that swayed from a ponytail like wheat in a summer breeze, and a flawless complexion that glowed against the stage's low-lying gaslights, the young woman's beauty imprisoned Drago like a padlock. In the sparkle of her violet eyes he saw something amazing—a unique essence of goodness that compelled him as he often compelled others.

She's even more beautiful than she was in my vision.

The girl flashed him a smile—and when it illuminated his world of darkness like a bright spotlight, the need to protect and possess her rose within him. But it didn't matter how he felt. He was here to banish a cruel curse cast upon her when she was a baby. And if he wanted to weave his unique spell around her, he needed to hypnotize her now.

A hush fell over the theater. Clasping his hands behind his back, Drago paced the stage like a caged animal. "For my next trick, I need a female volunteer from the audience."

Numerous hands went up. He ignored them. Once he unlaced his dark cape, he threw it into the wings. "I need a very *special* participant for this mystifying trick."

Pressing his forefinger to his temple, he pretended to use his powers of telepathy. Just then, the beautiful blond girl left her seat, accompanied by her dark-haired friend. They scurried to the theater's center aisle, apparently averse to the thought of being called on to volunteer.

"You there!" Drago thundered.

The duo froze in their tracks and wheeled around.

Pulling on her thick, blond ponytail, Rose—her name popped into Drago's head suddenly—blushed.

"You, my dear." He galloped halfway down the staircase at the side of the stage and extended his hand.

"Go on, Rose!" her friend encouraged. Drago was right about her name.

Rose smoothed her gingham dress. She joined him on the shadowed staircase, then took his hand. As Drago grasped it, an alarming chill raced up his spine. And when her pink lips spread into another shy smile, he found himself completely enchanted.

Leading her to center stage he said, "Please tell the audience your name, Miss."

"It's Rose Carlisle."

"Have we ever met before, Rose?"

"No."

"If you don't mind, I'd like to tell the spectators how old you are."

"I don't know how you could guess that, but very well," she replied in a sweet, clear voice.

He cleared his throat. "Today is your birthday, and you are twenty years old." The number surfaced in his mind as surely as he knew his own birthday.

Rose's jaw dropped open. She nodded vigorously. "How did you know?" Her friend, who had returned to her seat in the front row, mirrored Rose's stunned expression.

Drago felt his affinity for the doe-eyed beauty grow. Yet he urged himself to be careful—and to make her feel as comfortable with him as possible.

"It doesn't take a magician to see that you've attended this show without your parents' permission," he said. "Is that right, Miss Carlisle?"

The crowd chuckled lightly at the joke. Rose looked stunned. "I haven't seen my parents since I was a baby. But my adoptive parents don't know I'm here."

"I see," Drago remarked lightheartedly. But when he saw Rose clutching her hands together nervously, he sensed her pain ran deep.

"Have you ever been a magician's assistant?"

"No," Rose replied. "In fact, this is my first magic show."

"We'll have to make it one you'll never forget."

When he reached for her small, velvet hand, it trembled inside his at the suggestion.

"Promise me you won't be anxious," he said. "I would never allow harm to come to you."

She slid a glance his way—and they locked eyes for what felt like an eternity.

"I'll try not to be nervous," she finally promised. "What do I have to do?"

"Absolutely nothing. Just close your lovely eyes and remain in one spot."

Rose did as she was told. Drago took the opportunity to study her high cheekbones, dainty mouth, and hourglass figure. Though she was tall, her demeanor lent her a fragile air. She seemed to him a delicate, porcelain doll which could be broken easily if handled improperly.

Frowning, he tried to concentrate on performing his illusion. While Rose kept her eyes closed, he massaged the air in front of him with his fingertips. As he murmured something inaudible, he willed Rose's feet to rise slowly off the ground.

It appeared as if someone was pulling her legs out from under her. Eventually, her torso, limbs, and head reached a plane parallel to the stage and she was levitating in space.

The crowd gasped as Drago reached for a large silver hoop. He proceeded to pass the circle back and forth over Rose's stiff body. When he twisted and turned it in every direction, the audience gasped again. The trick, which he'd performed only once before, proved it had the power to intrigue.

"Are you doing all right, Rose?" Drago asked in a gentle voice.

She nodded. Her ponytail swung toward the wooden floor.

"Excellent." Drago passed the silver hoop to his brunette assistant, Katherine. "Ladies and gentlemen, I have a confession to make. The second half of this trick is new even to me. However, it's something I feel bold enough to try with Miss Carlisle's help."

Drago's assistant cast him an angry look. He continued on anyway. "Katherine, would you hand me that red silk drape?" he asked.

Clearly irritated, Katherine moved to the tiny prop table in the corner. Once she'd passed a large cloth to Drago, he unfolded it and draped it over the length of Rose's levitating body.

"Ladies and gentlemen," he said in a low tone. "Making a woman levitate in midair is one thing. But what if I made her . . . disappear?"

He whipped off the red drape and exposed nothing but air. Men in pinstriped suits leapt to their feet and women touched their hats in astonishment.

When the audience's enthusiastic clapping subsided, Drago removed his gloves. "Now I'll make our lovely Rose *reappear.* Just . . . like . . . that."

Snapping his fingers loudly, he moved to a cabinet in the middle of the stage. He opened the cabinet's door with an exaggerated gesture and there stood a pale-faced Rose. Grinning, Drago took her hand and helped her out. Together they walked to the front of the stage and were greeted with thunderous applause.

As he took one step away from Rose, Drago bowed to her as well. Her cheeks regained their color—and she looked at him as if he were the most wonderful man in the world.

Although leaving her was the last thing he desired to do, he had no choice. Drago came closer to her and pressed something into her hand. Then he mouthed the haunting words, "Wear this and come back to me."

Rose's hand closed around the item the handsome magician had placed in her palm. The curtain closed with a dramatic *whoosh*—and as she stumbled up the aisle, she unfurled her hand and stared at the object. It was a beautiful amulet that bore a silver chain and mysterious Egyptian engravings.

CHAPTER 2

One hour later, the rain stopped and the moon smiled over Coney Island. The lively amusement park exploded with laughter and lights, but the gaiety swirling around it in contagious circles was to be short-lived.

A creature—half beast, half human—lurked in the shadows between the carousel and the half-built Wonder Wheel. Awaiting its chance, the hulking figure, robed in black trousers and the remnants of a shredded white shirt, crouched out of sight.

On this starless night, along the broad strip of beach, it had the urge to claim a new soul in order to sustain its immortal existence.

The figure had lived for many centuries. Over the years, it'd been virtually everywhere . . . from the green valleys of Austria to the stone castles of Scotland and to the colorful bazaars of Marrakech. It had experienced history alongside emperors and had witnessed the rise and fall of kings. It had also mourned the death of loved ones.

Now the monster found itself here, in a city where the Statue of Liberty signified new opportunities.

No one knew the creature in America, at least not in its demon form. And that was precisely its intention. Recently, it had come to the end of one existence and had proceeded on to its next identity.

Why? Because it felt a certain someone drawing it here.

As the tepid June breeze lapped over the demon, the need to maintain its longevity swept through the creature with a relentless force.

Stepping from the shadows, it scurried up the steel construction planks of the Wonder Wheel. Moonlight spilled over the creature's savage face, cragged jaws, scaly skin, and razor-sharp claws. And because tonight was the anniversary of its making, the demon's height rose from its normal measurement of under six feet to well over eight feet tall.

The fiend's swirling black cloak danced around the tops of its knee-high boots. Suddenly, it caught the scent of a human.

"Clarence, you know I hate to wait in line." A girl's voice floated upward. "You go ahead."

From its hiding place on the half-finished ride, the creature watched the girl with narrowed eyes.

"I'll meet you by the hot dog stand in a few moments," she instructed. Breaking from the man's grasp, she blew him a kiss.

She was suitable for the demon's purpose—and even from thirty feet away it could smell her perfume, infused with roses, rolling in and out on the soft coastal breeze.

Now that the girl was alone, she picked up her skirts and strode beneath the base of the Wonder Wheel. Pulling a powder compact from her handbag, she proceeded to pat her face with the talc.

The creature leapt up to the structure's next level, moving as gracefully as a panther. Starved for a new soul, it studied the girl with steady eyes. All it had to do was catch her from behind and squeeze her so tightly that she would slump over, unconscious. Then the demon could proceed with what it had to do—what had kept it immortal for well over four hundred years.

Of course, no one was forcing the demon to claim another unfortunate victim. But an eternal existence had become all it knew—and it was time to sustain it.

The creature slid its cloak over its shoulder and fanned out its gigantic wings. *Leap now.*

Without warning, it crashed down on the girl and took her by surprise. The girl cried out but the demon quickly clamped a hand over her mouth to silence her. With its other claw, it grabbed the edge of its rippling cape and blanketed both of them with the heavy material.

Once the girl was enveloped in the fiend's arms, the creature squeezed her hard enough to compress her lungs. She gasped for breath and just before she died, the demon opened its mouth and commanded her youthful soul to stream like a tornado funnel into its own body.

CHAPTER 3

"You still haven't told me what Dragomir Starkov gave you tonight," Olivia Marconi prodded her best friend.

Rose touched a hand to her high-necked blouse. After she'd stuffed the amulet inside her handbag, she had dodged into the powder room to put it on. Now the necklace was hidden from view. And that's precisely where it would stay.

It was all too exciting for words.

"Well?" Olivia asked.

"It's our little secret."

"Wonderful." Olivia frowned as she went on. "If I didn't know better, I'd think you and that mysterious magician were married! Furthermore, I can't believe you dragged me to his performance."

Something commanded me to go. Shivering at the thought, Rose said, "*I* can't believe Dragomir Starkov paid so much attention to me."

"Don't be silly," Olivia said. "You're gorgeous."

"That's what a best friend is supposed to say," Rose teased her.

Olivia shook her head. "It's true."

"I guess Mr. Starkov doesn't mind how tall I am."

"Thank God you grew out of your gangly stage."

Rose *had* grown out of her gangly stage, but she still wondered what a devilishly attractive man like Starkov could want with her. She was very young—on the cusp of womanhood, in fact. And he was older. Smoother. More experienced.

Yet the chemistry that had burned between them tonight could have set the city on fire.

Rose strolled arm-in-arm with Olivia to the Marconi home, breathing in the fresh smell of rain. She'd come to live with the vivacious Italian family when she was a baby. Upon her parents' request, she was taken in by Lorenzo and Elena Marconi—friends of her mother and father before they'd dropped out of sight.

The entire scenario was set up to protect Rose. She would see her parents a year from now. While she could hardly wait, she'd be forever grateful to the Marconi family for adopting her. And she was especially thankful for the support of her best friend, Olivia, a girl whom Rose considered a real sister.

Her head remained in the clouds as she glanced at the Marconis' front door. Without her reaching for the handle, the door flew open and a distraught Elena Marconi shot out.

"Rose! Where on earth have you been?" Elena whispered hoarsely. *"The curse!"*

"I'm fine, Mrs. Marconi. Besides, the curse isn't supposed to take effect until my next birthday."

"One never knows. Come inside quickly!"

Rose's adoptive mother guided her into a cozy parlor where she greeted Anthony Marconi, Olivia's ill-tempered twin brother, and her adoptive father, Lorenzo. Then she saw Anthony's best friend, Patrick O'Leary. Stunned that all of them had waited late into the night for her, she clutched her stomach nervously.

Olivia leaned toward her and whispered, "Maybe Patrick is here to give you something. After all, he's been trying to court you. And it *is* your birthday!"

"Do you think so?" Rose whispered back.

Patrick had been charmingly persistent in his affections, but there was her curse to consider. What's more, she wasn't sure how she felt about any man besides Dragomir Starkov after their intriguing encounter.

Olivia took her by the hand and steered her deeper into the room.

"There she is!" Patrick beamed. He strode closer and took her by the shoulders. "We were worried sick."

"Because of the curse?" she asked.

"Of course," he said.

Damn my Aunt Morvina. As much as Rose tried to forget—even debunk—the spell the woman had doomed her with, it caused her to live in constant fear.

"Where were you?" Patrick asked.

"Olivia wanted to treat me to dinner on my birthday," she lied. "After supper, I ran into an old school friend. We were catching up . . ."

Olivia shot her a startled look at the fib.

"It isn't the wisest choice to roam New York City at night," he reminded her gently. "But, nonetheless, you're safe."

Patrick was kind, considerate, and handsome in a fair-haired, boyish sort of way. Yet his good looks paled compared to Dragomir's mysterious aura at the moment. The more Rose thought about how she'd flirted with the magician and how kind the Marconis had always been to her, guilt stabbed at her conscience. She hung her head and dove into the truth. "Olivia and I didn't go to dinner this evening."

"Where did you go, *cara?*" Mr. Marconi asked.

She sucked in a deep breath. "We went to a magic show."

"I beg your pardon?" Patrick's face twisted with confusion.

Rose should have known he wouldn't understand. He shared little of what she considered interesting: literature, the arts, and anything remotely mystifying. Still, she spread her hands apart in an effort to explain. "It's my birthday—and magic is something I've always been fascinated with."

Anthony scowled at her from beneath thick brows. Stuffing his fingers inside the small pockets of his vest and puffing out his burly chest, he said, "You wasted your time and money on seeing a charlatan . . . a crackpot?"

The question infuriated Rose. "Dragomir Starkov is no crackpot. He's a genius who performs spellbinding illusions. Just when you think you have his tricks figured out, he spins them around in the end."

From the look of distaste on Patrick and Anthony's faces, she knew she'd said too much. A moment later, Patrick urged her to sit.

"It's no matter," he said. "I, for one, am glad you enjoyed yourself on your birthday." When he took her hands, she noticed that his were clammy. "Rose, you're probably wondering why I'm here at such a late hour."

She nodded. *Please don't ask me if you can court me. I don't know how I'll respond.*

"Everyone has had the opportunity to give you your birthday gift, except me. I want to give you something special."

Rose's heart dropped. "Something . . . special?"

She swallowed hard as Patrick stood up. Elena plucked a flat, black box off the parlor table and handed it to him. In turn, he presented it to Rose.

"Rose Emily Carlisle," Patrick began.

Rose's pulse pounded like a bass drum.

"Will you accept this necklace as a token of my affection?" His moss-green eyes glimmered with hope before he opened the box to reveal a ruby necklace. The main, oval-shaped jewel was tiny and hung on a flimsy gold chain.

Although Rose was relieved that Patrick hadn't asked her anything more monumental, her mouth went dry. He was the best man she had ever known and she'd grown extremely fond of him. But tonight, when Dragomir stood before her, an icon of passion and mystery, she knew she longed for more of those sensations.

However, she told herself, *this is just a birthday gift—not a marriage proposal.*

"It's beautiful," she finally said. "Of course I'll accept your gift, Patrick."

Beaming like a boy who'd gotten the pony he always longed for, Patrick fastened the necklace around Rose's neck. She could feel its weight against the amulet hidden beneath her blouse. She tensed.

"I saved up to buy you this," he admitted, "and I'm glad I did. It looks stunning on you."

Rose embraced him. After she pulled away, he took her into the hallway, where they could talk in private.

"You seemed uneasy in there," he said.

Rose reached up and brushed back a lock of his blond hair. "I'm sorry. The magic show seemed so real that it threw me for a loop."

"I nearly asked you to be my girl a minute ago."

Her face went red. She didn't respond.

"Would that have been so horrible?"

"Patrick. I can't make any solid commitments until I'm free and clear of my curse. Besides, I can't blame any man for hesitating to court me—considering my spell."

He looked nonplussed. "I know you're terrified, but the more I think about it, your curse must be nonsense. How can there be validity to a prophecy made by an old woman who went to a tarot card reader?"

"This is my Aunt Morvina we're talking about!" Rose cried. "When my parents overlooked inviting her to my christening, she went to a tarot card reader who was also a witch. The witch cast a curse over me on Morvina's behalf—"

"—and she doomed you to meet with a terrible accident on your twenty-first birthday." Patrick paused. "I know the story by heart, Rose. Morvina made an unexpected appearance at your christening and terrified everyone with the news."

She stiffened.

"I know you believe in this spell whole-heartedly," he added.

"How can I not?" she cried. In fact, Rose could think of little else except her impending destiny. Dying at the tender age of twenty-one would mean she'd be cheated of any future. Perhaps that's why she was drawn to magic. It was her only hope for reversing her fate.

"I've lived in fear of the prophecy ever since Elena informed me of it," she went on. "Now I only have a year to live."

Patrick squeezed her hand.

"I dream that Aunt Morvina creeps into my bedroom and kills me in my sleep," she said in horror.

"Do you even know what the woman looks like?" He tried to draw out a smile.

"I've only seen one photograph of Morvina and she's gnarled and hideous. According to Elena, she cast herself from society when she developed crippling arthritis." Rose grimaced. As far as anyone knew, Morvina had become a recluse . . . a spinster wallowing in self-pity.

"But what does she have against you?" Patrick argued.

"I really don't know."

Patrick gave a shudder, yet he managed to say, "Not to worry." He stroked her cheek and then gathered her to him. "I'm going to protect you from that horrible aunt of yours. And when I'm promoted to detective, I'll make a more respectable suitor. Maybe you'll have me then."

She lifted her head and stared into his sincere expression. He looked so hopeful. *Dear Patrick.* She couldn't help but adore him.

"Nothing would make me happier than winning your heart," he said.

"I come with a lot of complications," she whispered.

"None that we can't work out." He smiled.

"We'll see," Rose murmured. She didn't want to think of her curse anymore tonight. Nor did she want to see more disappointment on Patrick's face.

They stepped away from each other as the Marconi family called them to the dining room for a late-night snack. As the small group chattered away into the wee hours of the morning, Olivia stole Rose away for a moment. They huddled at the base of the staircase while Olivia handed her something. It was a tiny music box, inlaid with African violets.

"You're a dear, Olivia, but you shouldn't have," Rose said.

"It's not from me, silly. It's from that *magician*."

Puzzled, Rose opened it, then wound it. It played her favorite Mozart melody.

Goosebumps sprang up on her arms as she held the music box under the gas lamp on the wall.

She turned it over and studied the inscription on its underside.

Happy birthday, Rose. I count the hours until we meet again ~ Dragomir.

"Where did this come from?" Rose's cheeks warmed.

"It was lying on your bed just now," Olivia replied. "I went upstairs to grab a shawl and I saw it."

Alarm and excitement swept through Rose. "Dragomir Starkov was in my home?"

"Apparently. There is something very frightening about that man. How does he know where you live?"

Rose shook her head, as if in a daze.

"From the look in his eyes," Olivia continued, "he wants to make you his—at any cost. I don't trust him, and neither should you."

Rose lowered her voice. "Olivia, I don't think I can stay away from him."

"You have to!"

"If I didn't know better, I'd think he hypnotized me tonight. It's as though I'm at his beck and call."

"That's nonsense," Olivia said firmly. Pausing, she looked around the foyer. "No one else saw the music box. Do you want me to dispose of it?"

"No!" Rose clutched the memento to her chest.

"Very well. Do as you please. But I think you're making a mistake."

Olivia stormed off, leaving Rose alone in the dim foyer. *Do I dare go back to the Sunshine Theater?*

Strangely, she didn't feel as if she had a choice.

CHAPTER 4

Rose re-traced her steps to the theater the next night. She could hardly wait to see Dragomir Starkov again. Unfortunately, she'd been forced to lie in order to get out of the house.

I'm supposed to be visiting Widow Greenburg, she considered during the streetcar ride. Rose felt guilty, but she couldn't stand missing out on anything. In fact, she'd always been curious to a fault. From the time she peeked into her schoolmaster's grade book, to the time her adoptive father caught her opening her largest Christmas gift late at night, her inquisitiveness had gotten her into trouble more than once.

As she strode up to the façade of the Sunshine Theater, her mind wandered to the trick the illusionist had performed on her. One minute she was levitating, the next she was inside that musty cabinet. And she had no idea how the ruse was accomplished.

Shaking her head, Rose purchased a ticket and ducked inside the venue. Maybe it hadn't been a trick. Maybe, just maybe, it had been magic in its purest form.

She took her seat in the last row of the auditorium and watched the other seats fill up. Both shows she'd attended were standing room only, so it seemed Mr. Starkov was doing very well professionally.

Still, the rumors flying around about him were sinister. More and more, people were claiming he drew his powers from black magic. Ominous music threaded throughout the theater. Suddenly, Rose wished Olivia had accompanied her. While the chatter subsided, she envisioned the marquee poster she'd passed in the lobby. It bore Dragomir's captivating image, complete with his piercing blue-green eyes, wavy brown hair, and sensual mouth topped by a thin mustache.

The tagline she'd read on the poster replayed in her mind: *I have one secret that explains everything I do. I challenge you to discover it.*

Rose could almost feel the magician's warm breath on her face. Her heart fluttered. The curtains parted and a sense of danger replaced her girlish excitement. She nearly rushed out of the theater—until Dragomir appeared.

She slouched in her seat as she watched his first few tricks. Nervously, she rubbed her fingertips over the necklace Patrick had given her. Her thoughts turned to the Egyptian amulet resting beneath her blouse and her cheeks grew hot to the touch.

Dragomir performed an hour's worth of amazing conjures—enough to convince Rose that he was capable of sending a compelling force her way. The hold he had over her frightened and thrilled her at the same time. And as the show came to an end, she found herself wanting to lock eyes with his dark gaze again.

Rose leaned forward in her seat, her pulse pounding wildly. Dapper in his impeccably-cut tuxedo and well-oiled hairstyle, Dragomir was about to perform his final illusion. The gaslights flickered. The entire audience sat motionless.

In preparation, the magician removed his black tuxedo jacket, giving Rose a view of his broad shoulders and slim waist. "Ladies and gentleman," he said in his trademark Romanian accent. "As many of you may know, I always close my show with my grandest illusion. But what you may not know is that I enjoy doing the unexpected. Tonight I'd like to perform something with the help of an unsuspecting audience member. This illusion has been inspired by my fascination with the human body—which we all agree is a material substance. *But in my world, it's a substance that can be transcended.*"

The magician paused, his eyes darting around the hushed theater. "I call this illusion the 'bait and switch.'"

Rose grasped the arms of her seat tightly.

"As I said, I need a volunteer for this trick. A *female* volunteer." Half a dozen hands shot up at Dragomir's request. Meanwhile, Rose forced herself to relax in her seat. There was no way the illusionist could know she was here.

He continued to peer at the audience. Silence enveloped the auditorium as Rose clutched the arms of her seat. *Will I be disappointed if he doesn't call my name?*

"I sense that a friend of mine is in attendance tonight. A rare beauty by the name of Rose Carlisle."

Rose gasped. *How did he know?*

Dragomir moved forward. "I see you in the back row, Rose. Will you please join me onstage?"

Although she was incredibly nervous, she stood and made her way down the dipping center aisle. Meanwhile, the audience applauded politely. Trance-like, she took his hand once she reached the stage and followed him to a cage with metal bars, situated at stage left.

The sultry illusionist put his lips to her ear before they turned to face the audience. "It's wonderful to see you again." She enjoyed a surge of anticipation. Then she glanced at Dragomir's intriguing profile. He was even more dashing than she remembered. His chiseled cheekbones created intricate curves on his otherwise smooth face, while an incredible set of curled lashes fringed the pools of his eyes. And the way his mustache set off his full lips nearly made her giddy.

Everything about him oozed elegance and sophistication. She felt like moldable clay in his able hands . . . willing to do whatever he asked. And she admitted to herself that he would intrigue her until the day the world stopped spinning.

"Rose, would you please step into the cage? And no, I will not keep you there to be gawked at like a zoo animal. You're much too lovely for that."

Only a mild stream of laughter rippled through the theater. There seemed to be a tension in the air that could be cut with a knife. Rose suspected that tension harkened back to the belief that Dragomir the Magnificent's illusions were becoming increasingly dangerous.

Before she stepped into the cage, her gaze wandered to the back of the theater. No one from the Marconi family had followed her here and Patrick was nowhere to be seen. She was all alone—and if she perished during the magic trick she'd leave behind a mystery as to her whereabouts.

Dragomir asked her a second time to step into the cage. Obediently, she lifted her skirts and cooperated. Next, the magician reached into his trouser pocket and withdrew an ornate key. He locked her inside the metal cage, then handed the key to his assistant, Katherine. The brunette gave Rose a quick sneer before Dragomir climbed onto a ladder and draped the entire cage with a large black cloth.

"Are you still there, Rose?" he asked in an authoritative voice.

"Yes, I'm here," she assured him, as fright streamed through her veins.

"Excellent. Now Katherine will lock me inside another cage on the opposite side of the stage."

Rose couldn't see anything. Therefore she had to rely on her hearing. She listened as Dragomir was being imprisoned. Then she heard Katherine drop a black cloth over his makeshift jail.

"I present to you the key that has imprisoned both participants of this magic act," Katherine's voice reached Rose. Rose presumed Drago's assistant was holding the object up. "Are you all right, Miss Carlisle?"

"Yes," she answered, certain that her voice sounded muffled behind the black cloth.

"Very good," Katherine replied. "To let you know, Miss Carlisle, I'm placing the key inside a tin box that I will set on a table located between the two cages." She paused. "Can you hear me, Dragomir the Magnificent?"

"Yes."

"Excellent," Katherine said. "On the count of three, ladies and gentlemen, I will reveal the contents of Miss Carlisle's cage while a crew member reveals the contents of Dragomir Starkov's cage."

Sucking in a deep breath she cried, "One . . . two . . . three!"

Both drapes were pulled aside—proving that Rose and Dragomir had switched places! Rose's heart drummed. She had no recollection of ever leaving her original cage, let alone journeying to the other one. The trick was nothing short of astounding.

While the crowd applauded furiously, Katherine plucked the tin box off the prop table and revealed its lack of contents. Then, smiling victoriously, Dragomir removed something from his other trouser pocket. It was the very key that had been used to lock both participants in their cages! He reached his arm through the spacious bars, put the key to the lock and freed himself. Next, he moved quickly to Rose's cage and unlocked her door as well.

Dragomir kissed Rose's hand before he encouraged her to take a step forward. "Ladies and gentlemen . . . the ravishing Miss Carlisle!"

She bowed sheepishly. As she accepted his hand once more, he stepped closer to her. "Meet me after the show," he whispered. His intoxicating voice made her heady. "It would honor me."

Dropping her hand from his, she scurried back to her seat, enduring comments such as: "She must be part of the show." "I saw him bring her onstage before." "An audience member is always in on the trick!" And, "There must be a trap door beneath both cages!"

But Rose knew better. She could attest that the stage under the cage was as solid as a rock—and that there had been no means of escape.

As she slid into her seat, the house lights illuminated. She sat frozen for a moment before she gathered her belongings. As she did so, she glanced at the man seated next to her . . . a man who was writing zealously in a small notepad.

"Are you a reporter?" Rose asked politely while the theater emptied.

The strongly-built man, whose face was marred with pockmarks, nodded. "I am. Richard Bellum's the name. And tomorrow morning, when this story hits *The Gotham Times*, I'll bet nobody will be able to get a ticket to see Dragomir the Magnificent."

"He was fabulous, wasn't he?" She blushed.

Richard Bellum smiled as he secured his hat. "If you care to read about yourself in the morning, Miss Carlisle, be my guest. For your information, Mr. Starkov's knowledge of your presence was one of the highlights of the show. Your look of surprise was too spontaneous to fake."

"Please don't put my name in the paper," she pleaded.

"Too late. All these people have seen you. And since the trick you participated in was the best of the night, other reporters will be writing about you, too." He paused. "For what it's worth, Starkov has obviously taken a fancy to you."

"I don't know about that, Mr. Bellum." She paused. "But I'll admit I've always wanted to be a journalist."

"You have, have you?" The reporter shot her a quizzical look. "Do you have any experience?"

Because she'd been lying a great deal lately, she decided to be honest. "No."

"It doesn't matter. We're always looking for able-minded reporters at *The Gotham Times*—and we're even open to pioneering females joining the profession."

"Really?" Rose asked excitedly.

"I could put in a good word for you if you come around tomorrow. Here's my card."

The stout man handed it over, then disappeared into the crowd.

For Rose, the thrill of making a connection was short-lived because Olivia appeared, red-faced. "Rose Emily Carlisle. What the devil are you doing here?"

"How did you know I was here?" Rose asked.

Olivia arched an eyebrow.

"All right. I would have looked for me here, too."

"Who were you talking to just now?" Olivia accompanied her into the lobby.

"A newspaper reporter. According to him, my name will be front and center in *The Gotham Times* tomorrow morning . . . and I'm not supposed to be here, remember?"

"How do you get yourself into these situations?" Olivia shook her head.

"What am I going to do?"

Olivia put a finger to her chin. "Since we can't afford to buy up all the papers in the city, I suppose you're going to have to tell Papa the truth."

Rose hung the handle of her umbrella on her wrist. "I guess you're right. And don't worry. When I get home I'll do all the talking."

"Let's go." Olivia turned toward the theater's front doors but Rose stopped her.

"Wait," she said. "Dragomir asked me to meet him after the show."

"He *what*?"

"Shh! Do you think I ought to?"

"Certainly not," Olivia huffed as she stuffed a torn ticket stub into her handbag. "After all, you're practically going steady with Patrick."

"Practically—but not officially. Meeting Mr. Starkov will be harmless."

"I hardly recognize you lately." Olivia frowned. "Your behavior—"

"Please go ahead without me." Rose interrupted.

"I don't know . . ."

"I swear I'll be fine."

Olivia lowered her tone before she departed. "I'll go. But remember what I always tell you: You are a beautiful girl, Rose. A girl any man could lose his head over. Be careful."

"I will. I promise."

Standing alone in the vacated lobby, Rose rubbed her hands together nervously. Olivia was right. Her behavior was bizarre—and now that she was standing here with no companion or chaperone, apprehension over accepting Dragomir's invitation swelled inside her.

A quarter of an hour passed. Without Olivia's moral support, Rose found it awkward waiting alone. She exhaled with relief when an elderly usher materialized from a side door. "Are you the young woman waiting for Mr. Starkov?"

She nodded.

"Would you follow me, Miss?"

She traced the usher's steps to a narrow alley outside the building. Thankfully, the rain had stopped. Now the summer air hung around her, thick and damp.

The usher stopped before a portal marked STAGE DOOR 2. "I'm to stay with you until Mr. Starkov comes out."

Rose stared at the unmoving door handle. Suddenly, she remembered the attack on the young girl in Coney Island. She doubted the elderly usher would be able to protect her if that fiend appeared. Hadn't the poor girl been squeezed to death like a piece of wrung laundry?

CHAPTER 5

Following the show, Drago escaped to the sanctity of his dressing room. He sank onto a stool and began removing his make-up without the aid of a mirror. His intense aversion to mirrors—and to reporters and their cameras—was understandable because Dragomir Starkov was a man who cast no reflection in glass and who vanished like a ghost in photographs.

He was an Immortal. And the time for the Victory was nearly upon him.

More powerful than a vampire, more human than a werewolf, Drago had been transformed into a rare lord of black magic by the fortuneteller from whom he'd received his powers 448 years earlier.

The teller responsible for his demonic immortality had been a master of the occult. But he hadn't known it until it was too late.

That fateful night replayed in his mind, even though he'd willed the memory away a thousand times.

When Drago was thirty, he found himself unmarried and the son his ill father relied on to run their family's farm. Harsh winters in the countryside made putting food on the table increasingly difficult. Frustrated, lonely, and fascinated by the dark side, Drago became passionate about magic. In order to help his family and perhaps change his life, he wanted to find out if it was possible for someone to render genuine magic. He decided to pay a visit to a fortuneteller to discover the answer.

"Make yourself comfortable, young man." An aged woman garbed in a purple head-scarf indicated the chair opposite hers. A crystal ball on a draped table separated them.

"You would like to know what the future holds?" she asked.

"Yes," Drago replied. I'll start off with that, he thought. After he paid the required fee, he leaned forward anxiously.

The woman moved her hand over the crystal ball. The object began to sparkle. As it turned dark, she cocked an eyebrow in alarm.

"Is everything all right?" Drago asked.

"It seems the forces of black magic are requesting a card reading."

He swallowed hard. "A what?"

"Most people play games with picture cards. I use them to tell the future."

"Will it cost extra?"

"Of course."

He rolled his eyes and slipped the old woman a few more coins.

Nodding with satisfaction, she removed the crystal ball from the table and produced a stack of ordinary cards like the ones Drago's family often played with. The colors were faded and the cards' corners were curled, but for some reason, they intimidated Drago tremendously.

The woman pulled in a breath. "What I do with these cards is unusual, so allow me to explain. As you know, there are four suits of cards. Wands, cups, swords, and pentacles. Each suit contains fourteen cards. The order in which the cards are drawn and laid out will indicate the path of your physical and spiritual journey."

As the fortuneteller put the stack on the table, anxiousness filtered up Drago's spine. She proceeded to cut the deck into two equal parts. Next, she shuffled the entire pile with her gnarled hands. After that, she repeated the steps twice more. Perspiration beaded Drago's lip. He watched the old woman draw the topmost card and turn it over clockwise—from left to right.

The woman's weary eyes lit up. "The Ace of Swords. It denotes male sexuality, the beginning of a powerful relationship, and forces that will surround you without your control."

"Seems like a decent card," Drago said, cautiously. "Except the 'forces beyond my control' part."

"It is a good card because it shows you will enjoy success in spite of all obstacles. In a word, you are invincible."

Next, the woman turned over the Knave of Swords. She raised both eyebrows. Drago noticed that her hands had begun to shake. "This card tells me you'll become a fearless man as well as a dangerous opponent."

Opponent in what circumstances? Anticipation swelled inside Drago. Perhaps his life would contain some excitement after all.

"Ah," she paused. "Together, the Ace and the Knave of Swords indicate hostile opposition."

Drago dropped his stare back to the deck.

The woman turned over the Queen of Pentacles. "This symbolizes your true love. She will be a generous, warm-hearted female full of curiosity and willingness."

Drago felt a stirring in his soul.

The teller laid out more cards that didn't seem to impress her. However, the subsequent card did. "The Magician!" she announced.

Drago studied the card. Marked with Roman numeral I, it showed an angel with wings. Strangely, the angel wore a demon-like face as it kept watch over a group of mortals. "The Magician?" he cried. "It's a perfect card."

"You like magic?" the woman asked slyly.

"I live for it. I came here to find out if it's possible to enact real magic."

Hunched over, the hideous woman narrowed her eyes. "Indeed it is." With hands that shook with the ferocity of an earthquake, the woman turned over the last card. "My God!" she gasped. "The Final Judgment."

Drago grew concerned.

"I've never witnessed this kind of reading," she said. "It seems you have enormous talent, young man. I, in turn, can give you the power you need to perform real magic."

"You mean it's possible without using tricks and deception?"

"Yes."

"How can you give me the power I need to do it?"

The woman pulled a silver coin from her skirt pocket. *"If you're willing to accept this gift, you will be granted abilities associated with black magic."*

His fingertips tingled at the idea.

"Your fascination with the unearthly led you here," the woman said slowly. *"To take that fascination one step further, this coin will give you the talent many people wish they had. Not the kind of cheap props and tricks."*

The hair on the back of Drago's neck stood up. This was too good to be true.

"What's the catch?" he asked.

The teller glanced around to make sure they were alone. *"Accepting the coin comes with a huge price."*

"Price?"

"You shall become immortal."

To live forever! Who wouldn't want to perform astounding feats of magic and live for all eternity?

Before Drago could say *"yes,"* the woman raised a hand to quiet him. *"Please know that remaining immortal will require you carry out a special deed. I cannot reveal what that deed is. But for the spell to work and for you to become immortal, you must agree to perform it on this day, every year."*

"I agree," Drago said hastily.

"Good," the woman said. *"When you leave this place you'll discover what the deed is."*

He nodded.

"Now, before I hand you the coin, you must understand that it will show you the past and the present only. The one and only time it shows you the future, you must go to that place immediately—and follow the chain of events it predicts."

"What chain of events?" Drago asked quickly.

"All I can tell you is that you'll be unable to alter the course the coin shows you."

A part of Drago suspected that the Gypsy was delusional—and that nothing would come of their encounter. But as he stuffed the coin

into his pocket during the long walk back to his family's farm, his painful transformation into a demon occurred for the first time.
Drago realized he'd just made a deal with the devil.

He reeled out of the memory with a scowl. Becoming immortal had been a terrible price to pay. Certainly, he'd made enough money to turn the Starkov farm around. But as the years rolled by, he was forced to watch loved ones die while he never aged.

Still, Drago couldn't change his decision and eventually, he grew hell-bent on raising himself to the status of the world's greatest magician. Over the centuries, the picture cards used by the fortuneteller came to be known as the tarot. What evolved also were the quality of Drago's acts and the sophistication of his audiences.

Despite his growing fame, he'd become introverted and secretive, delving into the realm of magic as a way to deal with the loneliness of his existence. Thankfully, his profession as a magician garnered him an impressive income. It also garnered him a certain kind of power.

Not only had Drago come to like his famed status, he needed it like a drug. After all, how could he ever feel alone with the eyes of the world watching him?

He adjusted his bow tie by feel. Now that he'd had the vision of the future that the fortuneteller had told him about, he sensed his immortality might be coming to a close. Countless Immortals had roamed the earth before 1912, yet there were only two left in the world—himself and another incredibly potent demon.

If Drago could defeat this last demon and stand triumphant in the Victory, he might be able to die whenever he wanted to.

That would be the best prize of all. I wouldn't need to suck out someone's soul to maintain my current identity anymore. Nor would I be required to invade a foreign body if I want to live as somebody else.

As Drago waited for the Victory to take place, it was extremely difficult keeping the monster below his surface a secret. Yet he must, if he wanted to possess Rose. When he'd envisioned the other Immortal's arrival in New York, Rose had appeared to him as well. And because he'd waited an eternity to find his soul mate, he had purchased the amulet of Tousret and the bracelet of Amenhotep as insurance against her curse once he learned of it.

Patting the bracelet inside his jacket pocket, Drago's lips quirked. It was an object he carried around with him at all times—as was the coin. One of the items had brought him to Rose; the other would allow him to save her.

Had she figured him out yet? Had she come to the conclusion that his magic came from the dark side? Did she know there were no explanations for his illusions?

Drago couldn't tell her the truth without scaring her away. The dehumanizing stipulation that had allowed him to live for centuries would force her to flee from him. And he was not a man who was willing to lose his true love. Not after all this time.

This was his chance to be with Rose. And he needed to win the Victory to make that happen.

He donned his black cape and opened the dressing room door. Surely he could forget his morbid history for a moment in order to bask in her presence. After all, she was his angel of light.

Rose, who had been fidgeting uncontrollably in the dark alley, willed her knees to stop shaking. She was drawn to Dragomir Starkov like a magnet. *I must be hypnotized or I wouldn't be standing in this filthy side street.*

Growing more and more nervous, she glanced at the closed stage door.

Can Dragomir help me with my curse? Rose was hesitant to tell him about it because she didn't want him to think she was a fan who'd crossed the line. Yet she sensed he *could* come to her aid.

She would simply have to choose the right time to bring it up.

She waited a few more minutes. The lateness of the hour and the strange smells in the alley brought nausea to her throat. She laced her fingers together tensely. Suddenly, an image of Drago surfaced in her mind. He would open the door any minute, bearing a bouquet of roses.

Premonitions had been popping into her mind more and more— but before she could mull this one over, the side door burst open. A figure silhouetted by the theater lights stepped forward. Smiling seductively, Dragomir Starkov exited into the tepid night. Still dressed in his tuxedo, he'd added a stylish cape and a shining top hat to his ensemble.

Rose glanced down self-consciously at her lace blouse and ordinary trumpet skirt—disappointed that she could do nothing about her plain attire now.

Dragomir bent from the waist. His gaze never left her face. With all the flourish of an accomplished magician, he pulled a bouquet of roses from the folds of his cape.

At times like this, the accuracy of Rose's predictions scared her.

"For you," he greeted in an enticing tone.

"Thank you," she murmured.

The usher excused himself.

"Happy birthday, Rose," he said, handing her the roses.

"You're too kind. But my birthday was yesterday. And you already gave me two gifts. The amulet and the music box . . ."

"How do you like the music box?"

She blushed. "It plays my favorite Mozart melody."

It was then, as the moonlight glittered in the depths of Dragomir's cyan eyes, that Rose first glimpsed his obsession for her. Stunned, she cleared her throat. "How did you get the music box inside my room?"

He drew his brows together. "You must never ask a magician such things."

He spoke so firmly that she dropped the subject.

"I'm glad you like your present, my *draga,*" he went on.

"*Draga?*" she echoed.

"In Romanian the word means 'darling.'"

She studied her feet. "But we hardly know one another, Mr. Starkov."

"You're right." He looked embarrassed. "Forgive my boldness. But please, call me Drago."

"Very well . . . Drago." His name on her tongue thrilled her.

"My apologies for making you wait in this wretched alley," he said. "It was the only way I could assure we'd be left alone by reporters and my fans."

"Where are your fans?" she asked.

"At the official stage door, on the other side of the theater."

"You don't like reporters?"

He shook his head. "They're like famished vultures, ready to nibble away at my illusions until all of my secrets are revealed."

"I never thought of it that way."

Silence ensued, exaggerating the fact that Rose was alone with a strange man in a dark alley.

"It's late," the gallant Romanian admonished. "May I escort you home?"

She hesitated. "You may walk me as far as Twenty-Third Street. I'll take a cab the rest of the way."

He nodded—and as they strolled along the bustling avenue, their striking appearance turned heads: Drago, with his polished good looks, and Rose, with the enchantment he spawned in her.

It was like a dream:

The warm breeze fluttering soft tendrils of hair about her face.

The fragrance of the roses wafting through the air.

And the feel of Drago's hot touch on her arm.

She felt very grown up. But after a few moments, she was compelled to make a confession. "I should tell you the truth, Drago. Following my appearance at your first show, I received a great deal of criticism."

He raised an eyebrow and chuckled. "Was it that sordid of a place to be?"

"*I* didn't think so," she said quickly. "But magic shows have a particular *reputation* among New Yorkers."

"What sort of reputation?" He seemed puzzled.

She hesitated. "People claim there is no such thing as real magic. They say magicians are charlatans. Isn't that preposterous? You, on the other hand, are different. Skeptics continue to be bewildered by your illusions."

"I'm glad."

Hesitating, she added, "Unfortunately, other people are accusing you of being a dark sorcerer."

To her surprise, he smiled. "And what is your opinion of my tricks, young Rose?"

"I think you're the most astounding magician I've ever seen. And if you *are* capable of real magic, people should refrain from criticizing you."

"You're refreshingly honest."

She looked at the ground. "Did I say too much?"

"Not at all. Over the years I have come to appreciate honesty. Now it's my turn to ask you something."

"Of course."

"Did you enjoy the show this evening?"

Her eyes widened. "Oh, yes! It was incredible. I suspect that you used more than one key, but I don't understand how you transported me to your cage. There wasn't a trap door in sight!"

"Ah," he said guardedly, "illusions are not always done with the proverbial trap door."

She went on. "I was also astonished at how you knew I was in the audience."

"How do you *think* I was aware?" The corner of his lip curled up mysteriously.

"My adoptive sister suggested you hypnotized me last night—and willed me to come back to you. Unthinkable, isn't it?" Once the words were out of her mouth, she erupted into nervous laughter. Drago, however, remained quiet.

"You're laughing, but how do you know Olivia is incorrect?" he finally said.

She stopped in her tracks and turned to face him. "How do you know her name?"

He made no reply, but took her by the shoulders. Exhilaration rippled up her spine.

"More importantly, did you hypnotize me?" she asked softly.

"If you're enchanted, maybe it can be attributed to the necklace I gave you," Drago said. "Are you wearing it?"

She blushed all over again. "Yes."

"Excellent. If you trust me, good things will come from it. As for your question about being hypnotized, I told you: a magician never reveals his secrets."

"Never?" she asked. "How can I trust you if you don't confide in me?"

"You're beautiful and intelligent," he said in a sultry tone. He moved in closer to her, their noses mere inches apart. "Perhaps if you agree to have dinner with me tomorrow evening, I'll explain one of my tricks."

She could feel his very soul sweep forward. And as his masculine scent encircled her, she leaned into him. "I don't know . . ."

"Please consider it. Say, Rockwell's at eight o'clock?"

"Yes," she heard herself murmur. Gazing into his bewitching blue-green eyes, she nearly swooned. If she were ever to wish for anyone to hypnotize her, it would be Drago. He was standing so close to her . . . would he kiss her?

Her stare shifted to his moist mouth and hollowed cheeks, and she had never wanted anything so badly in her life. To her disappointment, he took a step back—staring at her as if she were an object he was forbidden to touch. "I'll send a taxi around for you." He paused. "Before we part ways, Rose, I want to ask you something."

"Yes?" she asked, her cheeks still flushed from their close contact.

"Over the past three years, you received unexplained birthday gifts, correct?"

"Yes." She sucked in a breath.

"Did you wonder who sent them?"

The expensive dress. The pearl necklace. The charm bracelet. Rose remembered every one, and cherished them equally. "From you?" She could barely get the words out.

Another smile tugged at the corner of his mouth.

"But why? And how?"

Ignoring her questions, he simply said, "Even as a girl of seventeen you intrigued me. I realized you were much too young for any sort of relationship, but I never stopped thinking of you. You have no idea how far I've come to be with you."

"You knew me when I was seventeen?"

"Not exactly."

Confusion whirled in Rose's head. She felt dizzy . . . intoxicated. Yet she sensed it wouldn't do any good to ask Drago more questions.

Drago summoned a taxi with an ear-piercing whistle, then took her hands in his. "Another gift waits for you when you return home. This one celebrates your bridge into womanhood. It's unlike the other, extravagant presents, but I believe its simplicity will hold a special value for you."

Before Rose climbed into the cab, Drago paid the driver in advance, then planted a kiss on her cheek. After the motorcar pulled away, she watched his stately figure disappear behind her.

Jostling gently in the rear of the vehicle, she asked herself why she wasn't repelled by the magician's fixation for her. Then again, wouldn't any young woman on the brink of adulthood find the attention exhilarating? Not only was Drago incredibly handsome, he was financially successful and undeniably talented.

Following a ten-minute ride, the cab stopped in front of the Marconi home. Rose alighted and raced to the doorstep—to the spot where all her other birthday presents had been waiting for her in years past. There on the stone step sat a package. She ripped the brown parchment paper away in furious motions. Inside sat the tin box Drago had used in tonight's 'bait and switch' illusion.

When Rose lifted its lid, she spotted the key that had unlocked both cages.

Marveling at how Drago could have transported them here, Rose hugged the roses and the tin box close to her chest. All the while, her nerves prickled at the possibility that he had performed real magic.

CHAPTER 7

Rose.

Drago sat in the darkness and repeated her name in his mind.

Ironically, darkness had become a way of life for him. It encouraged him, propelled him. Even comforted him. After all, it was from the depths of night that he drew the strength to perform his illusions.

Drago was nocturnal—and when he awoke from a day's sleep, he was always forced to shake off the heavy fog of lethargy. If he didn't, fatigue would beat him down and snatch away his energy.

Of course, being a demon didn't mean that he was forbidden to go into the sunlight. He would not die a horrible, consuming death as would a vampire. It was just that he had become a demon at night all those years ago—which meant he summoned most of his energy after the sun set now. As part of his routine, he slept away the daylight hours in his tiny apartment located near the theater district. It was a place of refuge inside which he'd installed black window curtains. Drago owned grander accommodations of course, but he liked that this apartment was within walking distance of the Sunshine Theater. And he liked the sound of people around him. Furthermore, he needn't worry about visitors here. His manager, Archibald McMillan, and his assistant, Katherine, knew better than to disturb him at home—as did the apartment building's superintendent, Mrs. Kravitz. She was a lonely widow who seemed starry-eyed around him even though he'd never cast a spell around her.

This was Drago's schedule: he would rise every evening at six, prepare to leave for the theater, and then perfect his illusions once he arrived extra early for his eight o'clock show. Katherine had been with him for nearly two years and, thankfully, she asked no questions. They'd never enjoyed a love affair—and he couldn't figure out why she stayed with him.

Perhaps she remained to ride on the coattails of his success. Or maybe she was loyal because she hoped to share his bed someday.

It was no matter. Drago needed her only in the most practical sense.

Glad that the theater was dark today—as it was every Monday—he rose with the familiar fog of fatigue. After striding to the window, he glanced beyond the thick curtains. The last slice of sunlight disappeared over the skyline. He tried to remember a time when he could watch the sun rise and set in the normal span of a day. But that had been so long ago.

Now among the privileges Drago enjoyed was shape-shifting. Transforming himself into a cat, a dog, a bird—whichever creature caught his fancy. That's how he had been able to observe Rose these three years without being noticed.

He pined for her even now. How could he ever leave her behind when she grew old and died and he remained alive and young? Being a slave to eternity was the worst thing about his special powers.

Rose, of course, knew nothing about him. She had no idea that he was forced to move on from a place when people noticed he hadn't aged. Nor did she know that he'd amassed a staggering fortune during his 448 years as an immortal, or that money no longer interested him. Instead, what motivated him was stunning people with his inexplicable illusions.

That and winning the love of his golden-haired beauty.

Drago picked the lei coin off the bedside table. Romania's former queen appeared on the front of the object while a pair of fierce horses facing one another adorned the back. He studied the coin with frustration, as he often did. The enchanted coin lent him ability to see the past—yet glimpsing the future was one thing Drago couldn't do. Except for the time it had shown him Rose.

He wanted to see that image again.

Frowning, he said, "Show me the night I first saw Rose in a vision." The coin obeyed. After it glimmered, it projected a scene of him sleeping—then jerking awake. Then it flashed to him picking up the coin from the bedside table. When Drago gazed into it, he looked upon Rose's astonishing face. Subsequently, he saw her falling to her doom from someplace extraordinarily high—a place too obscured for him to make out.

Determination shot through him. *I need to prevent Rose's death.*

Once the coin went dark, Drago tucked it into his pocket. He insisted that the object—along with his special bracelet—stay in his possession at all times, except when he slept.

He checked his watch. His dinner date was drawing nearer but not fast enough. If it were possible, he would speed up the hands of time. Unfortunately, altering chronology was one illusion he wasn't capable of.

After Drago finished shaving, he dressed carefully in a three-piece suit with a pewter tie and a jacket cut low enough to reveal a solid vest. He wore his hair in a more casual style tonight. When he wasn't performing, he enjoyed running his fingers through it until it fell forward in wavy strands.

He checked his pocket watch one more time.

Seven thirty. Time to leave and meet Rose at Rockwell's.

He didn't doubt that she would be there. After all, he'd summoned all of his powers to hypnotize her by way of the Egyptian amulet. It was a state that would remain over her forever—unless he decided to dissolve it.

Although Rose wasn't aware of the coincidence, she dressed carefully in silver for her dinner date, too. She chose her most expensive dress—a pewter gown set off by a satin bow at the small of her back, and matching, elbow-length gloves.

And like Drago, she also took the time to try a new hairstyle. She rolled a curled fringe downward over her forehead and drew the rest of her mane up at the sides into a high chignon.

Once she'd whisked her favorite shade of raspberry lip stain over her mouth and stepped into a cloud of her iris-scented perfume, she was ready. Not wanting to be late, she made her way down the carpeted staircase to the house's foyer. The twist of a doorknob startled her. Anthony Marconi entered the house wearing his police uniform and his usual sour expression.

His frown deepened even more when he saw her. "All dressed up, Rose? Where are you going *this* evening?"

The smug and condescending Anthony was one member of the Marconi family Rose had never felt close to. He'd admitted once in a moment of rage that he resented her relationship with Olivia. He claimed that before Rose was in the picture, he and Olivia had been inseparable. Rose scoffed at the notion, saying that since he was so disagreeable, she marveled that he was even related to Olivia, let alone her twin brother.

Their relationship had remained icy ever since.

Years later, Rose considered it ironic that Anthony and amiable Patrick were friends.

"I'm having dinner downtown," Rose replied curtly. She pulled the lace curtains aside to see if the taxi Drago promised to send had arrived.

"Dinner? With who? Patrick, I hope."

"No," she murmured quietly.

Patrick was the son of impoverished Irish immigrants who had struggled to open a tiny bakery in the city's Lower East Side. He could never afford to take Rose to Rockwell's on his modest policeman's salary.

"Pardon me?" Anthony came to stand beside her.

She glanced into his look of disapproval and cleared her throat. "I said, I'm meeting someone for dinner and it isn't Patrick."

"You aren't meeting that *illusionist*, are you?"

Her chin dropped. "How did you know?"

Anthony raised his bulky shoulders. "The way you gushed on about him two nights ago was sickening. Then you proceeded to break my best friend's heart by turning your nose up at his birthday gift."

"I did no such thing!"

"What's gotten into you, Rose?"

"Nothing," she retorted. She didn't dare tell Anthony that she feared she'd been hypnotized by Drago. Nor did she think it wise to tell him that she had felt the world shift beneath her feet when Drago touched her yesterday. "It isn't any of your business who I have dinner with."

He studied her with defiance. Then he began to climb the stairs. "Patrick is courting you, despite your curse," he called down to her. "You should consider yourself lucky, instead of consorting with other men."

"Consorting?" she yelled up the stairwell. "Dragomir Starkov and I are just having dinner."

"The flame might burn out on Patrick's patience, you know," Anthony said over his shoulder.

"Some brother you are!" she shouted.

"*Adoptive* brother," he cried before he disappeared from sight.

Rose murmured something unladylike under her breath. As she continued to wait for the taxi, her nerves tingled. Her association with Drago was driving *everyone* to the edge.

Was she mad to continue on with him? She probably was, but she'd be damned if she'd let Anthony spoil a night she had been looking forward to all day.

CHAPTER 8

A quarter of an hour later, Rose accepted a chair from Drago inside the hushed atmosphere of Rockwell's. Settling in her seat, she noticed a red rose on her plate. Drago took the chair opposite hers while she brought the flower to her nose.

"Another rose for a Rose," he said charmingly. "I couldn't resist."

Her face heated.

He smiled at the sight of the Egyptian amulet around her neck. "It looks stunning on you."

"This is the first time I'm not keeping it hidden." She continued to blush.

"You're embarrassed." He observed. "Don't you enjoy being fussed over, Rose?"

"I don't deserve it."

"You do," he said as his eyes glimmered like a moonlit ocean.

She looked away.

Impeccably dressed and unbearably handsome, Drago wouldn't stop staring at her. Then, he reached across the tiny table and clasped her hand. Unlike Patrick's nervous touch, his was solid—and completely electrifying.

Rose took a quick intake of breath as he raised her fingers to his mouth and kissed them.

If she wasn't careful, this man could seduce her into doing very wicked things.

"A woman as lovely as you should think more highly of herself," he said.

"I'm hardly beautiful," she protested.

"Why do you say that?"

"I'm so tall. I was teased about it as a child."

He shook his head. "You're *statuesque*. There. You see? Magic is all about how something is presented."

Statuesque. She liked it.

Withdrawing her hand as inconspicuously as possible, Rose perused the menu. Then she stole a glance over it, into Drago's cyan eyes. "You have me at a slight disadvantage."

"Oh?"

"You know my birthday, but I don't know yours."

He settled back in his chair and sighed. It was obvious that he didn't like to talk about himself. "I was born on July twenty-fourth."

"Ah, what a coincidence! The birthday of my favorite author."

"Alexandre Dumas?"

"You enjoy his novels, too?" she asked.

"Absolutely."

They smiled at one another and discussed the genius of Dumas as they waited for the escargot to arrive. Drago explained that his fascination with *The Count of Monte Cristo* lay in the fact that its lead character, Edmond Dantès, walked among old acquaintances completely unrecognized after many years of incarceration.

"By changing his physical appearance and social status he was able to fool everyone," Drago said enthusiastically. "Dantès was an understated magician. Yet he couldn't deceive the greatest love of his life, Mércèdes. It shows that true love can transcend the test of time. Don't you agree?"

"Only if both participants are willing," Rose countered wisely.

Drago didn't seem pleased with her response.

She was grateful when the waiter appeared with the delicious-smelling snails. Famished, she began to eat, but noticed that her companion consumed nothing. "Aren't you hungry?"

The illusionist shook his head. "My performances usually start at this time and I'm accustomed to eating very little before them." He watched her devour her appetizer, then smiled at her empty plate. "Tell me, my charming Miss Carlisle, how is it a suitor hasn't snatched you up by now? Is there no one in your life?"

At first, the question seemed intolerably bold, but then again, they'd skipped over many polite formalities. "As a matter of fact," she replied as she dabbed her mouth with her napkin, "there is someone in my life. His name is Patrick O'Leary."

Wearing a curious expression, Drago rested both elbows on the edge of the tablecloth. "And what does this Patrick fellow do for a living?"

"He's a police officer."

Drago seemed impressed. "An honorable profession; there's no denying that."

Rose took a sip of the full-bodied wine. She was unaccustomed to drinking alcohol, so her head felt light very quickly. "Patrick is extremely proud of his work. He was recently put on the Coney Island murder case. In case you haven't heard, women have been attacked there three years in a row . . . on the same night."

Drago's expression remained stoic. "Yes, I read about it in the papers. Those poor girls. Assaulted by someone—or something. Do the police have any leads?"

"No," Rose glanced down. "But they don't think the murders were theft-related because there's never anything missing from the girls' handbags."

"The police are probably right," Drago said as he sat back in his chair. "I often wonder, is it difficult being involved with an officer of the law? What I mean to say is: don't you worry?"

She shook her head. "Patrick and I are not really *that* involved."

Drago cracked a smile.

The waiter arrived with Rose's lobster bisque—which looked just as delicious as the escargot. She took several spoonfuls before she turned the conversation back to Drago. He was drinking in her every move.

"When I asked you earlier about your birthday," she persisted, "I was hoping you'd divulge the year you were born."

"My, my. You are an upfront young woman, aren't you?"

She felt her cheeks grow hot again. "You said that before. Is bluntness something you disapprove of?"

"Not at all. And to answer your question, I am thirty years old."

Her eyes must have grown wide because her dinner companion threw his head back in laughter. To Rose it was a magnificent sound—and when his strong features softened in the moment, she felt herself being pulled beneath his seductive canopy like a helpless animal.

"Does thirty seem very old to you?"

"No," she lied. He *was* the oldest man she'd ever associated with, but she wouldn't dream of making him feel self-conscious.

After a brief pause, Drago sipped his wine. "I don't mean to appear mysterious, but I believe a magician cannot help the fact. I came to America three years ago—and began performing in a side show in Coney Island's Bowery."

Rose made a face and he laughed again. "I know. It's a horrible place. Thank heavens an agent spotted me and brought me to the Sunshine Theatre. The rest is history, as you Americans say."

It was Rose's turn to laugh. "We 'Americans' must seem uncultured to a refined European such as yourself."

"I'm European, but my beginnings were hardly refined. My parents were farmers and I helped tend to their fields for many years."

Rose's heart skipped a beat. This dashing, well-dressed illusionist seemed a far cry from a rustic plowboy.

"Does the fact that I come from nothing alarm you?"

"No," she said firmly.

"I must say, America amuses me," Drago drawled, his lips glossy from the deep Merlot. "The people of this country have a unique zest for life I find contagious."

Rose finished her fillet of sole. After she refused dessert, she and Drago waited for the waiter to deliver the bill. Drago leaned in to the flickering candlelight. "Tell me, did you find your last birthday gift?"

Her expression brightened. "Yes. However did you manage to get the key and the box all the way to my doorstep? Did you send it ahead with someone?"

Drago made a *tsk*ing sound.

"I know. A magician never reveals his secrets." Rose pouted. "But you promised to let me in on one of your secrets if I agreed to have dinner with you. You're not going back on your word, are you?"

"I always keep my promises, Rose. In order that I may do so, you must accompany me to my workshop. Are you willing to be alone with me for a few moments in the basement of the Sunshine Theater?"

Caution escalated inside her. Only Anthony knew she was at dinner with Drago. What if dark secrets lay in wait for her there?

His eyes twinkled. "I can assure you it's perfectly safe. I won't turn you into some wild animal—or make you disappear. For very long, anyway."

Against her better judgment, Rose agreed to accompany him. Obviously pleased, Drago settled the bill and stretched a hand in her direction. She accepted it, and as they exited the restaurant with all eyes on them, excitement barraged her.

CHAPTER 9

Drago emerged from the cab in front of the Sunshine Theater with Rose on his arm. His regret at having to lie to her about his age was quickly replaced by his delight at being alone with her.

Nerves humming, he unlocked a side door and led her down a narrow flight of stairs—to a shadowed basement with a low ceiling. Once he illuminated the gaslights, he watched her take in his sea of props with awe. Wooden boxes of all shapes and sizes awaited their next chance to be onstage, while a slew of draped birdcages littered the room.

Rose maneuvered around several card tables, brushing her fingertips over their felt-covered tops. "Do you spend much time in here?"

"I come here every day—right before my show," he replied. "It's important to perfect my illusions down to the last detail."

As he watched her, Drago considered how sophisticated she'd become since he'd first seen her in his vision. Gone was her girlish lack of confidence. Now, her seemly neck and womanly curves lent her a timeless beauty.

She stopped in front of one of Drago's works in progress and questioned the piece with her violet eyes.

"I know it looks daunting," he said, "but it's really about illusion."

She looked uneasy anyway. "It's a guillotine."

"It is—and I promised to show you how one of my illusions is done, didn't I?" Removing his jacket, he joined her in front of it.

She held her breath, then said, "Perhaps you can show me something that doesn't involve chopping someone's head off."

He smiled as her eyes flashed a host of emotions his way: fear, doubt, and above all, interest. She flicked a pink tongue over her dry lips and Drago felt a pang of arousal.

"Wise choice," he replied. "This illusion isn't perfected yet."

Exhaling with relief, Rose continued to meander around the dimly-lit workshop. As she moved, Drago decided it was time for him to reveal a bit more about himself and his strange existence. "In my eyes, magic is the crossing of a special boundary—the boundary between reality and illusion. It's the closest thing we have on Earth to another dimension."

She stopped. "Can magic re-direct someone's fate?"

"Perhaps," he replied cautiously.

"In that case, maybe there's something you can help me with." Color rose in her fair cheeks. "But first, I want to know if the talk about your being in league with demons and supernatural forces is true."

"What do you think?" As he spoke, he rolled up his shirtsleeves and unfastened his tab collar. Rose, too, was forced to remove her wrap due to the stifling summer heat. When she leaned back against a large wooden cabinet, Drago walked toward her and pinned her against the structure by stepping in close and leaning over her.

He sucked in a breath, entranced by her beauty. Beneath the glow of the gaslights, her lily-white shoulders shimmered and the soft rise and fall of her creamy cleavage captivated him. He eyed the Egyptian amulet that rested in the cavity between her breasts—and it was all he could do to resist pulling her into his arms for a passionate kiss.

"Frankly, I don't know what to believe," she said in a whisper.

He took her hand.

"I've seen your illusions first-hand," she added, "and I'm more confused than ever."

"Confused? Perhaps I'll show you something to clear your mind."

She seemed relieved.

He took a step back. "When a magician performs a trick he suggests something extraordinary to his audience. Take for instance, the infamous 'bullet catch' trick."

Dropping her hand, he reached over to a small table and retrieved a velvet bag from its ledge. By loosening one of its drawstrings, he opened the cinched bag and removed a gleaming silver pistol.

Rose gulped. "Is that a real gun?"

"It's very real." Drago stroked the metal of the firearm. "Would you like to examine it?"

She did just that. Then she handed the pistol back to him.

"During the bullet catch trick," he explained, "the firearm is loaded with gunpowder and ragging while a bullet is stuffed inside the barrel with a ramrod. But the trick is: the ramrod takes the bullet out when it's extracted. Therefore the bullet is never really inside the gun when it's fired. The magician, who appears to be anxiously waiting to be shot across the stage by his assistant, hides a stooge bullet inside his mouth all the while. The shot is fired and the magician reveals the bullet he supposedly caught between his teeth to a very impressed audience."

"So," Rose considered, "every magic trick is just that—a clever farce? A fraudulent act meant to fool the audience?"

"Yes. Are you relieved, or disappointed?"

"I'm not sure," she said softly.

Drago wasn't ready to tell her that *his* illusions were real. No doubt she would flee and deem him a sinister wizard.

"But you're so good at what you do," she protested. "No one seems to perform their tricks better. Perhaps you'll share one more secret."

He stepped in again and lifted a hand to her cheek. It felt like silk against his palm. "Very well. I shall reveal one more. This one pertains to you, my dearest Rose. I wanted nothing more than to find my soul mate. And when you appeared to me in a dream, you stole my heart."

She rasped a breath inward.

"Your astonishing beauty is unparalleled—as is the purity of your heart. You have no idea how long I've waited to meet someone like you."

Dazed, she stared at him. Her eyes gleamed like the petals of an orchid. "I'm intrigued that you saw me in a dream, but that isn't the kind of secret I was talking about."

"I know."

She tilted her face to the side, as if to prepare for the kiss she knew would come. When her eyes fluttered shut, Drago seized his chance. His stare shifted from the perfection of her complexion to her raspberry lips. Running a finger along the delicate bones of her jaw line, he snaked his other hand around her tiny waist and gathered her close. With a quick intake of breath, his lips came crashing down over hers for a kiss that, oddly enough, wasn't a kiss of two strangers. Instead, it was so scorching, so intimate, and so connected, it felt as though they'd known each other forever.

Desiring to possess every inch of her, Drago used his tongue to invade her sweet mouth. It twisted and turned with hers in hasty fervor—and he found that she tasted more delicious than he remembered melted caramel tasting . . . more savory than the finest cut of meat.

Driven by his pent-up lust, he gripped the exposed nape of her neck, damp with perspiration. And as he plundered her mouth, he felt grateful that Rose hadn't withdrawn from him. In fact, she seemed to relish their burning chemistry.

He pressed his abdomen forward, certain that she could feel the uncontrollable jut of his shaft. Her firm but curvaceous body responded by heaving forward. Their tongues made contact and entangled again—stoking the fire that'd ignited between them.

Rose moaned against Drago's mouth before she drew away, gasping for air. With cheeks flushed beneath the tendrils that had escaped her coif, she looked embarrassed. "I can't believe I allowed you to kiss me like that."

"I hope it wasn't unpleasant," he said.

She put her gloved fingertips to her mouth.

"I, for one, will never regret kissing you, Rose. You're very special to me." He took her hand away from her face and raised it to his lips. Kissing one finger and then another, he offered her a smile.

She didn't return it. "You scare me when you talk like that."

Regardless of her mesmerized state, it's obvious she maintains a degree of self-will.

"Please forgive me," Drago said solemnly. "Frightening you was never my intention. It's just that your beauty makes it difficult for me to resist you."

She pulled her hand from his grasp and plucked her wrap off the table.

"I hope you'll agree to see me again," he said.

"I . . . I don't know," she paused. "It's late and I have to go."

"I'll see you safely home," he replied, hoping that despite her self-consciousness, he'd gotten a little closer to capturing her heart.

CHAPTER 10

The more Rose reflected on her encounter with Drago, the more she wanted to burst. Giddy and guilty at the same time, she simply had to tell someone about the kiss they'd shared last week. Titillating—and so deliciously sexual—she swore it stole her innocence away.

"Olivia," she said in a rolling gush, "I need to tell you something."

Olivia, who was brushing her teeth at the vanity, nodded.

"I let Drago kiss me."

Olivia nearly choked on her paste. "Are you mad, Rose? The fact that you snuck out to have dinner with a stranger was bad enough, but allowing him to kiss you?"

"I didn't sneak out to have dinner with him."

The petite brunette rinsed her mouth before she swung around and placed her hands on her hips. "Yes, you did. Anthony told me."

Rose rolled her eyes. "Anthony! He has it out for me lately."

"He cares, that's all."

"Sometimes I wonder." Rose leaned against the wall and fondled the thick braid hanging over her shoulder. "I know I shouldn't have agreed to meet Drago that night, but I couldn't resist."

Olivia cocked her head to the side. "You keep saying that."

"It's time I showed you what he gave me the first night I met him." Rose straightened up. "Come closer."

Olivia did and Rose unclasped the top three buttons of her night-gown to reveal the Egyptian amulet.

"It's beautiful," Olivia said. "But why are you showing it to me now?"

"I think Drago used it to hypnotize me."

"Really?"

She nodded.

"Gracious, Rose! Do you know what you're getting yourself into with this man?"

"You don't understand," she replied with an eerie quality to her voice. "I feel commanded by him."

"Are you serious?"

"Completely. The worst part is he makes me want to do such dirty things—and then I feel guilty about it."

"Listen to me." Olivia took both of Rose's hands. "You're not under a spell. You're just infatuated. You need to forget about this mysterious magician. No one seems to know anything about him. It's as if he appeared in New York City from another galaxy."

Rose smiled. "He's not from another galaxy. He's from Romania, where he left all of his friends and family behind. He's thirty years old and his favorite author is Alexandre Dumas. As is mine. So you see? He's hardly a stranger to me."

Olivia exhaled with frustration. "He's practically an old man!"

"He is not," Rose protested.

"Anthony used his position in the police force to look into Starkov's background." Olivia said. "Do you know what he came up with?"

"What?" After Rose pinned her braid into a chignon, she walked to her wardrobe.

"Nothing," she heard Olivia call out from behind her. "He came up with nothing. Doesn't that worry you?"

"Not at all." She shrugged as she pulled out her clothes. "Drago admitted that he comes from humble beginnings. Perhaps he wanted to make a fresh start here in the States. Besides, lots of documents fail to come through Ellis Island."

"Forget Starkov's lack of credentials and forget his good looks," Olivia pleaded. "Isn't there something else about him that frightens you?"

Rose stopped in the middle of getting dressed and turned to Olivia. "There *is* something odd about him. He speaks as though he's from a different century. And when he kissed me, I felt the earth move. How does he *do* that?"

"Forget your libido for a minute." Olivia continued to protest. "He doesn't seem normal, Rose."

"Maybe not,"—Rose's expression turned solemn—"but I think he can help me with my curse."

That silenced Olivia.

For her job interview, Rose chose a fashionable apricot day dress with a mini-train and a braided collar. A fitted jacket and matching gloves completed the ensemble.

After she dressed, she looked at Olivia. "I wasn't going to tell you, but Drago shared one of his illusions with me last week."

Olivia's eyes brightened. "Tell me all about it!"

She shook her head. He hadn't sworn her to secrecy, but Rose didn't wish to betray his trust. "I can't tell you more than that, but the point is: Drago isn't a warlock or a sorcerer of the dark arts. He swears there's an explanation for every trick he performs."

"Do you really think there is?"

"Yes."

Olivia sighed. "It seems you've got it bad for him, Rose. If I can't talk you out of avoiding him, promise me you'll be careful."

Grateful that Olivia cared so much, she gave her a smile. "I promise. Now, how do I look for my interview at the paper?"

"Very professional. *The Gotham Times* will be lucky to have you as a journalist's assistant."

"Richard Bellum is interviewing me himself. Turns out he needs a helper. I only hope I'll be promoted to bona fide reporter someday."

"You know you don't have to work at the newspaper. My father offered you a post in his import company."

"And it was very generous of him. But I think I'll leave the pasta business to the true Italians." Rose laughed. "Besides, you know me better than anyone. I've always been a truth seeker. Do you remember when Frank Del Gado stole your lunch sack in fourth grade and said he didn't?"

Olivia giggled, too. "Of course I remember. You investigated his whereabouts, interviewed the other children, and didn't give up until you got him to admit he was guilty."

"Exactly. And I've used those skills to research Richard Bellum. Let's see." She ticked off the facts with her fingers. "He's worked for the newspaper for three years, is an avid collector of historic artifacts, and smokes like a fiend."

"Well done!" Olivia clapped her hands together. "Now you need to uncover more about Dragomir Starkov."

Rose rolled her eyes. "That may be more challenging."

"Best of luck," Olivia said. Glancing down at the clock pendant pinned to her blouse, she gave a little start. "Now off you go! The Printing House Square isn't close by and you don't want to be late for your interview."

Rose hastened into the bright daylight and considered her conversation with Olivia. She was honest when she promised Olivia she would be careful. On the other hand, she lied when she claimed Drago didn't frighten her.

The worst part was she yearned for more of his magical wiles.

Drago awoke with the taste of Rose on his lips. Moonlight streamed through the cracks of the dark curtains and he wondered if he'd been too bold with her in his workshop last week. Had he scared her off with his forwardness? But wasn't that impossible? She was, after all, under his spell.

What she couldn't have faked were her moans of delight when he kissed her. Furthermore, he could read her body language. She was ready to become a woman. And his kiss had set her every sense aflame.

To win her over, Drago decided he must do something about her beau, Patrick O'Leary. He'd known about Patrick before, but he'd feigned ignorance at dinner. He wanted to hear what Rose had to say about her ardent suitor.

Drago pulled himself out of bed and reached for his tuxedo. No doubt this Patrick was a man with many allies—so Drago needed to be careful.

I won't allow any real harm to come to him.

After all, the young man was innocent enough. Still, Drago could certainly arrange for the policeman to become disenchanted with

Rose. How? *By convincing naïve O'Leary that she has become interested in me instead.*

It was deceptive, yes . . . but the burning need to have Rose was an utmost priority. It pulsated through his veins like an insane craving.

As the newly-married Greek couple next door broke into one of their heated arguments, Drago shaved. Every line and groove of his own face was familiar . . . even memorized. Yet his inability to cast a reflection bothered him to no end. He was tired of paying barbers to cut his hair in the latest, ridged style, away from the mirror, during closed hours.

Once he finished dressing, he splashed cologne over his cheeks and smoothed his hair with a palm-full of pomade. Then he exited his ninth-floor apartment. As he galloped down the stairs, he wondered what kind of man Rose desired *emotionally*. It was something he was looking forward to discovering.

Stepping out of the building, he joined the bustling pedestrians as they moved along the sidewalk. Then he closed his eyes for a moment, knowing that if he concentrated hard enough, he could literally compel Rose to come to tonight's show. And this time he would urge her to bring her unknowing suitor.

CHAPTER 11

"What would you like to do this evening to celebrate your getting hired at the paper?" Patrick asked, his green eyes full of pride at her accomplishment.

"Maybe we should celebrate here," she replied.

While Rose sat with Patrick in the Marconis' parlor, the aroma of sizzling garlic reached them from the kitchen. She was about to rise and help Elena prepare dinner when a strange sensation washed over her. She put a hand to her temple.

Come to the theater district, a voice commanded. *Bring Patrick with you.*

"What on earth?" she said sharply.

Patrick grasped her hand. "What's wrong?

Do as I say, Rose.

"There is it again," she cried.

"What?" Patrick look perplexed.

Rose quickly shook her head. He wouldn't believe she'd heard a voice, so she decided not to tell him. While Patrick sat there studying her face, an internal war pulled her in opposite directions. She wanted to see Drago's show, but she knew it might be dangerous. Yet, in the end, the stronger force got the upper hand.

"Patrick, since you're always saying you'd like to take me out, I've changed my mind," she broached the subject as best she could.

Confusion shadowed his face.

"Tonight I'd like you to escort me to the magic show Olivia and I attended on my birthday."

His eyes flashed with displeasure. "You mean Dragomir Starkov's show . . . the one you lied to everyone about attending?"

"Yes," Rose replied. "I want you to see that he's no crackpot."

He dropped her hand and stood. Obviously frustrated, he began pacing the length of the room in long strides. "I don't understand. What is it about this magician you find so enthralling?"

Now it was her turn to look flustered. "I don't find *him* enthralling. I simply enjoy watching his fascinating illusions." The look on Patrick's face, however, told her that he wasn't buying her story. She decided to try a different approach. "You're clever, Patrick. Perhaps you'll be able to come up with a good explanation for the tricks."

He ran a hand through his hair. "You're missing the point, Rose. I have no interest in figuring out any of Starkov's cheap tricks. I'm a skeptic when it comes to magic. I don't believe in anything that I cannot see, hear, touch, taste, or smell. To me, nothing is real until it's actually proven to be."

Rose knitted her brow. Patrick was no fun at all. Besides, she *must* see the show tonight. If Drago was trying to contact her, she knew her attendance was of the utmost importance. "What do you have against magicians?"

He sighed as he sat next to her. "I don't have anything *against* magicians. My suspicious nature is rearing its head."

Rose folded her hands in her lap, her eyes downcast. "I suppose that's what makes you such a good police officer."

"Maybe." Patrick seemed to be buying into her flattery. "Look. I did a background search on Dragomir Starkov. *There is no record of him anywhere.* No registration of him entering Ellis Island and no record of him residing anywhere previously."

"He isn't a ghost." She laughed.

"But don't you find his ghost-like existence disturbing?"

"Some people want to make a fresh start. Maybe Drago changed his name in the process."

"Drago? You two are on a first-name basis, are you?"

Rose softened her expression. "You have nothing to be jealous about."

His face flushed. "Rumor has it that this mysterious illusionist is in league with the devil."

Her lungs hitched at the suggestion. Had the forces of black magic given Drago his seductive powers? She couldn't fathom it.

"For heaven's sake," she said. "The Salem witch hunts have been over for centuries. Dragomir Starkov is a very talented magician. That's all. And frankly I believe your ignorance is rearing its head along with your suspicions."

"Do you?" he asked sourly. "How?"

"By speaking of things you haven't seen first-hand."

She knew from Patrick's expression that she'd made a good point.

"Very well," he conceded. "I'll take that as a challenge. I'll accompany you to the show, then we can discuss Starkov's viability."

Olivia rushed into the room. "Two tickets just arrived."

"Tickets?" Patrick echoed.

"Yes, a messenger handed me these." She subsequently passed them to Patrick.

His face drained of color. "What the hell? They're for Dragomir the Magnificent's eight o'clock performance at the Sunshine Theater."

Rose's heart beat to an insane rhythm.

"How did he know we wanted to go?" Patrick clenched his jaw.

"Magic," she replied softly.

Patrick and Rose said goodbye to the Marconis before departing for the auditorium. The windless, muggy night air pushed at them before they found themselves inside the Sunshine Theater. Patrons droned on excitedly about Drago's astounding talents as Patrick located their seats in the second row. Stepping aside, he allowed Rose to shuffle across to seats B7 and B8.

Just before the curtain rose, Patrick glanced around. "All of these people are obviously under this man's spell, just like you."

A rousing overture signaled the start of the show, so Rose gave him a "Shh." The heavy, burgundy curtains parted with a gentle sway and an empty stage was revealed. Just then, a familiar voice sounded from the rear of the theater.

Rose turned in her seat to see Drago moving gracefully down the center aisle. The audience gasped—then erupted into a chorus of confused murmurs.

"Ladies and gentleman, my name is Dragomir Starkov, better known as Dragomir the Magnificent. I'm beginning my show this way to prove an important point. We, as humans, should never expect the expected. Rather, we should free our minds and open them up to the possibility of *what can be.* Trust me. It makes for a more satisfying life."

Once he reached the barrier of the stage, Drago trotted up the side staircase with tantalizing elegance. As she watched him, Rose couldn't help but notice how his muscular legs flexed beneath his snug-fitting trousers and how the cut of his jacket emphasized his wide shoulders.

He made a very attractive figure on stage.

She glanced at Patrick to gather his impression of Drago—only to see him glowering.

"Why doesn't he just get on with it?" He hissed without taking his eyes off the stage.

"It's all part of the theatrical anticipation," she whispered, "to prolong the wonderment of what he'll do next."

Patrick crossed his arms defiantly and watched the majority of the show with a scowl. When it came time for Drago's final illusion, he looked as if he couldn't wait to go home.

"Only one more trick," Rose said gently.

"Ladies and gentleman," Drago announced, "My lovely assistant, Katherine, will now wheel in the apparatus I require for my final illusion. This is a trick I haven't practiced frequently, but I assure you it's perfectly safe. You'll know what I mean once you witness it."

He did a tiny bow toward the crowd then turned his attention to Katherine. She positioned the twelve foot high, draped apparatus just behind him. With the flourish of a professional, Katherine whipped the red drape off the structure. Rose gasped. It was the guillotine she'd seen in Drago's workshop!

"Please don't ask me or Patrick to volunteer," she murmured under her breath. But it was too late. Drago had already singled Patrick out. "You, sir. Would you be so kind as to join me onstage?"

In response, Patrick pointed a finger toward himself and mouthed the word: "Me?"

"Yes, you. The man in the seersucker jacket. I believe your name is Patrick O'Leary. Is that right?"

Patrick nodded, then looked at Rose. "I'm going to prove this fellow is a fraud."

Finding herself speechless, Rose watched him hasten up the steps and take a spot next to Drago.

"Thank you for participating, Mr. O'Leary," Drago said. "That is your name, isn't it?"

Mouth agape, Patrick nodded.

Without wasting any more time, Katherine bound Patrick's hands with a rope while Drago explained the stages of the trick for the audience's benefit.

"As you can plainly see, Katherine is incapacitating Mr. O'Leary. His head will then be placed inside the guillotine. You must remember that the device was, and still is, the only official method of execution in France. Personally, I view it as the ultimate death machine. Rulers such as King Louis XVI and his beautiful wife, Queen Marie Antoinette, lost their heads to its razor sharp blade in 1793."

Drago paused as he checked the rope's knot. He nodded with approval. "And we can only wonder, what were those unfortunate royals thinking as they marched to their deaths? Did their entire lives flash before them? Did their regrets burn at their souls—too late to undo?" He paused. "Maestro, a little marching music for Mr. O'Leary."

A solemn drum roll ensued. Wide-eyed, Patrick moved behind the frame of the guillotine at Drago's instruction. A moment later, he was seated straddle-style over its narrow bench. Katherine helped maneuver his head into a nestled position.

Rose glanced at the blade suspended above him. The way it caught the light sent her stomach into a roil. What was about to happen?

Common sense told her there was no such thing as real magic. Yet her entire body hummed with fright.

The crowd remained on edge as a transparent screen descended over the stage, leaving the three people behind it in shadowy outlines. Drago, now garbed in a black executioner's mask, grasped the rope that governed the rise and fall of the blade. Rose went into full-panic mode. Would Patrick be harmed—or even killed? Should she leap out of her seat and stop the trick?

The dangerous obsession she'd witnessed in Drago's eyes made her think he was capable of violence.

Before she could stand up and protest, Drago leaned over and said something to Patrick. Then, with a wild slicing noise, the blade dropped to meet its cruel ending point. Screams filtered through the crowd as what appeared to be a head rolled off and fell to the floor. The body it had been attached to was gone!

The buffering screen lifted. Drago strode forward, grasping a head of lettuce. He removed the executioner's mask, then raised the round object above his head. In response, the crowd exploded in applause.

"Thank you, ladies and gentleman," he said, as a sly smile spread across his face. "Are you wondering what happened to our brave Mr. O'Leary? If the usher at portal five will open the door to the lobby, you'll see that he's perfectly intact."

The usher, looking as surprised as anyone, pushed the door open. In stepped Patrick. Face flushed with rage, he raced forward, holding his neck with one hand "You bastard!" The severed rope hung from his wrist. "How dare you threaten me, then scare me out of my wits!"

Before anyone had the chance to stop him, Patrick leapt onstage and began pummeling Drago to the ground.

"Patrick!" Rose bolted out of her seat and charged up the staircase. The two men at center stage were in the middle of a violent brawl—and no one was making a move to stop them. "Somebody get the police!" she called out.

Falling to her knees, Rose tried to pry Patrick off Drago. But it was no use.

As the men rolled about with ruthless ferocity, blood began to fly. Rose stepped out of the way. Praying that the brawl would stop soon, she clutched her chest. Luckily, an officer bounded up the main aisle and blew his whistle.

"What's goin' on 'ere?" the cop asked in an Irish accent. When he reached the stage, he halted. "Is that you, young O'Leary?"

"Yes, it's Patrick!" Rose responded. "Stop them, officer!"

"See 'ere, ya two maniacs. Stop yer fightin' or I'll arrest ya both." The red-faced officer managed to pry Patrick away from Drago.

When the enemies stood apart, they wiped the blood from their lips with the backs of their hands.

"Who started this nonsense?" the policeman asked.

Patrick remained silent. Drago, on the other hand, pointed at his opponent, his breath too ragged to speak.

"Is it true?"

Ashamed, Patrick hung his perspiration-soaked head. But then he seemed to get his second wind. "This lunatic nearly killed me. And he has every intention of stealing my girl away!" He started at Drago again with clenched fists.

"Hold on there, young man. Let's get some fresh air, shall we?" The policeman didn't wait for an answer, but took Patrick by the jacket lapel and started to yank him away.

The audience remained fixated in their seats, entertained as much by the brawl as they had been by the magic.

"Rose," Patrick called over his shoulder, "let's go."

She stood frozen for a moment. *What should I do?*

She longed to comfort Drago and Patrick both, but her need to be with Drago overshadowed everything else. She stared at him. His smoldering stare bore into her soul, speaking a thousand words, though he never opened his mouth.

"I'm staying," she murmured in Patrick's direction.

"You're what? Rose, you don't know what that bastard said to me just before he pretended to kill me!"

The officer rolled his eyes and whisked Patrick out of sight. Hushed words of surprise and criticism followed them as the crowd began to filter out of the theater as well.

Now that she was alone with Drago, Rose moved to him. "Are you all right?" She placed a hand to his bruised and battered face. Her eyes welled with tears. "I need to know what you said to Patrick."

He said nothing. Instead, he took her hand and pressed it to his swollen lips. "Come with me," he whispered with passion and urgency.

CHAPTER 12

A slew of reporters that hadn't been allowed in until then attempted to get close to the stage. In the meantime, four ushers barred the side staircases.

As Drago dodged the camera flashes, he shielded his face with his hand and grimaced. Racing into the wings with Rose alongside him, he shouted, "Get their film, Archibald!"

Ducking questions from Katherine and avoiding murmurs from the stage crew, who claimed that the guillotine trick was nothing like it'd been rehearsed, Drago managed to escape with Rose out the side door.

The alley was filled with shadows and the smell of rancid trash but, thankfully, it was void of people. Drago grasped Rose's hand tightly and directed her around the corner. They spotted a throng of reporters and on-lookers at the front of the theater, lying in wait.

"I grant interviews to reporters on one condition," Drago said darkly. "No photographs." He pulled Rose in the opposite direction from the crowd. "We'll go to my apartment."

Had Rose lost her mind? She'd dragged Patrick to the theater tonight only to snub him in public. The reality of it convinced her that she had no control over her actions.

She wouldn't be surprised if Patrick never spoke to her again. And to make matters worse, she was in the center of Drago's media frenzy.

It took five minutes for them to reach the sanctity of Drago's apartment building. Never before had Rose been so happy to see a common redbrick structure with tin molding. Still grasping Drago's hand tightly, she followed him up a flight of stairs to apartment 9G.

After Drago slipped his key into the lock, she stepped inside and gathered her collar about her throat. She'd never been alone with a man inside his home and knew nothing about how to behave. Drago seemed to sense her unease. He offered her a smile as he removed his jacket with slow, pain-filled motions.

"Excuse me while I tend to this gash under my eye. Make yourself comfortable on the divan."

Rose nodded, but she was too nervous to sit down. She began to pace around the sparsely furnished flat. The spotlessly clean parlor spilled into a tiny kitchen, complete with an icebox and a coal-burning stove.

Curious as to Drago's likes and dislikes in food, she meandered to the kitchen's cabinets and took the opportunity to peek inside. They were completely bare!

Isn't that just like a bachelor? At least she assumed it was.

She settled on the upholstered divan. Instead of displaying personal photos, the walls of the apartment were covered in framed marquee posters of Drago's shows.

Does Drago have any family or friends? And why is this place darkened by drapes of velvety black? It seemed an odd color for curtains.

Unable to relax, Rose's mind harkened to the background check Patrick had ordered for Drago. There was no doubt he was mysterious—and unfortunately, the impersonal apartment offered no further insight about his past.

Patrick. Rose knew she'd broken his heart tonight. Would he ever forgive her?

With trembling fingers, she removed her hat and fidgeted with the drawstrings of her handbag. It was infernally hot inside the apartment and the ridiculous layers she was wearing were unnecessary. Deciding she couldn't stand the stifling fitted jacket and three-tiered jabot any longer, she removed them just as Drago re-entered the room.

His eyes gleamed at the fact that she was removing her clothing.

In turn, Rose's eyes zeroed in on his swollen lips and the blood-soaked bandage that topped his cheek.

"Your friend packs a powerful punch," he said as he sat next to her.

"You made him furious. What did you say to him onstage—before the guillotine's blade fell?"

Drago shrugged, sending stray pieces of brown hair to his cheekbones. "It was nothing. Your suitor despised me from the moment he set eyes on me, so I played with him a little."

"That wasn't very nice." She was sure there was fire in her eyes.

"I know, and I'm sorry." He exhaled. "I'm just glad you chose to come with me and not go with Patrick."

A wave of rage rose inside her. "Chose you? Do you think I am here of my own free will?"

Surprise lit Drago's face. "What are you talking about?"

"Don't play dumb with me. You hypnotized me—and spoke to me from far away."

"Why do you think that?"

"Don't try and deny it."

"You're upset—"

"Nothing but unpleasantness has happened since I met you. I'm overwhelmed by this sense that I have no control over my actions. And the rift you've caused between me and Patrick is horrendous. It's all because of my attraction to you—"

His eyes narrowed. "You're attracted to me?"

"Couldn't you tell by our kiss?" She buried her face in her hands and started to sob.

Gently, he put an arm around her and allowed her to cry for a long while.

After she stopped, she looked at him somberly. "You don't understand. You're all I think about."

"Does that mean you'd rather be with me than Patrick?"

"Yes," she said quietly.

"I think that's what's infuriating Patrick the most."

"I hope he'll forgive me for hurting him," she replied. "But I need to know. Am I under some sort of trance, Drago? One you are responsible for?"

He spread his hands wide. "You are an intelligent woman. I believe you'll figure it out."

"Enough riddles!" she exploded. "I want the truth. Did you hypnotize me into falling in love with you?"

Happiness washed over his face. "You're in love with me?"

"You're so exasperating!" She began to cry all over again. "Yes, I am. But I don't know if my feelings for you are *real*."

With a slow, sultry motion, Drago leaned in and began to kiss away her hot tears. "Your feelings are very real, Rose."

Her eyelids grew heavy and her eyes fluttered shut against his touch.

"They're real because I love you in return. And I'll never let you go."

"You still haven't given me an answer," she said hoarsely.

"If I did hypnotize you, do you want me to lift my spell?"

His warmth enveloped her—and because she knew deep down that she would never feel alive without him, all she could do was answer honestly. "No."

Apparently, that was what he needed to hear. Urging her head upward, he covered her mouth with his. Body aflame, she parted her lips and let his tongue glide forward. Its sweet taste intoxicated her—and as his hand dropped from the curve of her neck to the roundness of her breast, she pressed against it to make his grasp firmer.

In a single scoop, Drago lifted her off the divan and carried her into his bedroom. After he laid her on the bed, he lowered the gas lamp's flame to a dim glow. Then he stood to remove his shirt and when he joined her on the mattress, another surge of desire shot through her.

"My rosebud. I want you more than any other woman I've ever known. Without you, food has no taste, music holds no gaiety, and life has no meaning. Will you let me show you how much I love you?"

She could only whimper a response. A slip of air separated them and she could smell his masculine scent sweep forward. Reeling with anxiousness, she reached for him and he caressed her lips with his again. Rose put a hand to the angle of his jaw and felt it clench and unclench as his experienced tongue rolled in and out of her mouth.

She never knew a kiss could offer so much satisfaction. What carnal delights awaited her when she was finally naked in Drago's arms?

Naked? My God! Reality rushed over her. What on earth was she doing in this apartment, with this man who was so much older and more experienced than she?

As if he'd read her thoughts, Drago said. "Don't worry, Rose. This will be our little secret."

Before she knew it, he was unbuttoning her lace blouse. As his deft fingers moved over the fabric, he continued to devour her with hot kisses. Meanwhile, Rose's desire for him made her throw her cares to the wind, fueling her willingness.

That sense of empowerment stopped her from freezing with self-consciousness when he exposed her breast.

"Christ," he said gruffly at the sight. "You're so damned beautiful."

She blushed and looked away.

"As you've guessed by now, I'm a bad man," he murmured, just as gruffly. "A man who wants to make love to you hotly. Wickedly."

The words couldn't have enflamed Rose more. As he took her peach-colored nipple in his mouth and teased it with his tongue, she suspected that she'd lose her virginity this very day. And she could think of nothing more pleasurable.

She stared at Drago's face as he worked his magic on her flesh. His lips were moist and supple and his dark skin glimmered in the light.

Releasing his mouth from her nipple, Drago hungrily eased her other breast free of the thin camisole. Then, with a flick of his fingers across both nipples, he made them rise. The sight caused him to moan louder. And by gathering both of her breasts in one hand, he was able to lap his tongue back and forth over her stiff buds while she writhed beneath him anxiously.

After a moment, he glanced up at her and she felt herself melt under his smoldering gaze. "Don't be nervous, Rose," he urged. "I won't hurt you."

When he slid one hand beneath the folds of her skirt, he found the creaminess between her thighs. She, in turn, felt his thick staff surge forward against her leg. Her heart thundered in her chest but she didn't dare look down at the bulge in his trousers. She was inexperienced, to say the least, but with this princely Romanian, she was more than eager to learn.

His nostrils flared with passion as he stroked the tops of her thighs. "My sweet. I won't break the barrier of your chastity, but I want to touch you . . ." After he caressed the silkiness of her blonde fleece, his fingers got completely lost in her flow of passion.

Rose sucked in a breath. His touch felt incredibly sinful. *Should I stop him?*

In reality, that was the last thing she wanted to do. Refusing to think about what a wayward girl she was being, she closed her eyes. Drago continued to fondle her damp folds and she heard him moan again.

"You're not ready to taint." His gravelly voice was at her ear. "But when you are, I hope you'll give yourself to me willingly. It'll be a night you won't forget."

Rose gulped with excitement. The length of his stone-hard penis protruded against her leg again. As she tried to swallow away a sense of fright, she avoided looking down. *That* was going to fit inside her someday?

"You can touch me too, if you'd like," he said.

Before she could respond, Drago reached for her hand. On its journey to the mysterious region of his groin, her hand brushed over the layer of hair on his chest and the rise of his chiseled pectoral muscles. Still grasping her fingers, Drago guided her reach to his thick cock and instructed her as to how to stroke it to a full charge, through his trousers.

"There . . ." his breath quickened.

The experience overwhelmed Rose. Her eyes grew wide—and she wondered if she was doing it all correctly. Fortunately, she didn't have to wonder long, thanks to Drago's intense grunts.

When it was apparent that he couldn't stand the anticipation any longer, he rolled his body on top of hers and kissed her fully on the mouth. The kiss—hot enough to ignite the tiniest speck of gunpowder—kindled their connection even more. Drago rocked his staff forward, and when he pressed it against her center, Rose yearned to feel it between her bare thighs.

"Nothing could bring me greater pleasure than claiming you," he said in a primal tone. "You'll let me know when you're ready, won't you?"

Driven by lust, she was about to scream out, "Now! I'm ready now!" when a knock at the door rudely interrupted them.

"What the devil?" Drago barked.

"Mr. Starkov?" A woman's voice reached them in the bedroom.

"Jesus. It's my landlady," he told Rose. "Wait here."

Drago answered the door without a shirt. "What can I do for you, Mrs. Kravitz?"

"Mr. Starkov. Pardon the intrusion, but we have a problem. A crowd has gathered at the front stoop of the building. Reporters are strewn all over the place, chanting your name. I was tempted to go out in my bathrobe to give them a piece of my mind but . . ."

Drago hadn't unlocked the chain attached to the wall, but had cracked the door open a bit so Mrs. Kravitz could see part of him. "No need to do that. I'll take care of the situation."

The elderly busybody made no move to leave. Instead, she seemed perfectly content to stare at the patch of his bare chest visible through the door's opening. "Of course, when Stanley was alive," she rattled on, "I would have sent him to take care of such matters."

"Yes. Please go back to sleep, Mrs. Kravitz."

She stood there.

"Good night, madam."

"Oh!" She gathered the collar of her chenille robe around her wrinkled neck. "Then good night to you."

Before Drago made his way back to the bedroom, Rose studied the items on his bedside table. There was a beautiful, golden bracelet bearing colorful Egyptian designs and a worn, foreign coin. *How strange.* She was tempted to pick up the coin, but she busied herself with ordering her appearance instead.

When Drago returned, his foul look scared her.

"Did you hear that?" he thundered. "Those vultures discovered where I live!"

"Vultures?" she echoed.

"Reporters."

"I should go, Drago," she said as she rose off the bed.

"I guess you should, but we need to get you out of here without being noticed. We don't want to see your face in the morning news-paper."

No, we don't. The backlash Rose received after seeing Drago's first show was bad enough. Now she wanted to avoid further reproof.

She watched him pull on his shirt and button it before she moved to the window. Brushing aside the dark curtain she said, "There they are."

She craned her neck to see down to the front stoop of the building. It was covered by a swarm of enthusiastic reporters. "Obviously I can't leave the way I came in," she remarked. "Where should I go?"

Drago rolled up his shirtsleeves and planted a quick peck on her cheek. "Follow me. I have an idea."

Before leaving the tenement, Rose grabbed her belongings and took one last look around. *Will I ever have the chance to be alone with Drago here again?* If he could bend the path of fate—as he already proved he could—somehow he'd ensure it.

Stepping into the hallway, he led her around the corner. Without speaking, they treaded through another narrow corridor until they reached a dumbwaiter meant for transporting groceries and garbage.

"Only one of us can go up to the roof in this small lift," he said.

"Why can't I take the stairs?"

"You might encounter a reporter, or worse, Mrs. Kravitz."

"Will it hold my weight?" Her stomach was a bundle of nerves.

"I think so."

That wasn't what she wanted to hear.

Riding the lift up to the roof would be possible even though Rose possessed a debilitating sense of vertigo. Whenever she looked down from a high distance the phobia immediately kicked in and she became paralyzed with fear.

Before she knew it, she was being encouraged into the contraption by Drago's strong grip. He smiled and wrapped the heavy cords around his hands. "Don't worry. I'll distract the crowd somehow. In the meantime, you need to find your way down the back fire escape, all right?"

"I can't, Drago. I'm afraid of heights."

He kissed her swiftly. "You must. I promise we'll see each other again very soon."

She shot him a feeble smile as he pulled on the ropes. Seconds later, he disappeared from view. Squeezing her eyes shut, Rose jostled around in the rancid-smelling dumbwaiter for six more stories. She held her breath until it came to an abrupt stop on the roof level, where she was able to step out into the warm night air.

Horrified, she inched to the edge of the building, her heart racing. Daring to look down, she discovered that the crowd had developed into an angry mob.

"Drago! Drago!" they chanted impatiently.

She had no idea how Drago intended to break up the chaotic scene, but she was determined to find out.

Lifting her skirts, she serpentined around crates and sun chairs to reach the opposite side of the rooftop. Just as Drago promised, a flight of wrought iron stairs suspended in layers led to the street below. Fear gripped her as she placed one foot on the first step. The fire escape wobbled in and out of view surreally. Rose knew the sensation was part of her vertigo, but the knowledge didn't help dispel her fright.

She glanced about wildly. There wasn't an alternate way down.

Telling herself she could do it, that she *had* to climb down the fire escape, she grabbed the handrail. After closing her eyes, she felt around for the edge of the step with her toes. *There!* She'd taken her first step down.

Opening her eyes, she began her descent. When she refused to look below her, she found it easier. After what felt like an eternity, she managed to reach the dark alley. The achievement filled her with pride.

Once her legs stopped trembling, she ducked around a trash bin and peered at the crowd of reporters. They'd quieted. Moonlight bathed their faces as they craned their necks upward. *What on earth are they looking at?*

Unnoticed, Rose inched around the building's corner and glanced up, too. High above the street lamp was a man suspended in space. Squinting her eyes, she realized the man was Drago—and that he was walking between his apartment building and another tenement on a laundry line!

Will he fall and hurt himself?

As he stepped over pieces of brightly colored clothing that flapped in the evening breeze, Rose's heart leapt. *He's nine stories above the ground*...

Miraculously, Drago never faltered. When he reached the other building, he looked down at the crowd with a mischievous grin. He even caught Rose's eye and held it for a moment.

An instant later, he disappeared before everyone's eyes—and a dove took his place.

CHAPTER 13

The next morning, the entire city was abuzz about Dragomir Starkov's disappearing act.

"I was right there," Richard Bellum attested as he stood by Rose's tiny newsroom desk. "For the life of me, I can't explain how Starkov vanished from the clothesline!"

Rose nodded. She was astounded too, but not to the same degree as Richard. The more time she spent around Drago, the more convinced she was that he was capable of anything.

She watched Richard pace before her. She'd only been working with him for a short while, but she suspected that she could learn a lot from him. He was hungry for the truth, just like her. But in Drago's case, Bellum's hunger made him the most audacious kind of reporter.

"What exactly did you see yesterday?" she played along.

Richard frowned. "Dragomir Starkov disappeared right before my eyes. And the dove . . . I'm assuming he had someone release it from the rooftop, but I can't be sure."

Drago's magic was really beginning to bridge the gap between illusion and reality. Nobody could explain it. She'd mentioned the Salem witch trials to Patrick. *Isn't this how they started?*

Her blood chilled at the thought.

"It was the damnedest thing I ever saw!" Richard pounded his fist on the desk. "That's what makes Starkov's challenge all the more maddening."

"Challenge?"

"You know, the tagline he puts on every marquee."

Rose thought back to what she'd read on Drago's poster: *I have one secret that explains everything I do. I challenge you to discover what it is.*

The proposition was excellent publicity, but it was also driving a lot of people to frustration.

"Are you determined to find out all his secrets?" Rose asked Richard. She wanted to know how far he'd take his curiosity.

"Damn right, I am," he replied. "Follow me. I want to show you something."

Rose followed him across the newsroom to his office. After yanking on his desk drawer, he pulled out a folder bearing past stories *The Gotham Times* had published. "The monster that attacked the three Coney Island women left the first two comatose. Then it literally crushed the third girl's lungs and all of her bones."

"What those women suffered was horrible," she remarked as she scoured the articles he'd handed to her. "But how do their attacks correlate with Drago?"

Richard heaved out a breath. "I think those women had some sort of spell woven around them. Some kind of *magician's* spell. Maybe this demon wanted to kill the first two women, but was interrupted. Furthermore, this demon was seen at Coney Island. A ten-year-old boy claims he witnessed the monster turn into a *bird*."

Rose remembered reading about it at the time. However, she'd chalked up the child's claim to his imagination. But now that Drago may have turned himself into a bird . . .

"The kid didn't say what kind of bird the demon morphed into. Maybe it was a *dove*," Richard said, his dark eyes flashing.

"Are you insinuating that Drago was involved in these attacks?"

"If someone puts two and two together, it only makes sense," he insisted.

She crossed her arms. "I don't believe it."

"Look," he said, stepping forward. She noticed that Richard would have been a handsome man except for the army of pockmarks that marred his cheeks. "The attacks started a few months after Starkov moved to New York City."

"There is a record of him coming here?" she asked. "I thought there was no documentation at Ellis Island."

"There's no formal documentation, but I've tracked Drago's past myself. The only thing I managed to pinpoint is the year he began working at Coney Island."

"That's not enough proof."

Richard paused. "But it's interesting to know the police consider Dragomir Starkov suspicious enough to investigate, too. Isn't it?"

"With all due respect"—Rose crossed her arms—"I think you're grasping at straws. Besides, Drago would never hurt anyone."

"No?" Richard replied. "He pummeled your boyfriend into a bloody mess last night."

She shot him a contemptuous look. "They both walked away alive."

Ignoring the comment, Richard slid into the chair at his desk and hoisted his feet up.

"And let me make it clear," she said. "Patrick is not my beau."

Leaning back, her boss smiled smugly. "Do I sense an attraction to this Romanian mystery man instead?"

"No," she stammered. *Either way, it's none of your business.*

"If you're falling for him," Richard urged, "I suggest you end your relationship right away. This Starkov fellow is sinister, even dangerous. You'd be wise to stay away."

I can't stay away.

When she didn't respond, Richard stared at her again. "Still unwilling to heed my warnings? Let me show you something else. Something that will convince you Dragomir Starkov is a man to be feared."

Bellum took her by the arm and guided her out of his office. Down the hall they went, to the photo lab of the newspaper. Once they entered it, he reached into a cabinet and withdrew a large envelope. "I developed this myself," he said as he thrust a hand inside the envelope. "Afterward, I was so shocked that I hid this photo away until I can decide what to do with it."

A nervous knot formed in Rose's stomach.

"Before I reveal my little secret," Richard said, "let me tell you that during the fanfare of Starkov's tightrope act on the laundry line, the police arrived—as did Starkov's manager. Starkov must have some members of the NYPD wrapped around his fingers because Archibald McMillan confiscated all the reporters' film. Except mine. I fled before he saw me."

Slowly, Richard twisted the photo around so that Rose could view it. When she looked at it, her eyes fluttered shut in a panic. Stammering something inaudible, she put a shaking hand to her mouth. Richard helped her into a chair and brought her a glass of water.

"I can't believe it," she said. "I just can't believe *he's not there.*"

"I took the photo through the window of a neighboring building—while Starkov hovered over the street on the laundry line."

Rose glanced at the photo again. The line was sagging from somebody's weight, but there was no magician in sight. "There has to be some logical explanation for this," she finally said as she sipped the water. "Maybe the wind . . ."

"Not possible. I'm sure it's one of Starkov's tricks, but I can't figure it out."

Rose pushed herself out of the chair and handed Richard the empty glass. "Have you shown this to anyone else?"

"No."

"Please don't. We need time to contemplate what to do with it."

"Look, Rose. I know you and Starkov are closer than you're admitting. I'm sure you want to protect him."

She nodded.

"But there is no 'we' in this decision. I'm your boss and I want you to get close enough to him to blow this whole thing wide open."

She recoiled in disgust. "You want me to *spy* on him?"

"If you want to call it that." He put a finger under his collar and tugged.

"I won't do it."

"I think you will." His eyes narrowed. "Because it will be your first, official reporting job."

CHAPTER 14

Rose hesitated outside the Marconi home. Her resentment for Richard built as she grasped the iron newel on the front railing. Her boss wanted her to spy on Drago, but she hadn't given him an answer yet.

"I can always quit the newspaper," she'd said before she stormed back to her small desk and pretended to work.

Now, looking up at the façade of the Marconis' brownstone, a chill filtered through her. *Patrick is here. I can feel it.* He was the last person she wanted to see, but she knew she had to.

Just how angry would he be at her decision to leave the theater with Drago last night, instead of him?

With a dry lump in her throat, she entered the house and made her way to the front parlor. Patrick was standing by the window. He had his back to her, while Anthony was reclining on the sofa. The breadth of Patrick's shoulders emphasized his narrow waist and his blond hair edged attractively over his collar, but the sight of him didn't charm her today as it usually did.

She greeted him.

"Rose." He wheeled around and revealed a battered face awash with rage and frustration. "As you can see, Starkov broke my jaw last night! I just got out of the hospital—and now you owe me an explanation!"

When he began to take quick strides toward her, she became afraid of him—more afraid than she'd ever been of Drago. But she didn't show it. They stood practically nose-to-nose while Patrick's moss-green eyes blazed with indignation and the massive bruises he'd received from Drago deepened in color.

"Anthony told me you didn't come home until late last night."

"Thanks, Anthony," she muttered angrily.

"What were you doing with that crackpot late into the night?" Patrick asked. His voice sounded strange—and then Rose realized that the right side of his jaw was wired shut.

"I wasn't doing anything with him," Rose said. She wasn't about to tell him they had been in the throes of passion.

"Anthony said you smelled of cologne when you returned. You were with *him*."

She shot Anthony an enraged look. "It's none of your business."

Her adoptive brother surged to his feet. "I was worried about you, Rose. What were you thinking? Going about New York City with no chaperone—with that lunatic?"

"It's none of your business," she repeated. "And I'm surprised at you, Anthony. You've become quite the snitch. Only police officers appreciate those."

"We've had our differences in the past," Anthony retorted. "But you know I care about you."

Rose flashed him a doubtful look.

"That's a low blow," he continued.

She made no reply.

"Rose. Just answer the question," Patrick urged. "Where did you go with Drago?"

She turned to him. "We had no choice but to run from the reporters. Drago has an aversion to the press."

Patrick's eyes seemed to sink back inside his head. "It doesn't matter where you went. The point is you're not to go with that sorcerer again."

"Sorcerer?" Rose asked stoically. "Aren't you being melodramatic, Patrick?"

"Have you seen the papers?" He cried. "The man vanished into thin air!"

"He says that all of his tricks can be explained."

"He's probably been feeding you a whole line of bullshit," Patrick brooded.

"Take that back!" she said.

"I'm sorry. But I don't want you to see him again!"

"You can't tell me what to do, Patrick."

"I'm concerned," he said as he moved closer. He tried to take her hand, but she retracted it. The action seemed to cause him pain.

"This conversation is over," she said.

Patrick continued to glower—and she realized she'd never seen him this mad.

"It's over when I say it's over," he said sternly.

She looked him directly in the eye. "You're not acting like yourself."

"I wonder why." Sarcasm edged his voice. "Maybe it's because I've been publicly humiliated—and refused by you, without being given a chance."

Guilt escalated inside her. They'd been friends for a long time and she hated to spoil that friendship, but she had no desire to be courted by him.

"Don't you care that Starkov hurt me last night?" Patrick shouted. "Fractured my jawbone?"

"Of course I do . . ." her tone softened.

"Dragomir Starkov pounded me like a madman, Rose!"

"You struck him first."

He winced at the truth.

"I'm sorry if I humiliated you," she said quickly. "I'm also sorry that you got hurt."

Anthony walked over and put a hand on his friend's shoulder. "Rose has apologized, mate. Let's go."

Patrick seemed to come to his senses. He stepped back. Tugging on his vest, he looked embarrassed as he ran a hand over his hair to smooth it. "I'm sorry too, Rose. I didn't mean to raise my voice. I just wanted to prove a point."

"I'm going to say this as kindly as I can. I don't care for you the way you care for me." Rose's eyes began to mist. "I'm going to return the necklace you gave me."

Her gaze switched to Anthony as she said, "I'll go to my bedroom and get it right now."

Turning on her heel, she heard Patrick throw something against the wall. She flinched from the loud crash but kept walking.

"You wouldn't be so loyal to Dragomir Starkov if you heard what he said to me during his magic show!" he yelled behind her.

Shoulders tensed, Rose tried to shut the door before she heard another word. But she caught, "Drago claimed you'd never be mine! Even if he had to murder someone and take you from this world to do it!"

Rose was horrified at the words. As she rode a streetcar to the Sunshine Theater, she became more and more afraid. Had Drago really threatened Patrick that way? *Does he actually mean to kill Patrick—and then me?*

She gave her hat a straightening. *I won't leave until I get the truth.*

The streetcar clattered and rumbled while a conversation between a middle-aged man and woman snagged her attention.

"I can't believe what the papers are saying about that *magician*." The woman folded her hands primly in her lap.

"What magician?" the man asked.

"Dragomir Starkov."

"I've heard of Harry Houdini, but I haven't heard of him."

"Houdini, while he's talented, is merely an escape artist," the woman, who Rose presumed was the man's wife, replied with an air of importance. "On the other hand, Dragomir Starkov has talents only the devil could deal out. He wills animals back to life and transports himself to a different location right on stage. He even disappears into thin air."

"Unfortunately, Josephine"—the man patted her chubby arm—"the press sensationalizes everything."

Josephine, a solid woman with frizzy red hair, held up a copy of *The Gotham Times* and shook it. "My dear husband, it says right here that Starkov vanished off a clothesline as though he'd never been there. If you're such a genius, tell me how he did it."

Hemming and hawing, the man shrugged. "Must have been mirrors, I'd say."

"Mirrors, Murray? Nine stories up?" The woman folded her beefy arms across her bosom.

"I dunno. It's a mystery."

Josephine pointed to the newspaper again. "Apparently, Dragomir the Magnificent has been wooing a young woman. That girl must be crazy! If I were her, I'd be terrified. One argument and she might go up in a puff of smoke."

The couple laughed while Rose slouched in her seat. *I'm not crazy. I'm being controlled by the amulet Drago gave me.*

The streetcar stopped in front of the theater. Rose jumped off and knocked on the side door. When there was no answer, she remembered what Drago told her about the time he spent in the basement workshop.

"I come here every day—right before my show."

Rose glanced at her pin watch. It was six-thirty. She knew he was here.

Someone who looked like a member of the stage crew exited the building. Exhaling with relief, she stopped the door with her foot and hastened inside. Cheeks flaming, she descended the staircase to the basement—where the sounds of tinkering and Drago swearing under his breath filled the air.

Rose entered the workshop, but Drago didn't seem to notice her. When he finally swiveled around, his mouth quirked with surprise and concern.

"Rose," he greeted. "What are you doing here?"

"I came to discuss something with you."

He stalked her way and her pulse thumped wildly. Under his dark gaze, it would be so easy to fall into his arms. But what was it he'd said inside his apartment? *"I'm a bad man."*

Gad. She couldn't believe how the statement flushed desire through her, even now. Still, she needn't melt like ice cream on a hundred-degree day. It was important to find out why Drago had threatened Patrick.

"You really shouldn't be here," he said gently.

"I've been doing a lot of things I shouldn't lately," Rose admitted. "Such as trusting you."

He raised an eyebrow. "That hurt." After a moment he said, "Did you see any reporters outside?"

"Forget the reporters, Drago. They seem to come with the territory." She paused. "If they want to learn something, nothing will stop them."

His brows drew together. "Perhaps." Then he smiled. It was the same sultry, mysterious smile that made her go weak at the knees. "All right. Now that you're here, discuss away."

She turned away from him and walked around the workshop. "I know you're preparing for tonight's show, but you never answered my question."

"What question?"

"I want to know what you said to Patrick onstage."

She stole a look over her shoulder. Drago remained silent as he ran his hands through his hair.

"Please tell me," she said softly.

As they locked eyes, distress brought out the fine wrinkles across his forehead.

"You broke his jaw, Drago. The least you can do is admit the truth."

His frown deepened, but still he didn't answer her.

She went on. "Very well. I'll tell you what Patrick claimed you said."

Drago was listening intently.

"Apparently you said you'd do anything to keep me from him." She paused. "Even commit murder."

Drawing in a breath, Drago said, "He's right."

She gasped. "You can't mean it—"

"Come sit with me, Rose."

He indicated the stool. She sat. And after he pulled up a second stool, he reached for her hand across the worktop. "It's time I told you everything about the amulet you're wearing."

She tensed. The necklace was hidden beneath her dress. She hadn't taken it off since the night he'd given it to her.

"I have always wanted to get my hands on it. It possessed a dark history before it fell into the hands of a Romanian Gypsy tribe, a tribe that protected it for many years. Some of those Gypsies were my father's relatives, so I felt compelled to track the necklace down.

Once I did, I bought it from a private dealer. It's familial, powerful, and sentimental all at the same time."

"That explains why you had it," Rose said. "But why did you give it to me?"

"I wanted it to blend in with the other gifts I gave you."

"Blend in?"

"I didn't want you to question it."

"I've always suspected you used it to hypnotize me."

He nodded thoughtfully. "As I said, the necklace has a dark history. It also has the special abilities of a talisman. *The power to control and the power to re-direct someone's fate.*"

"What if I remove the necklace right now?" she asked.

He shook his head. "The spell it casts is permanent, even if you manage to take it off."

"Permanent?"

"If you must know, the amulet's hypnotic spell can only be lifted when I say it's time."

She locked eyes with him. "If this is true love between us, I don't need the necklace to want to be with you. You should lift your spell."

Drago jerked his head away. "Not yet. The amulet and its control are my way of protecting you."

"Protect me from what?"

"It's going to ensure that you do what I want."

"Which is?"

"Carry out an act I saw in a vision."

Her face flamed with frustration. "I don't understand."

"This has been overwhelming for you, Rose—and I don't want to scare you further."

"I can handle whatever it is. I'm twenty years old."

Drago returned his dark stare to hers. "About that. If Morvina resurfaces, you'll need all the protection you can get on your twenty-first birthday."

"You know my Aunt Morvina?" Her pulse accelerated.

"I know something about her."

Rose cocked a brow. "What, exactly?"

"That she is evil and heartless."

"*How* do you know, Drago?"

"Please don't ask me that."

She frowned and studied the tools that lay on top of the table. "Does the amulet fit in with the threat you made to Patrick?"

"I didn't mean that I will kill *him*."

"Who, then?" she asked.

"Morvina, if she comes close to you."

Rose squared her shoulders. She knew it was time to be brave and ask Drago everything. "What about the threat you made to take me from this world, if necessary. What did you mean by that?"

A heavy silence hung between them. Finally, Drago said, "Were people stunned by my disappearing act yesterday?"

"Yes," Rose said. "My boss is especially curious about it. He took a photo of you, but there is no trace of your image."

Urgency flashed in his eyes. "What has he done with this photo?"

"Nothing, yet."

Drago reached for her hand and gripped it. "You must get that photograph, Rose. It's of the utmost importance."

"I can't," she cried. "I saw Richard lock it up."

"Richard? Richard Bellum?"

"Yes."

"Christ! That man has been a thorn in my side for months. Even more reason for you to confiscate the photo." He paused. "I assume you've seen it?"

"Yes."

"And it startled you, right?"

"Yes."

Drago released her hand. The revealing glance he gave her made her blood freeze. "How do you know I didn't enact real magic on the laundry line?"

Stunned, the possibility of what he said came crashing down on her. "A . . . are you saying what I think you're saying?"

"My manager confiscated all of the reporters' film last night—except your boss's, apparently," he informed her. "We didn't see him take my photo."

Rose gripped her fingers tightly. "Why are you so worried about it?"

He sucked a breath. "If you must know, I don't show up in photographs—or mirrors."

She raised her hand to her mouth. "Are you some sort of ghost?"

"A ghost? No. I'm a warlock."

"Good God!"

Drago rose and paced before her. "I'm putting myself at risk by telling you this, but you'd have found out sooner or later."

Rose's nerves began to fray like the seams of an ancient garment.

" 'Warlock' is actually a weak term for what I am," he explained. "I'm a powerful lord of black magic. And if I desire, I can take you from the here and now into another lifetime."

The revelation tilted Rose's world off its axis. She'd always been fascinated with magic, but seeing it this close frightened her like nothing else. Shaken to the core, she asked, "Take me into another lifetime? You mean time travel?"

He nodded grimly.

Struggling to breathe, she fanned herself with her handbag. "I don't believe it."

"It's true," he said. "When a vision of Morvina came to me, I saw you in the same vision."

"That's how you know about my aunt—and my curse?"

He nodded solemnly.

Horrified, she murmured, "It explains all the birthday gifts . . . and why you want to protect me."

"I was a magician for many years in Romania," Drago explained. "And using my powers here in America was the only way to find you."

"Don't you mean it's the only way I would come to you?"

"Yes," he said quietly. "If you're under my wing, Morvina can't hurt you."

"I don't know who to be more afraid of."

"I'd never hurt you. I fell in love with you in my vision."

Denial and terror mingled inside her. She turned away. "I need time to process this."

He grimaced. "There's more. You need to know the details of the amulet, before you hear them from somebody else."

Without meeting his gaze, she braced herself.

"The necklace belonged to an Egyptian princess named Tousret. When Tousret took a lover named Amenhotep who was a priest from her court, the action sealed both of their fates. The Underworld God, Anubis, willed Tousret to kill Amenhotep. Then Anubis forced her to turn the knife on herself as punishment. Now any female who dons the necklace is doomed to murder her lover, then commit suicide."

"What?" Rose screeched. "How could you do this to me?" She leapt off the stool and made for the door.

Drago stopped her with a thrust of his arm against the portal. "A bracelet made by Amenhotep's fellow priests can neutralize the prophecy. Counteract the dark forces." He paused. "I have it."

The bracelet in his bedroom.

The information made her feel a little better, but not much. She tried to yank the door open, but the pressure of his hand was too strong.

"I know something about you, Rose. When we met, you secretly hoped my powers were real. Hoped they could alter the path of your curse."

"Maybe I did—"

"Now that you know the truth, I can help you with Morvina's spell."

She stopped pulling on the doorknob. "Y . . . you can?"

"In my vision, I saw the accident you're going to face. But if you cooperate with my plan, you won't die."

"What plan?"

"There's no need to frighten you now. I'll tell you when your twenty-first birthday draws closer."

Rose's breath became ragged and she sagged against the door. *Is Drago my only hope for survival?*

"You aren't going to die," Drago assured her, "at least, not because of the amulet."

"I don't understand."

"The necklace won't put you in danger because it'll allow me to direct you. Moreover, I'll be wearing the bracelet of Amenhotep on your birthday."

She looked at him. Tears lined her face. "This is all so confusing."

He stroked her cheek. "I can't tell you everything right now. But you need to trust me. Do you, Rose?"

She knew she should run out on him right then. He'd lied to her. His magic couldn't be explained. It was deceptive of him, yes. Yet, she realized why he'd been untruthful. He was here to guard her.

Finally, she replied, "I trust you."

"Good," he said. "Now whatever you do, don't tell anyone about this conversation."

Her hands shook.

"If I'm going to shield you from Morvina,"—he knitted his brows—"the fewer people who know about my powers, the better. You can't tell anyone I enact genuine magic. There's much at stake here."

She hesitated.

He continued to frown. "Promise me."

"I promise."

He squeezed her arm. "I mean it, Rose."

"You have to know that I'm scared, Drago. I don't want to deceive anyone."

"Not even Morvina?"

She made no reply.

"If you give away my identity, the police will seize me and I won't be able to protect you from her."

Goosebumps blanketed her arm. "I swear I won't tell anyone you're a sorcerer."

He gathered her to him. "I realize this is mind-boggling information. And I know you have no loyalty to me, especially with my dark powers. But my capabilities aren't meant to scare you. They'll be a godsend, you'll see." He paused. "You have to trust me."

Why does he keep saying that?

"I need to prepare for my show now. Say you'll come to the theater tomorrow night. After my performance."

Ultimately, she agreed.

"Until then, my sweet Rose. And remember: mum's the word."

CHAPTER 15

Morvina despised New York City. Perspiring beneath her jacket, she paced in front of an open window. She hated the automobiles' incessant honking and the voices she heard day and night. July in this city was stiflingly hot and repressively humid. And the energy of the place never slowed down.

The combination of these things made Morvina pine for the mountain breezes of her homeland. She planned to return there when this was all over.

After I destroy Rose.

Morvina threw her head back in laughter. *Rose has no idea I'm this close to her. Close enough to hear her talk about her hopes and her dreams.*

On another peal of laughter, Morvina considered another juicy secret. *No one knows I'm an enchantress . . . an enchantress who's resorted to occupying someone else's body.*

As one of the last two remaining Immortals, she intended to defeat Dragomir Starkov in the Victory. And she required the strength and the endurance only a male body could provide.

She looked down at her hands. Hairy, large. *A man's hands.* Sighing, she took a turn around the room. She'd chosen her male victim very carefully. Now, staying hidden inside this new identity was exhausting. But that's one of the things demons were capable of. If they wanted to become a new person at any given time, they could possess and occupy any foreign body they chose.

"The beauty of evil lies in its ability to take various forms." She whispered her motto as she studied the photographs adorning the parlor walls. She put a fist up to one photo in particular. *Rose*. With her pert, etched nose, glossy lips and rare, violet eyes, she was undeniably beautiful. Unfortunately, Morvina's plan to destroy Rose couldn't be executed until the girl's twenty-first birthday.

"*Patience*," the enchantress said under her breath.

Rose's torment over knowing that her twenty-first birthday would be her last had been Morvina's only source of satisfaction over the years. That's not to say Morvina hadn't dreamt about killing her niece in violent ways. Poison. Pushing the girl from a window so she'd smash against the pavement. A fatal gunshot wound from a distance would have been satisfying, too.

But these were just entertaining scenarios Morvina envisioned in order to pass the time. She'd have to wait until Rose's curse was realized to see Rose dead.

However, it was extremely hard to wait.

Morvina hated her niece, it was true. In fact, she'd resented Rose from the instant she wasn't invited to Rose's christening. But Morvina's loathing went deeper than that. Morvina had been a sorceress for centuries and she'd been privy to a premonition that Rose would grow up to be extraordinarily beautiful. Something Morvina never was.

In fact, her appearance had been the one thing she couldn't change in the beginning. She began with a body gnarled by arthritis, but following each attack she exacted in her demonic state, she gained the ability to morph her appearance into a better-looking woman. With every drop of blood Morvina extracted from pretty girls, she acquired more beauty and youth.

At this point, I'm almost as stunning underneath it all as I want to be. But not quite.

Rose held the key to Morvina's final improvements. Once Rose died and Morvina sucked out her soul, Morvina would transform into the perfect woman.

Someone who will live forever as the world's ultimate beauty. But first, she had to defeat Drago in the Victory to ensure her immortality . . .

Rose entered the newspaper office in slow motion. The clatter of the typewriters and the hum of the presses rang in her ears like deafening church bells. She'd been awake all night, agonizing over the information that had poured out of Drago. He'd begged her to keep his warlock identity secret and to steal the photograph Richard had taken of him. In the meantime, her boss was demanding all the information she was willing to give.

I'm certainly not going to tell Richard that Drago is a lord of black magic.

Rubbing her bleary eyes, she sat at her desk. Perhaps a little nap wouldn't hurt . . .

Before she could rest her head and close her eyes, Richard charged over with his hands stuffed in his pockets.

"Come to my office," he commanded.

Once she was settled inside his work space, he shut the door. "Did you polish the story about the sweatshop shutting down on East Eighty-Second Street?"

"Yes," she answered. "I finished it yesterday."

"Good." He puffed on his cigarette. "You know, Rose, the pressure's on."

She stiffened. "Excuse me?"

"Phillip Cameron just secured an exclusive interview with Harry Houdini. You know what that means . . ."

"Not really." She feigned ignorance.

"It means that this department needs to produce an exposé on Dragomir Starkov as soon as possible. If I don't come up with some scorching inside information, I'm gone. You will be gone, too."

Rose's heart nearly failed to beat. "Fired?"

"Oh, yes." He glanced at her. "I hope you're going to tell me that you stayed up all night in order to coax some ripe information out of your suitor."

She glowered. "Dragomir Starkov is an expert at keeping things to himself."

"Does that mean you *tried* to coax something out of him?"

"It means that he prefers not to talk about anything personal," Rose replied. "Maintaining a mysterious aura helps him to keep his secrets close to the vest."

Agitation replaced the gloom in Richard's expression. "I couldn't give a whit what this magician 'prefers'. Keep working on him. I've found out all I can about him and now I'm at the end of my rope. You, however, can use those warm, purple eyes of yours to chip away at his frosty exterior."

"I won't be your snitch, Richard."

"You're terribly naïve about the way this world works, Rose. Besides, if you want to be an effective reporter, you have to be willing to do what it takes."

She pursed her lips together.

"So you refuse to kiss-and-tell, eh?"

Rose exploded out of her seat. "Why do men have to be so crude?"

Richard shifted his stance. "I'm sorry. But my job is in the balance."

"I understand that, but I wouldn't feel right revealing information Drago doesn't want exposed."

He raised an eyebrow. "So you *are* privy to inside information."

Why did I say that? "N . . . no," she stammered.

A knock at the door made her jump.

"Saved by the coffee boy," Richard said, as he allowed a runner into the office. The boy, who appeared to be no older than fourteen or fifteen, set a clattering tray on the desk. Richard slipped the runner a few coins before the lad disappeared in haste.

Rose sat and watched her boss doctor up two cups of steaming coffee with cream and sugar. Richard handed her one of the cups.

"As I said, I can't dig up any more dirt on Drago myself. But maybe you can." he said.

Rose took a sip of the steaming drink. The scalding liquid burned her tongue and she started to choke. Tears streamed down her face. An alarmed Richard tried to pat her on the back.

Gasping for air, Rose unclasped her cameo and unfastened the first two buttons of her blouse. When she finally stopped choking, she sat back in her chair and accepted a handkerchief from Richard.

"Good God," he said. "That scared me." As he watched her dab her eyes, his gaze fell on the amulet visible from her opened blouse. His eyes widened. "Christ, Rose! Do you know anything about that necklace you're wearing?"

She put a hand to the stone and traced its familiar outline. "It was a gift."

"From Dragomir Starkov, I presume," he asked.

She looked away, still trying to catch her breath.

"Cut the malarkey, Rose."

She'd be smart to play dumb. "I don't remember. I got so many gifts for my birthday."

Richard planted himself on top of the desk. Concern shadowed his face. "You need to take that necklace off at once."

"No." Panic stung Rose's already raw throat.

"But you're wearing the cursed Amulet of Tousret!"

"I know all about its history."

"Then why the hell are you wearing it?"

"It's complicated."

"Complicated, my ass. I mean my foot." Richard paused. "Damn it. I'm still not used to working with a woman."

She scowled at him.

"Anyway," he went on in a hurry, "I'm assuming Starkov gave you the amulet to manipulate you."

"How do you know about the amulet anyway?"

"You can tell by the artifacts in my office that I'm interested in rare objects. While I was doing research for an article on cursed jewelry, I came across the story of the amulet. Do you know who owned it originally?"

"Yes," she said. "An Egyptian princess."

He seemed impressed. "What you may not know is that the amulet was unearthed from the sands of Egypt by an archeologist named Sir Harris Farrington. Farrington gave the necklace to his daughter. Thank God he also discovered the bracelet of Amenhotep. Do you know about the bracelet?"

Rose nodded.

Richard went on. "Luckily, the archeologist's daughter survived the curse. Through the years, the bracelet was placed in the British Museum, where it was eventually stolen. Later it was rumored that the amulet and the bracelet were reunited only to be purchased by a private collector. Now I know that that collector was Starkov."

Rose squirmed in her seat.

"If I had to guess," Richard said, "he used the amulet to spellbind you. You'd better be careful."

"What if Drago has the bracelet?" Rose asked. "Won't it counteract the amulet's prophecy?"

Richard shrugged. "So the legend goes, but if I were you, I wouldn't count on it."

She stood up. "Why are we talking such rubbish? I'm sure the amulet isn't cursed."

"Then you'll have no problem taking it off," he said slyly.

She looked nervously at her feet.

"What kind of hold does this man have over you?"

A very powerful one.

"Listen. I may not be able to compete with a magician's hypnotic spell, but knowledge is power, right?" Richard said. "Dragomir Starkov came to New York City three years ago and started to work in the Bowery at Coney Island."

Rose turned her nose up the way she had when Drago told her about his former place of employment.

"I know. The Bowery is a stink hole, but I want you to accompany me to the sideshow tent Drago performed in years ago. I'd like you to meet Felix Huxtable, the fellow who ran it then and now swears Drago enacted real magic. Says he caught Drago commanding an old Romanian coin when he didn't know he was being watched. This coin flashes glimpses of the past, like a pictograph."

The coin. She'd seen it in Drago's apartment along with the bracelet.

"No one can enact real magic," Rose said in Drago's defense. "I say Huxtable is a drunkard. Or maybe his eyes played tricks on him in the dingy shadows of the Bowery."

Richard shot her a cold look. "All I know is that if you want to continue working here, you'll accompany me to the Bowery on Saturday night and talk to this sideshow mountebank yourself."

Richard stormed out of the office and Rose felt like throwing a typewriter at his head. Part of her didn't *want* to know any more dark facts about Drago. But of course, part of her did. That's why she'd agreed to go with Richard to the Bowery just now. Although she knew Drago was capable of performing genuine magic—and that he'd come to New York three years ago after envisioning her Aunt Morvina's return here—how could she explain that to Richard?

Bellum saw journalism as a cut-and-dried way to inform the public. What was his motto again? Oh, yes. *No stone left unturned means no story left untold.*

It was essential that she learn everything she could about Drago so that she could protect his remaining secrets from Richard and the rest of the world. So, in turn, he could protect her from Morvina.

The rest of Rose's workday lagged terribly.

Finally, the time arrived for her to keep her midnight rendezvous with Drago at the Sunshine Theater. That night, the taxi he'd sent round for her arrived at the Marconi brownstone. Under the shroud of tattered clouds, Rose managed to steal out of the sleeping household. Her nerves tingled.

A silver moon hung high in the sky as she made her way to the exterior stage door. This time the alley appeared even more ominous because she was alone.

She knocked. Her heart wormed its way up to her throat. A vision flashed before her—a vision of her and Drago making love. She hardly had time to touch her flushed cheeks when Drago opened the door and allowed her entry. Rose looked at him. All her misgivings melted away. He was handsome enough to spin scalding fire through her. And when he gazed at her with those blue-green eyes, he made her feel alive—as if she hadn't lived a day until she met him.

Quickly, he gathered her in his arms for a hot kiss. Rose clung to him as if it were their last embrace. As she kissed him back with equal fervor, she smiled as the whiskers of his thin mustache tickled her face. And as his scent filled her with a palpable desire, she wanted to tell him that she was ready to make love.

Still, shouldn't Drago take the lead in this forbidden encounter?

When he guided her into the main auditorium, the empty stage loomed before them at the end of the sweeping aisle. The sight caused the hair on Rose's arms to stand on end.

"Is anybody here?" she whispered in a quiver.

"We're completely alone." He gave her a wry smile. "Go ahead. Yell if you like."

"Hello!" she screamed at the top of her lungs. Smiling in spite of herself, she said, "Your turn."

He let go of her hand. Raising his arms to shoulder-height, Drago spun in circles. "I love this woman!"

She laughed. The sound of his booming voice made her relax a bit. "Do you have a key to the theater?"

He nodded. "I enjoy perfecting my illusions here late at night."

His cyan eyes glittered at her while his dark skin glowed in the gaslight. His looks and his sensuality surpassed Rose's wildest desires. It felt amoral to be here alone with him, but it also felt right.

"I'd love to watch you practice your magic sometime," she said softly.

"I have a better idea." He drew her close. "Perhaps you'd like to be my new assistant."

"Assistant? What about Katherine?"

Drago frowned. "I fired her."

"Why?"

"As my shows get more and more sophisticated, I need someone I can trust. Tonight Katherine questioned one of my tricks. She's never done that before."

"She doesn't know about your genuine abilities?" Rose asked.

"No. But I'm afraid she's getting dangerously close to finding out."

Rose drew her brows together. "I don't know, Drago. I just got my dream job at the newspaper."

He stepped back. "I don't doubt your writing talents, Rose. And I commend you for your ambition. But your boss is a bastard."

"All the more reason to prove myself."

"An admirable goal, I admit. But I've said it before: this Richard Bellum is a thorn in my side."

"He wants me to give him information about you. He said my job depends on it."

"He's holding that over your head?" Drago thundered. A moment later, his sour expression softened. "I know you won't divulge anything scandalous about me because you promised not to."

"Even if people thought you were a warlock, or whatever you call yourself," she said, "they wouldn't know how to respond."

"I know how they'd respond," he said darkly. "They'd have me arrested or killed."

Rose cringed at the thought. She was under the spell of the amulet and being without him wasn't a viable possibility.

"What do you think about being my assistant?" He offered her a grin. "Keep your position at the paper if you like and work with me at night."

She studied his face. He never smiled fully, only quirked his lips in a sideways tug. But those mystifying grins made her knees wobble. "Do I have time to think about it?"

"I fired Katherine, remember? I need you."

When she continued to hesitate, he said, "Rose. I've been offered full billing at the Herndon Hippodrome."

"The Hippodrome?"

"Yes."

Drago was on his way to becoming the greatest magician who ever lived. But if the rest of the world discovered his sinister secret, his career would be ruined and he wouldn't be able to protect her from Morvina.

She supposed she could maintain both jobs, like he'd suggested, as long as she delayed Richard's exposé by pretending to be digging up dirt on Drago.

"Consider me hired," she said.

"Let me show you how much I appreciate it," Drago purred.

Prickles of delight raced over her as he flicked his tongue along her neck. And when a trail of heat spiraled up her spine, she nearly exploded with lust. "I'm ready to be yours, Drago."

"Are you sure?" he asked in a husky tone.

She remembered how it felt to have his hard body lying on top of hers. And she desperately wanted to experience it again. "I've never been more certain of anything in my life."

His heart beat anxiously against her chest. When she pulled away, he was grinning again. "Then tonight I'll be the luckiest man on earth."

Slowly, Drago inclined his head and brought his lips to hers. Sweeping his tongue forward, he prompted her mouth open with it. The hot contact escalated Rose's excitement. And while their tongues collided, soft moans of pleasure floated out from somewhere deep inside her. Here she was with a man who intrigued, baffled, and comforted her, all at the same time. She knew she'd never meet anyone else remotely like him.

"I love you," he whispered as his fingers got lost in her hair. Knocking her hairpins loose, he tugged at her curls until her mane slipped down in heavy locks. He took a tiny step back. "God almighty. You are the most beautiful woman I have ever seen."

Rose barely registered the compliment. She was too busy trying to memorize everything about Drago—from the spectacular hue of his eyes to how his arousal felt against her skirt. Her soul stirred in his embrace and if God ever chose to part them, at least she would have these things to remember him by.

"Please," she said. "Make love to me now."

"Come with me," he commanded.

Grasping her hand, he led her backstage. They ascended a spiral staircase which took them up to the balcony level of the theater. Drago guided her along a shadowed corridor and opened a door at its very end.

Rose stared into a plush box. Draped in green and gold curtains, the small room boasted a pair of high-backed silk chairs and a long damask-covered bench. She surmised that this was the most expensive box in the theater.

"It's lovely," she murmured as they stepped inside.

"Only the best for you." Drago drew the curtains that overlooked the stage, then twisted a gas sconce up to a low glow. Without saying another word, he took her hands, lifted them above her head, and pinned her against the wall. Rose's eyes fluttered shut as his mouth crushed hers. She thrust the top half of her body forward when his free hand dropped from her face to the fullness of her bosom.

"Open your eyes, Rose," he whispered against her lips, "I want you to really look at me."

Their stares locked for an intense moment before he kissed her again—wildly, deeply. The way it provoked her stripped away the last shred of reserve she had. Her tongue tangled with his in a kiss that drew out a groan from Drago and whetted her hunger for him.

Drago was wonderfully complex, strong, and unyielding, and she wanted him to be the first man she gave herself to. The *only* man.

Standing this close to him, Rose realized she was almost as tall as he was. In school, she'd always towered over most boys—and her height had stolen some of her confidence away. But Drago didn't seem to mind it. His hips moved against hers and when his rock-hard arousal pressed closer, heat rolled through her with the force of a bonfire.

Cheeks flushed, she returned his hot, breathless kisses. Suddenly, she had the urge to feel his sex. She tried to wriggle out of his grasp, but it was too tight.

"Yes," Drago broke contact with her mouth. As if he read her mind, he said, "Touch me."

He released her hands from over her head. Then he directed one to his groin. "There." With his hand covering hers, he showed her how to massage his shaft through the fabric of his trousers. Thick and erect, his penis became even stiffer. In fact, it felt like a cement pole against her palm.

"God, yes," he moaned.

Rich and low, his voice excited her.

Next, Drago rocked into Rose and found her breast again. Although she was inexperienced, she began to move in tune with his body, reacting to the way he caressed her curves.

He seemed to enjoy fondling her through her dress, until an impatient growl escaped his throat. Quickly, he peeled off her jacket and unhooked the tiny buttons of her blouse. Left in nothing but her corset and skirt, Rose gave a little cry as he dipped a hand inside the corset's boning and searched for her nipple. Bowing his head, Drago lapped at it in scalding circles.

She never knew anything could feel so amazing.

When Drago lifted the bulk of her breast higher, then took its bud into his mouth, she inhaled sharply. To her delight, he sucked it until moisture saturated her undergarments. She was dying for him to touch her *there*. She said breathlessly, "I'm so wet."

Rose's admission fueled Drago's desire even more. "Christ," he said. "Let me feel you."

His hand found its way under her skirt. Hooking a finger around the edge of her panties, he pulled them aside. Then, looking up at her with a lustful expression, he spread her sex apart and located her hidden pearl. His fingers, slick with her wetness, stroked her as gracefully as a delicate doe moves through the forest.

Rose's core was so sensitive and Drago's fingers were so experienced and manly that she couldn't help but whimper like a child. As he dipped his fingers in and out of her, she pressed against them. But when he encountered her female barrier, he stopped.

"Should I break your chastity, Rose?"

"Yes," she pleaded hoarsely.

He did. Searing pain raked her body at first, but then pleasure replaced it. She reached for his shaft again. This time Drago heaved against her hand while her petals swelled around his fingers. A pressure and a rhythm built like a wave raging toward the shore. Finally, her clitoris beat and throbbed.

"My God," she whispered when the intense vibration stopped. "Did you feel that?"

"It was your first climax, my darling. But it won't be your last."

Excitement rained to every part of her body as he guided her to the damask bench. Once he'd splayed her across the bench's length, he gazed down at her as if she were a nymph offering herself to the Gods. Strangely, that's what she felt like. She was willing to do anything Drago suggested and do it wholeheartedly. Not only did she sympathize with his lonely existence, she related to it. It was as if neither of them had ever belonged to anyone in particular, and now they'd found one another.

Drago was dressed in a loose linen shirt and dark trousers. Rose's heart galloped as he yanked his shirt out of his beltline and unbuttoned it to reveal the sight she'd beheld in his bedroom. Bulging biceps. An abdomen cut with muscle upon muscle. And a small, concave belly button that topped a remarkable line of tendons that streamlined into his trousers.

Could anything be more delicious?

As he leaned one hand on the edge of the bench, he removed his pants and undergarments. That's when Rose glimpsed his jutting erection for the first time. Gulping, she watched his thick, vein-wrapped penis grow longer, in the moment. The tip of it—which was covered in smooth foreskin—glimmered in the gaslight.

Smiling, he dropped forward on both hands. And while his massive forearms framed Rose's head, she received a whiff of his scent. He smelled of fresh soap and spice—like the most delectable man on earth.

"I'm going to take you slowly," he whispered against her collarbone. "So that we can revel in every minute."

She clasped his head in her hands and directed him to look up at her. Their eyes locked. Gliding her hands through his hair, she smiled, too. Several strands fell loose over one eye, free of hair tonic and stiff balms. Rose preferred it this way. The casual style made him far less fearsome and more boyish.

"I'm ready," she whispered.

Drago dropped his stare to her bare breasts. As his tongue slid past his full lips, it led the way to her nipples. He spent a long time swirling them into sharp peaks. The sensation built her passion even more. Squeaking out moans of ecstasy, Rose noticed that Drago's cock was still as hard as stone.

While he removed all of her clothes and peeled away her panties, she felt her blood rushing through her veins. But now that she was naked, she was embarrassed enough to close her eyes.

"No need to be shy," he murmured. "You're radiant."

Flicking her eyes open, she managed a smile. He returned it, then pushed her legs apart gently. "Stay open for me," he instructed. Shifting, he moved lower so that he could see her dampened folds. "Christ, Rose. You're pink and wet and perfect."

Sliding a finger into her moisture, he caught a drop on his fingertip, then tasted it. Inflamed, Rose thought she'd go mad. Warm and moist, his shaft brushed her thigh. Considering that he was ready—

and that he'd completely readied *her*—this was going to be a magical moment.

Drago guided his penis into her folds. He was large and she was tight and at first, the discomfort made her wince. But because Rose was so ripe, a blinding wave of lust banished all the pain. He thrust deeper. Her legs trembled—and as his weight flattened her breasts, sounds of their mutual desire mingled in the air.

Her folds undulated around his erection. She let out a gasp. He grasped her buttocks and thrust harder.

While she clutched Drago's bare back, Rose pinched her eyes shut and clung to him. The way their bodies molded together relayed feelings without speaking a word.

Drago gave her pumps as deep as his kisses. The theater box rang with grunts of delight. "Damn it." He tore his lips from hers. "I can't hold out any longer!"

She wanted to say, "I'm reaching that place again, too," but the words caught in her throat.

He plunged furiously now, and when he arched his back, his torso rippled enticingly. While his chest glistened with sweat, he cried out loudly and spilled his semen deep inside her.

When he slumped forward, she blinked against the stillness of the moment. He gathered her to him and stroked her tousled hair. "That was the best moment of my entire life."

"It was mine, too," she said.

Joy raced through Rose and she couldn't help but smile. Drago made it sound as if he'd been alive for hundreds of years, but he was only thirty.

They lay still for a long time, their harried breathing pronounced in the silence. Once Rose's breathing calmed, she inhaled remnants of cigars and heavy perfume that lingered inside the box. From this perch, patrons of the theater watched with fascination as Drago performed his complex illusions. He was creating quite a name for himself and she felt privileged to be here with him.

On that note, she wondered if he'd brought other women to this spot. It really didn't matter. She just wanted him to know that what they'd experienced was special to her.

Drago repositioned himself so that he could face her on the bench. She rested her cheek on the crook of his bent arm and whispered, "I want to tell you something."

He leaned over and kissed the top of her head.

"I wouldn't be here, alone, with just any man," she said.

"I pass no judgment. Because—" he lifted her chin so that she could look into his eyes "—you're my rosebud."

"I would go anywhere with you. Do anything *for* you."

"And you're my *draga*," he murmured into her hair. "My once-in-a-lifetime-love."

A hint of panic stabbed at her. She only hoped his magic could keep that lifetime from ending on her twenty-first birthday.

CHAPTER 16

Rose tiptoed inside the Marconi house at two-thirty in the morning.

In a blissful state, she crept into the dim foyer and noticed the parlor light glowing. When she peered into the parlor, she spotted Olivia asleep in an armchair, a magazine open across her chest.

When Rose turned to ascend the staircase, she stepped on a creaky floorboard. Olivia snapped awake and Rose froze.

Olivia marched toward her and thundered, "For Pete's sake! Where have you been!"

Before Rose could utter a word, Olivia adjusted the rollers in her hair, then pointed a finger at her. "No," she said. "Let me guess. You were with that illusionist."

Rose's lips set in a straight line. Olivia knew her too well.

"I didn't tell Mama." Olivia paused. "Don't I deserve a 'thank you'?"

"Thank you," Rose said quietly.

"Your sneaking around needs to stop," the dark-haired girl whispered sharply. "Mama was half out of her mind tonight."

"I thought you said you didn't tell her."

"When she came into your bedroom to give you something, she discovered you weren't there."

"I didn't mean for her to worry," Rose said in a soft voice.

Olivia's face flushed with frustration. She stayed mad for a minute longer, but eventually dropped her stern expression. "I persuaded her not to call the police before I ushered her back to bed."

"You're a pal," Rose remarked. "I appreciate you putting all my fires out. And thanks for waiting up for me."

Olivia nodded.

"Well. Good night."

Olivia placed her hands on her hips. "Not so fast. I want details!" She pulled Rose into the parlor.

The girls huddled together, laughing and talking while the few details Rose shared heated her anew. She'd never forget this evening with Drago—magical hours during which he'd stolen her virtue and captured her heart.

Unfortunately, the girls' chatter woke Anthony. He stumbled into the room wearing a scowl and yanking the sash of his bathrobe into a knot. "Damn it, you two! Thanks for interrupting a good dream."

"Dream? Were you fantasizing about Angela Bosco?" Olivia teased.

"The pretty girl who just moved in next door?" Rose raised an eyebrow.

"Maybe I was," Anthony replied. "And for your information, she's no girl. She's a *lady*."

Silence filled the air, until Olivia burst out in laughter. For once, Anthony joined in—until Elena Marconi entered the parlor.

Her silence snuffed out everyone's laughter.

Elena locked eyes with Rose. Her nostrils flared. "Olivia and Anthony. Back to your rooms."

"Yes, Mama," they replied in unison before they scurried away.

Fidgeting with her hands, Rose stood. "I'm sorry we woke you. And I'm sorry you were worried about me."

"I *was* worried. And for good reason." Elena paused and indicated that Rose should sit down. "Don't lie, Rose. You snuck out to meet that magician."

Deciding that her adoptive mother needed to know about her feelings, Rose said, "I can't tell you much about Drago except that I love him."

Fright turned Elena Marconi's face pale. She made the sign of the cross. "Rose, I have to tell you how concerned I am. Anthony says no one knows anything about this Drago. And Olivia informed me that he has *compelled* you somehow."

"He did hypnotize me," Rose said calmly, "but I'm not sure I'm acting under a spell anymore. That's how strongly I feel for him."

Elena looked unhappy. "I'm sure that's what magicians do."

Rose's cheeks heated.

"If you think you are in love with him, then there's something you ought to know."

Rose lifted an eyebrow.

"Stay here," Elena instructed.

Rose watched Elena pad out of the room. Amid the silence, she noted the time: nearly three thirty in the morning. *At least I don't have to work tomorrow.*

Her adoptive mother reappeared, accompanied by her adoptive father. Rose noticed that Elena cradled some sort of scrapbook or photo album in her arms.

As the couple neared, she noticed that the silver streaks in Elena's hair had multiplied and that the crow's feet around Lorenzo's eyes had deepened. Of course, she would have noticed these things earlier if she spent more time at home. "Is everything all right?" she asked.

Lorenzo came to stand by her. He affectionately rested a hand on her shoulder. "It's time you learned where you really came from, *cara.*"

Elena sat beside Rose but didn't open the album. "Lorenzo and your real father have been best friends since childhood. That's why your birth parents entrusted us with your safety. It's something we don't take lightly."

Lorenzo sat in a nearby chair while Elena drew in a breath. "Everyone in this family loves you, Rose. We consider you part of our *famiglia.*"

"*E io apprezzo tutto quello che hai fatto per me,*" Rose replied. At least she'd learned a little Italian over the years.

"I know you appreciate everything we've done for you," Elena said gently. "And we'd do it over again."

"You're the family I never had." Rose fought back tears. "The good news is I get to see my real parents in a few months."

To Rose's surprise, Elena didn't smile. "That is a wonderful thing," she said, "but it's our job to keep you safe until then."

"You're worried about my curse coming true. I understand that."

"Yes." Lorenzo paused, then nodded to Elena. "But there's something else you need to know."

As Elena slid the photo album across Rose's knees and opened it, Rose's heart pounded violently. Looking at the images was like looking in a mirror. Rose was the spitting image of her mother. Her father was also as fair-haired and tall as they.

"Your mother and father were—gifted," Elena began.

"Gifted?" Rose echoed.

"Don't confuse her, Elena. First, she needs to know who her parents actually are," Lorenzo insisted.

"*Sì.*" Elena pointed to the first photo. "Your parents are Malcolm and Florence Hayes, the famous psychics and spiritualists."

Rose had heard of them! Her interest in magic had prompted her to read a lot of newspaper articles about them, but she'd never seen any pictures. She'd learned that twenty years ago, Malcolm and Florence Hayes had been mind-bending celebrities working in the realm of the paranormal. With their incredible talent, they took New York City by storm and had become internationally famous by holding private fortune-telling sessions and séances for prominent people: presidents, diplomats, outlandish movie stars, and wealthy businessmen alike.

"How could Malcolm and Florence Hayes be my father and mother?" Rose asked as her gut wrenched. Surprise overtook her and now her thoughts tumbled together, ensnaring her in a maelstrom of emotions.

"Carlisle was your mother's maiden name," Elena clarified. "Your parents had an incomparable ability to see the future. They amassed a fortune doing it, and you'll live like a princess once you're reunited with them."

"That's what they want for you," Lorenzo added. "But it will have to wait because what they saw terrified them enough to concoct this plan."

Rose's back prickled.

"The idea was for us to take you under our wing," Elena said. "To hide you away from your Aunt Morvina after she was banned from the christening and had you cursed."

"Why didn't my parents want *me* to know who they were?" Rose asked.

"They didn't want you to come looking for them. It would alert Morvina."

Rose's shoulders slumped forward. "If what my parents saw was so terrible, what made them think they could alter what would happen?"

Elena placed a hand over hers. "They hoped desperately that they could."

"Did my parents tell you details of the tarot card reader Morvina went to when I was a baby?"

Elena drew her close. "Rose. Your mother *was* the tarot card reader."

Rose's blood ran cold. "What?"

Elena nodded forlornly.

"No!" Rose broke away. "I don't understand!"

"Rose—"

"I love both of you dearly but you lied to me. I thought Morvina went to a tarot card reader following my christening because this reader was also a witch. The witch cast the spell over me—a spell that will send me to my death on my twenty-first birthday."

Elena sucked in a breath. "Let me explain. As sisters, Morvina and your mother used to be on good terms. One day, Morvina overheard your mother talking to your father about a vision your mother had at the turn of a tarot card."

"What vision?" Rose asked.

Elena's lips twitched. "She saw you falling to your death on your twenty-first birthday."

"*Falling* to my death?" Rose gave a shudder. *My vertigo.*

"Morvina offered to take you and hide you away in order to protect you. She insisted that she could prevent your fall from happening, but your mother hesitated. You see, Morvina suffers from crippling arthritis—and I suppose your mother questioned her ability to take care of you. Ugly words ensued, including Morvina's claim that she was more proficient at spiritualism and fortune-telling than your mother. 'I, too, have the gift,' she said. 'But I've never been given the chance to prove myself!' Afraid of what Morvina might do, your parents banned her from your christening. Morvina, who dabbled in black magic, cast her own spell over you—to doubly ensure that you would meet your demise."

"Morvina is the real witch I've always heard about?" Rose asked.

"Yes," Lorenzo answered.

"Why didn't you tell me this from the start?"

"We thought it best not to scare you. Having a witch as an aunt and a tarot card reader for a mother could frighten a child," Elena said.

"I've always been suspicious of Morvina." Lorenzo shook his head. "When she was twenty-five years old, she appeared out of nowhere, claiming to be your mother's lost half-sister. Because your mother was put in an orphanage by parents she didn't know, she believed her."

A new cloud of anxiety engulfed Rose.

"If you want to change your destiny," he continued grimly, "you need to hear what else your mother saw in her vision."

Rose turned to Elena who spoke quickly. "She saw a horrible creature, a demon. She predicted this demon will arrive in the form a magician or an enchanter and bring death and destruction. *Your* death."

"You think this dark figure is Drago?" Rose's voice was shrill as she gripped the photo album.

"Yes," her adoptive parents said in unison.

"It can't be! He talks about nothing but saving me."

"Perhaps that's what Dragomir Starkov says." Elena wrung her hands. "But how do you know he's not an evil product of Morvina—sent to seduce and persuade you to follow his lead?"

"I'll never believe it!"

"This is what demons do!" Elena cried. "They are fallen angels who lure humans into wicked acts—so they'll sin and become fallen, too."

"My dear Rose," Lorenzo stood and his wife did the same. "You think you're in love. But enchanters can charm you into thinking just that. They make you believe things and then it's too late."

"No!"

"This is your life we're talking about," Elena said firmly.

"I'll be safe with Drago."

Tears sprang to Elena's eyes. "We want to believe you, but we cannot take that chance. That's why we forbid you to see Dragomir Starkov again."

CHAPTER 17

Shock, sadness, and anger assaulted Rose like a firing squad.

Clutching the photo album, she raced up the stairs with it. When she encountered Olivia at the top of the landing, she practically plowed her down.

Olivia followed Rose to the bedroom the girls shared and shut the door. "I shouldn't have been listening, but I was. My God, Rose. I'm so sorry."

"How could your parents have lied to me?" she asked.

"I suppose they did it for your own good."

"I don't know if Drago is the evil demon they spoke of. All I know is that I can't bear to be without him."

"Hush now." Olivia sat on the bed and smoothed Rose's hair. "When this is all over—I mean, when you come out of this alive, you can see him again."

Rose brushed her tears away with firm strokes. "You don't understand, Olivia. I *have* to be with him. It's like the need to eat, drink, and sleep. It's a necessity."

"That's how young people feel when they're in love," said Olivia gently.

"You, of all people, know this is different. You saw me the night Drago called me onstage. I've been drawn to him ever since."

"Yes, but you heard what Papa said. Enchanters do that . . . in order to make you pliable, for their own purpose."

"It's no use talking about it." Rose went back to crying. "I love you like a sister. But I want to be alone right now."

"All right," Olivia said as she stood up. "But please don't go against my parents' wishes. They have your best interests in mind and you owe them a debt of gratitude."

Sitting in his apartment, Drago lamented over the fact that he was no psychic. He hadn't been given the ability to see into the future when he'd gained his astounding powers. However, thanks to the coin, he could see the present. And right now, he was staring into the image of Rose's world falling apart around her.

Stuffing the coin into his pocket, he pounded his other hand on the kitchen table. The bottle of wine he'd opened helped a little, but his blood still hurled through his veins like a windstorm.

Holy Hell. Rose can't see me anymore.

To add fuel to the fire, he sensed that Morvina was closer than ever. Although he'd built his own powers by drawing out only parts of people's souls every year upon the anniversary of his turning, he'd never killed a human or invaded another person's body.

It meant that he probably wasn't as powerful as the other remaining Immortal.

For the first time in a long while, he gave a shudder. The violence the Immortal had displayed when it murdered the last Coney Island victim meant that he or she was completely ruthless.

Soon he'd have to battle that creature—and Morvina.

Drago snatched up the wine glass he'd refilled and stormed to his bedroom. Settling on top of the covers, he closed his eyes. Before he attempted to will Rose to him, he took a sip of the wine then set the glass aside. Next, he retrieved the lei coin from his trouser pocket.

"Show me the woman I love," he commanded.

The coin's surface glimmered and projected an image of Rose lying in her bedroom. Outside her door, he could see Lorenzo Marconi locking her in.

"Damn it!" Drago rasped.

Should I open the lock with my telekinetic powers? Or should I let Rose stay where she's safe, at least for now?

Blowing out an exasperated breath, he told himself to calm down before he did anything. He decided to check on Richard Bellum. In the past, the coin had helped Drago prevent the reporter's investigations from going too deep.

"Show me Bellum."

The silver lei displayed an image of the aggressive reporter speaking to Felix Huxtable, Drago's old boss in the Bowery.

In the wavering scene, Bellum pushed his boater hat back on his forehead. "And you're sure you saw Dragomir Starkov conjure up flashes of the past with his coin, Huxtable?"

"Yeah, yeah." The side-show shyster shifted his fat cigar from one side of his mouth to the other. "I saw Starkov speak to it and magic happened right then and there. Never saw anything like it."

"You know, I believe you," Bellum said.

Huxtable grunted.

"I'll be bringing a young woman around tomorrow night. I want you to tell her the same thing you told me," the reporter instructed.

"Why?"

"Because Rose Carlisle holds the key to my future as a reporter. She's going to help me blow this story wide open." Bellum paused. "People are going to be talking about this real-life sorcerer for years."

"Well, no one came round here asking me about Starkov until you. Of course, I told people about the coin but they never believed me."

"I presume you tried to get the coin from Starkov?"

"Yeah, but he stuffed it in his pocket and ran off before I could. Never liked that shifty Romanian."

"I never liked you, either," Drago muttered under his breath.

Bellum turned to go. "I'll bring Rose to see you at midnight."

"Hate to say it, but it'll cost you." The hustler managed to choke the words out between cigar puffs.

"Cost me?"

"I was just starting to make money off Starkov's performances before he left me high and dry. I intend to make something now."

The Bowery image waved and the coin suddenly went dark. Drago rested his head against the headboard. He flipped the object over between his fingers. *Will Rose be able to escape from her room tonight? If so, I need to protect her from Bellum and Huxtable.*

"If you slimeballs think you're going to expose me," he growled out loud, "you have another think coming."

In the tunnel that led to the Bowery, the tip of Richard Bellum's cigarette burned a bright red. He had glanced at his watch three times in the last minute. Now he took an uneasy look around and lifted his jacket collar up against an apprehensive chill.

The Bowery, which was the seediest part of Coney Island, stretched along the amusement park's boardwalk. It was home to shoddy music halls, carnival con artists, bawdy theaters, and curious patrons who wanted a closer look at anything amoral. Muggings and knife-fights had been known to occur in this very tunnel.

Of course, being a reporter who chased after the sensational hardly made Bellum better than those hoodlums, but he considered it a half-step up.

Why the hell aren't you here, Rose?

A few minutes passed, then a bottle clinked and rolled forward in the tunnel. Wearing a frown, Rose materialized a few seconds behind the bottle. "I nearly tripped and killed myself!"

"And I've been growing gray hair waiting for you here," he cried. "What took you so long?"

"You don't want to know," she said.

With an impatient harrumph, Richard threw his cigarette to the ground and snuffed it out with his shoe. He looked up and down the tunnel. "Come on, Huxtable's waiting for us."

As she followed her boss into the heart of the Bowery, Rose wished she'd brought along a perfume-dipped handkerchief. Stinking of beer, cigars, and body odor, the place was completely unfit for a lady. Of course, Rose had been no lady when she'd stolen out her bedroom window and shimmied down the enormous elm adjacent to it twenty minutes ago. But she couldn't care less.

Trying not to dwell on the punishment she would receive upon her return, she accompanied Richard past a row of penny arcades. They stopped at a group of red-and-white tents. Carnival games abounded around them, but the booths seemed a far cry from the innocent ones at the other end of Coney Island—booths Rose had visited as a child. Felix Huxtable stood in front of the center tent. Colorful posters adorned the ramshackle structure, advertising such oddities as a bearded lady, a snake charmer, and a fully tattooed man.

Huxtable, who was busy hawking the show to passersby, stopped in mid-sentence when he saw Richard Bellum. "Did ya bring my money?"

Begrudgingly, Bellum slipped the carnie a few dollars. Rose frowned yet said nothing. Apparently this was how it worked in the depths of the Bowery.

"Step over here," Huxtable instructed as he stuffed the payment into his trouser pocket. "Yer holding up traffic."

When the man removed his visor, Rose took a moment to sum him up. He had a ring of black hair that didn't match his graying eyebrows, and his jowls were meatier than a bulldog's. Paunchy, short, and dirty, the fellow reeked of corruption and cheap whiskey.

Pushing down the bile that slid up her throat, Rose extended her hand for Huxtable to shake. "I'm Rose Carlisle."

"Yer the lady who wants to know about Dragomir Starkov?"

"Yes," she replied in a hushed tone. *If Drago happens to see me here, it will look bad.* He might think she was going behind his back.

"What do ya want to know about that slippery Romanian?" Huxtable asked.

"Can you tell me how Mr. Starkov came to work for you?"

Grunting, Huxtable sucked in his enormous belly, only to let it sag free an instant later. "It was three years ago, on a summer night much like this. Seein' as how I'm the best manager in the business, Starkov sought me out. Although he claimed he'd been a respected magician in Romania, he said he wanted to start from the ground up here in the States. Made me suspect he was running away from somethin'."

"Starkov commanded a following even here in the Bowery?" Bellum asked.

"That's right." Huxtable pulled a fresh cigar from behind his ear and lit it. "He started off as a sideshow act, but his tricks were always damned impressive. Levitated people. Had a dog jump through a hoop only to make the animal vanish midway. And he could guess a customer's birthday, every time.

"After word of Starkov's talent spread," Huxtable said, "he abandoned me go to one of them fancier theaters along the Boardwalk. And when he needed an assistant, my daughter, Katherine, started working for him."

"Katherine is your daughter?" Surprise vibrated through Rose.

"Yes, and she was happy working for that cad until he threw her out like yesterday's trash. I have a mind to pound a lesson into Starkov's foreign brain . . ."

"So you're bitter enough with Drago to talk to us?" Rose asked as calmly as she could.

"That's a good way of puttin' it." Huxtable paused. "The point is I'm a master at spottin' a fake. But the more I watched Dragomir, I came to realize he's in league with the devil."

Rose raised an eyebrow.

"His tricks can't be explained." Huxtable seethed.

"Are you hoping we expose Dragomir Starkov as some sort of warlock or sorcerer?" Richard asked.

"It's why you're here, isn't it?" Confusion washed over Huxtable's unshaven face.

"Miss Carlisle is torn over her feelings for Mr. Starkov," Richard said. "Seems she's fallen in love with him."

Huxtable moved closer to Rose. His body stench and rancid breath nearly knocked her off balance. "You're a female reporter, ain't ya, doll?" he asked. "A rare breed. Shows you've got courage. I'd say you aren't afraid to know *everything* about Starkov. Am I right?"

"I want to know about the Romanian coin he carries around with him."

Huxtable's eyes lit up. "Pulled it out one night, stealthy-like. Didn't think no one was watching him. But I was. I crept up behind and saw him talk to this coin. It flashed glimmers of light, then revealed Starkov and what he did in the past. The past as in a hundred years ago—when people were travelin' around in horse-drawn carriages with their servants. Even odder, Starkov *didn't look no different.*"

Now Rose knew Huxtable was full of hot air. Either that or he was suffering the ill-effects of the beer. "You were drunk," she accused.

He looked hurt. "I was sober that night, doll."

"You're nothing but a money-hungry man out to seek revenge on an employee who abandoned you," she spat.

"That's my father you're talking to!" a voice cried out behind them.

Rose and Richard wheeled around to see Katherine, Drago's former assistant, emerge from one of the tents.

"How come I didn't put two and two together?" Richard asked.

"I gave you the surname 'Heath' when you interviewed me, Mr. Bellum."

"Your stage name?" He rubbed his chin.

"Yes."

One look at Katherine's red, swollen eyes told Rose the brunette had been crying. She'd made an attempt to catch her hair up in a chignon, but large, unruly pieces escaped it. Her mussed hair and rumpled dress gave Rose the impression that the girl hadn't taken the news of her termination well.

"I'm sorry I spoke to your father that way just now," Rose apologized. "But what he claims is too fantastic to be true."

"I also saw Drago talk to that blasted coin." Katherine said. "He would pull it out, sometimes late at night. He always murmured quietly enough to avoid being heard and he always turned away from me, but I could tell something unnatural was going on."

"Why didn't you expose Starkov then?" Richard asked.

Katherine's face flushed. She studied the ground.

Rose's heart plummeted. *She's in love with Drago.*

These people were coming dangerously close to discovering Drago's dark secret. What would happen if his genuine powers were out in the open? Katherine wrapped her arm around her father's shoulder and lifted her chin defiantly. "I want both of you to leave."

"We'll leave," Richard said. "Rose has heard all she needs to."

"I heard all I need to as well," Katherine remarked in a strange voice.

"What do you mean by that?" Rose turned around.

"I overheard you and Drago talking inside the Sunshine Theater last night."

Rose gasped. "You were there?"

Anger flashed in Katherine's brown eyes. "I was gathering my things from the dressing room."

"What did you hear?"

"I heard Drago begging you to be my replacement."

Rose's eyes narrowed. "He didn't beg me. He asked me."

Glaring, Katherine remained silent.

"Drago is moving his act to the Herndon Hippodrome," Rose said, "so he desperately needs an assistant."

"He had me." Tears threatened to spill down the girl's freckled cheeks.

"Drago and I have come to know each other well," Rose explained.

"I guess he's moving on to bigger and better things."

"I'm sorry, Katherine. I truly am."

"It doesn't matter. What's important is that I heard you and Drago discuss his abilities to enact real magic. That's why he wants you to be his new assistant."

Rose's heartbeat stuttered.

"Is this true?" Richard asked sharply.

"I don't know what you're talking about." Rose avoided Richard's hawk-like stare and Katherine's accusing eyes.

"I heard what I heard," Katherine stated.

Rose shook her head. "You heard wrong."

"Just get out!" the scorned girl said.

Bellum took Rose's arm and led her away. Once they reached the end of the row, he released her. "Steady there. I thought you were going to pounce on that woman like some rabid animal."

"She hated me the minute she laid eyes on me."

"How do you know?"

"Women sense these things."

"Maybe she was jealous of the attention Drago showed you. It was obvious he fell for you right away."

Had the entire audience noticed it?

"But that's irrelevant," Richard went on. "The important thing is Katherine corroborated her father's story about the coin. What's more, why the hell didn't you tell me about Starkov's genuine powers?"

Since Drago wasn't here to defend himself, it was left to Rose. "There is no such thing as real magic, Richard."

He grabbed her by the arm. "I want to know everything Starkov told you."

She wormed against his grip. "Let go. You're hurting me!"

"Spill the truth, Rose. Our jobs depend on it."

A noise sounded behind them. Rose and Richard whirled around. Standing atop a half-wall, Drago loomed over them like an imposing skyscraper. He curled his hands into fists and glared at Richard.

"Starkov?" Bellum went pale.

"It takes a real weasel to bring a woman to the Bowery then manhandle her."

Drago looked incredibly appealing in a dark jacket over light trousers, both cut expertly to fit his muscularity. He tugged his ascot cap lower on his forehead, leapt to the ground and stalked toward Richard. The sight of his long duster rippling behind him made Rose's pulse jump.

Bellum backed up.

"Why the hell do you persist in writing about me?" Drago roared.

"It's my job."

Shoulders hulking, Drago shook his head. "You're paid to write reviews of my shows, not bare my private life to the public."

"I'm paid to give readers the stories they want."

"Where I come from, journalism—and being a gentleman—must mean different things." He reached out and grabbed Bellum by the lapels. "Stay out of my life!"

Richard shrank. "I only want to show people that your talents are like nothing they'll ever see again."

"Let the public come to its own conclusion. And don't ever try to manipulate Rose into doing your dirty work again."

"Y . . . yes," Richard stammered.

"In fact." Drago's face grew crimson, "I'll give you a chance to redeem yourself. I want you to recommend Rose to the editor-in-chief of *The Daily Gazette*."

"What? The largest newspaper in New York?"

"Yes. I want you to write her a recommendation and then I want you to tear up the photo you took of me on the laundry line."

Richard shot a pained look at Rose. She looked away, her face hot.

"If you don't do these things," Drago fumed, "I'll hunt you relent-lessly—and I won't stop until you're either fired . . . or dead."

"You're threatening my life?"

"You catch on quick, Bellum. But on second thought, maybe I'll make you *disappear* . . .

Drago stared deeply into Richard's eyes. The reporter shut his eyes and jerked his head away. "Don't try to hypnotize me!"

At that, Drago released Bellum with a ferocious push. Bellum stumbled back and slammed his head against a brick wall. Pressing a hand to his bloody wound, he yelled, "You're finished in this town, Starkov! I guarantee all your secrets will be exposed!"

"Shut up, Bellum." Drago clasped Rose's elbow and said, "Let's go."

Rose took in a long breath. "I'm not going anywhere with you."

CHAPTER 18

Resentment blazed through Rose. "Thanks for showing up when you did, but now Richard knows I told you about the photo."

"That's the least of our worries."

She anchored her hands on her hips. "You're right. My biggest worry is that Richard may not welcome me back to *The Gotham Times*. What's more, you threatened his life!"

"I can't have him exposing my secrets."

She made no reply.

Drago stared at Rose with shock. "You're angry?"

"Anger is what you get when you presume to fight my battles for me."

"You need protecting." He gathered her close.

She tried to wriggle free but his embrace was too tight.

"I might need protection, Drago, but not all the time."

"You mean too much to me for me not to guard you."

She studied the anguish in his eyes, then let out a heavy breath. Drago *had* come at a good time. Who knows what Richard would have resorted to in order to get the information he desired?

Shuddering, she sagged against his solid chest.

"Let's talk about this somewhere else," he suggested. "My motor car is right over there."

To avoid people's curious stares, she nodded and allowed Drago to take her to the waiting vehicle. Parked along a road at the top of a sandy incline, the stunning Garford shone as if it still graced the showroom floor.

Drago opened the car door. Once Rose settled on the tufted passenger's seat, he joined her inside. Shifting the car into gear, he maneuvered it along the glistening streets of New York, wearing a scowl.

"I think you have some explaining to do," he said above the engine's roar.

Her heart drummed. "You're wondering what I was doing at the Bowery in the first place?"

He nodded.

"I wanted to find out everything Richard knows about you. I was there for a meeting he set up between me and Felix Huxtable."

"Despicable man," Drago growled.

"Most despicable," Rose agreed. "After showing me how bitter he is that you cut him off as manager, he told me about the coin you talk to."

"What exactly did he say?"

Rose relayed the information, ending with Huxtable's claim that he saw the coin flash images of Drago alive a hundred years ago. "*That's* when I knew the man was going too far."

"The coin gives me my powers," Drago said. "I keep it with me except when I sleep."

Emotion washed over Rose's face. "I don't want anyone telling lies about you."

Grabbing her hand, he pressed an urgent kiss to it. "I love that you're looking out for me. I've never had anyone do that before."

"I don't know if Richard will tear up the photo, Drago."

Drago's scowl returned while Rose's nerves jostled. *Should I tell him who my real parents are—and that the Marconis believe he's the demon my mother saw in her vision?*

Deciding the information could wait until he calmed down completely, she remained silent.

"Hopefully, I scared Bellum into a paralyzed state," Drago said. "But, I have more important things on my mind."

He gave her a look, dark with desire, and Rose's body tingled in response.

"I loved seeing you naked in my arms at the theater," he said in a sultry timbre. "And I liked feeling your soft skin against mine."

She wet her lips at the seductive admission.

With an abrupt turn of the wheel, Drago yanked the car into a deserted alley and parked it in the shadows. He killed the engine then heaved Rose toward him. When his mouth found hers, he plundered it with hot kisses. The sensation of his hands exploring her body made her cry out.

"I want you right now," he said gruffly. "I've thought of little else all day."

Rose murmured something breathless in return. She'd yearned for Drago—even had her first erotic dream about him, under the covers last night. Now, the desire to repeat their encounter in the theater box crackled through her like lightning.

Drago tugged her into the rear of the motor car. Bearing down on her over the rear bench, he impatiently pulled at the buttons of her dress. Once he caught a glimpse of her breasts, he fondled them and kissed them alternately.

Waves of passion and hunger swept through Rose. Drago's erection swelled and hardened between her thighs and as she reclined across the narrow bench, his warm breath stoked her craving for him even more. She moaned as his expert hands roamed her curves, found her sweet spot beneath her layers of undergarments, and twined her lust into a frenzy. Sweat beaded his brow—and as he murmured his unending love for her, he caught her eyes with a smoldering look.

Panting, Drago unzipped his trousers and buried himself deep inside her slick folds. Meanwhile, neither of them broke eye contact. Rose gave a little cry as her core opened and closed around his penis. He pressed harder against her cleft. It was just the right amount of force and her excitement soared.

"Christ," he murmured against her neck. "You feel so good."

As he raised himself on locked elbows, he rocked his slim torso forward.

"I can't stand to be without you," he whispered.

As she grasped his upper arms, she admitted that she felt the same way.

Lowering his mouth to hers, he caught her lips with another scalding kiss. Over the next few minutes, he pumped his way to their mutual climax. Rose's folds contracted over and over and she found herself disappointed when the moment ended.

Struggling for breath, Drago pitched forward. "We would have fogged the windows if they'd been rolled up."

He laughed as Rose smiled. "I can't stay mad at you very long." She paused. "Let's never argue again."

"Agreed." He pressed delicate kisses across her forehead. "I panicked when I looked into the coin and saw the vision of you in the Bowery."

"I can take care of myself," she said as she sat up and covered herself with her dress.

"Ordinarily you could, Rose. But in my vision I caught a glimpse of a black, unearthly figure following you."

"A black figure?" she asked. Could it be the creature her mother saw in her prediction?

"I couldn't see the figure's face," Drago said while he pulled himself to a sitting position, "but something very evil is coming closer to you, Rose."

"Morvina," she murmured. Feeling the color drain from her face, she looked directly at Drago. "I learned something important tonight."

He nodded.

"My adoptive mother revealed to me who my real parents are."

"Who are they?"

"Malcolm and Florence Hayes."

"The famous psychics and spiritualists?"

Drago recognized the names as she thought he would. "Apparently, my mother held a tarot card session about me," she rushed on. "She saw a vision of me falling to my death on my twenty-first birthday. And in this vision, a dark figure was the cause of my accident."

"A dark figure?"

"A *demon*." She looked into his perfect features, features that were so sublime they had to be a divine product. He couldn't be a fallen angel.

"And the Marconis, as sweet as I'm sure they are, think this dark figure is me, I presume?" Drago asked suspiciously.

"Yes. That's why they forbid me to see you."

"That explains what I saw in the coin." He scowled. "What you just described to me . . . the vision of you falling. It's the same scene that came to me three years ago—when I saw the future for the first and only time."

She braided her fingers through his. "Is that when you bought the Egyptian amulet and the bracelet?"

"Yes." He glided his fingers along her face then cupped her chin in his palm. "After I purchased them from a private owner in Europe, I traveled here in a hurry. I did it all as soon as I saw your extraordinary beauty—and witnessed the creature that wants to destroy you."

"Your coin. That's how you knew Morvina was coming to New York City." It finally dawned on her. "She's a witch who cast her own curse over me."

"Her own curse?"

"Yes. She created a damnation spell—to ensure I would fall to my death on my twenty-first birthday. Morvina *wanted* my mother's vision to come true."

"Christ." Drago glowered.

"I don't think I'll ever convince Elena and Lorenzo that the dark figure is Morvina and not you."

"Now that I'm in New York City, I wish I could see her clearly," he said. "But her new identity is throwing me off."

"New identity? She is that powerful?"

"You have no idea how potent witchcraft can make a person."

"Can't you look into your coin and see who she's disguised herself as?" Rose asked with urgency.

"I wish to God I could." He helped her up to the front seat and started the car.

Lulled by the motion of the car, Rose fell asleep in no time. She awakened when the vehicle came to a gentle halt. "Where are we?"

Drago turned the engine off and stretched his arm across the back of her seat. "We're at one of my other residences."

"*One* of your other residences?"

He indicated the house with a wave of his hand.

Rose looked out her window and gawked at a magnificent mansion. Preceded by a winding driveway and grand gates, it was centered inside a circle of towering elms. The mansion shimmered invitingly in the dark. From its ornate gables that framed endless rows of windows, to its shining gray brickwork that showcased its vast array of rooms, the house possessed all the glamour and elegance expensive taste could buy.

When Rose stretched her gaze beyond the mansion, she realized that it was perched on the end of a jutting embankment. The embankment, in turn, hovered over the crashing waves of the ocean, next to a hamlet.

"We're on the edge of Long Island," Drago informed her. "In East Hampton."

"It's beautiful, but I thought you were taking me home."

"I won't allow anyone to separate us." His nostrils flared. "If you go back to the Marconis', that's precisely what will happen."

"I may have broken Elena and Lorenzo's hearts by sneaking out tonight, but they'll worry when I don't come back."

He took her hand in his. "You're a grown woman now. And you needn't worry about sneaking around without permission anymore."

What he said made sense.

"I want you to stay here with me," Drago whispered.

"Live with you in sin?"

He laughed. "No. Of course not."

Her shoulders came crashing forward with relief.

"I want you to marry me. So that we can be together every minute of every day."

Her heart sang as he got out of the car and opened her door. Sinking to one knee, he grasped her left hand and looked up at her wide-eyed. "Will you marry me tomorrow?"

Rose's hand quivered in his. "Yes!"

Drago pulled her out of the car and lifted her off the ground. "Welcome to your new home, the future Mrs. Rose Starkov."

After they shared a passionate kiss, Drago and Rose jumped back into the car and streamed up the driveway to the mansion. Drago insisted that Rose stay put as he rushed around to her side of the automobile and swept her into his arms.

"You don't have to carry me across the threshold until tomorrow." She smiled broadly.

"It's good practice."

He fumbled with his keys and pushed open the massive front door with his foot. Then Drago transported Rose into the mansion's foyer. She'd never seen anything so splendid. The marble floor shone like precious jewels while an enormous staircase lined in pale English oak rose, split into two sides, and met at the top. Beneath the bottom of the staircase sat a massive sunken drawing room furnished exclusively in white and cream.

It seemed a house suited for opulent parties—and Rose could easily envision butlers serving champagne to lively guests garbed in sequins and feathers.

"I come here infrequently," Drago said behind her. "One groundskeeper and two maids see to the upkeep at the end of the month. That's the extent of the servants." Encircling her waist, he spun her around to face him. "Tonight we're all alone."

"Hmm," she purred.

"On second thought," he said with a devilish look in his eyes, "this empty place might bore you . . ."

She swatted him playfully on the arm.

Drago whispered against her neck, "Good. I can suggest lots of things we can do now that we're by ourselves." With that, he gallantly whisked her up the staircase. Once he passed a spacious landing, he kicked open a set of double doors. A massive bedroom greeted them—a bedroom that overlooked the sharp edge of the hamlet below and hummed quietly with the ocean's crashing waves.

Decorated in shades of violet and lavender, Rose found that it suited her completely. She nuzzled her head into the crook of Drago's neck, never wanting their embrace to end.

Smiling, Drago spread her across the oversized bed. "Do you like the house?"

"Yes," she responded.

"What do you think of the bedroom?"

"I love it."

"I had it styled to match your eyes."

The notion made Rose pull him into her arms.

CHAPTER 19

Drago could barely get himself to stir the next morning. Fighting the fog in his head, he reached for his pocket watch and forced his eyes to focus on its hands.

One p.m.

He and Rose had slept away most of the day, tired from lovemaking, exhausted from their dark encounter in the Bowery. But as fatigued as he was, Drago smiled at the sight of Rose's warm body in front of him.

I can't believe she agreed to marry me.

Drago clutched the hand she'd threaded through his. Then he studied its fine veins and satiny skin. The wedding bands he planned to purchase in the nearby shops today would be modest at best, so he'd have to wait and buy Rose a magnificent diamond ring when they returned to New York.

He dreaded going back to the city but his new show was slated to open in a few weeks. Even he had to admit that his pride over being the world's greatest magician was beginning to cloud things. Yet, in his defense, he'd never been great at anything except magic.

Fortunately, Rose would be with him in New York. He knew that having a relationship with her meant isolating her from everything she held dear, yet it was the only way to protect her from Morvina.

In the silence of the afternoon, he closed his eyes and listened to her soft breathing. Giving a grunt, he entwined his legs with hers. His half-erect shaft bumped against her backside and a surge of erotic pleasure shot through him. After he kicked back the bed-sheet, he stared at her heart-shaped ass topped with an adorable pair of dimples. It was perfection—and all Drago wanted to do was stroke between her legs and bury himself deep inside her core.

With a tug at her waist, he pulled her closer. Rose stirred beside him but didn't wake fully. Moaning, she reached backward and cupped his face. He felt her entire body come aflame when he caressed the flair of her hips and pressed his lips to the column of her neck. Reaching down, he slid his fingers inside her center. And from behind, he readied her for a long time.

Feeling his erection rise, he grasped it and guided it inside her. Urged by his shaft's almost painful throbbing, Drago plunged and built up friction. And as he pumped, his temples pulsed. Making love to Rose was an insatiable craving. He'd never felt this way about any woman. He could honestly say that he loved everything about her— and knowing that he was marrying her today heightened his desire for her even more.

Drago reached around and gently played with Rose's breast. As he tweaked her nipple into a rosy point, he felt the moisture flow between her legs. Wetting his lips, he skimmed the slope of her back with his fingertips before he wrapped one leg over her graceful hip to intensify his thrusts.

"God, you're glorious," he whispered.

"I love you," she murmured over her shoulder.

Nearing release, Drago clutched her desperately. Visions of her rounded derrière and the sensation of her arousal drenching his sex brought him to an astounding climax.

Breathless, he said, "You're amazing to wake up to."

Rose responded by reaching for his hand and squeezing it.

"Today is going to be the happiest day of my life," he said into her shining hair. Then his smile dropped. It would only be the happiest day of his life on two conditions. *If* he could fight off the lethargy that came with daylight. *If* he could bring himself to go inside the chapel.

Late last night, Rose had made Drago promise she'd have a church wedding. Unfortunately, churches didn't typically welcome demons.

Before Drago woke Rose, she'd been dreaming of him. Imagining his hewn physique in nothing but a magician's cape, in fact. The image brought a smile.

She stretched her arms above her head after they made love and gave a lazy yawn. "I can't wait to marry you."

Drago brushed a locket of hair off her forehead. "You make me happier than I've ever been."

She sat up and scooted against the headboard. "I'm glad you're going to keep your promise to make me a respectable woman."

He threw his head back in throaty laughter. "Didn't I tell you? I've changed my mind. You will live here as my courtesan. My concubine for all time."

"I wouldn't care as long as we never left this house."

He laughed again, his eyes creasing at the corners.

She studied the man she was so desperately in love with. He had grown a shadow of a beard, and his tousled hair, which shone attractively with golden-brown streaks, had grown longer lately, too. Still, what enticed Rose most about Drago was the way his stare portrayed the hope that Rose would always be content as his wife. That's what she really loved about him. He would never stop taking care of her and protecting her.

"Since we're marrying today," Rose said excitedly, "I want to know everything about you."

"Hmm . . . I'm so interesting," Drago quipped. "Where to start?"

She rolled her eyes.

"All right," he propped his head on one hand. "I've always been interested in magic."

"Always?"

"My family never had any money, so my father would perform magic tricks to entertain us on long, cold nights." He paused. "Now that I think of it, the diversion it brought was my first glimpse at magic's power."

"That explains a lot." Rose smiled. After awhile she said, "I've always been interested in the unexplained, too. What do you think makes people so fascinated with illusions?"

"People say they want the laws of nature to be explained," he replied. "What they really want is to discover the truth about magic."

"The truth?"

"The public isn't content to be deceived by ordinary tricks anymore."

"You mean audiences want to believe it's *not* a trick?"

"Precisely." Drago nodded. "They want to believe that magic exists and can do great things."

Rose fingered his hair. "That's where you come in."

"I suppose."

"You can do it all," she reminded him.

"Conjuring. Mentalism. Sleight of hand. Mesmerism, yes. Curiosity draws people closer to me—to see if my abilities are merely gimmicks."

Rose considered what Drago said. "It's frightening to think what will happen to you if someone reveals your biggest secret."

"Hopefully, the public will never become that clever," he remarked dryly.

"You know so much about the world—about people. Sometimes I think you're older than your years."

He frowned. "I've lived many lifetimes in one."

Rose touched the amulet nestled above her breasts, then traced its outline. "If we're going to be married, I want to be honest with you. This necklace frightens me."

His eyes flashed like a sea under a tempest. "Don't be afraid. According to Romanian beliefs, protecting someone is what an amulet is supposed to do."

"Then I'll wear it until you tell me to take it off," she said tenderly.

Drago leaned in for a kiss. Rose greeted it with her entire body.

When he gathered her to him, he said, "I love you more every day."

She wrapped her arms around his waist and tightened their embrace. It was true that she'd given up everything for Drago—her, family, job, and friends. That's why, at this point, she could only hope that fate had designed her to be with him and no one else.

"We need to buy you a wedding dress," Drago murmured into the waves of her hair.

"Can't you just conjure up something for me to wear?" she teased.

He chuckled. "That wouldn't be any fun for you. I want you to pick out something special."

"Where on earth will we find a wedding gown?"

"Maybe in the village."

An hour later they found themselves on the charming streets of East Hampton. Clapboard houses rose beyond the brightly painted shops that lined the town's main avenue. And the entire town seemed immersed in an idyllic sort of trance.

Rose ate a late lunch at a picturesque café. Claiming he wasn't hungry, Drago watched her pick at a sandwich and a bowl of soup. After the hearty meal, she pulled him along the row of stores. Then she got excited when she spotted a dress shop at the end of the street.

Arriving at it, she pointed to a gown in the window. "That's the one."

"It's beautiful." Drago said. "But is it meant for a bride?"

"It may be a tea dress, but I love it. Besides, it's my best option in this tiny village."

He smiled. "Then I love it, too." After he kissed her on the cheek and handed her a wad of money, he urged her to go inside and try it on.

The shopkeeper helped Rose change into the white garment. With its fashionable empire waist and taffeta skirt, the dress boasted elbow length sleeves, a cross-draped bodice and a flowing lace overskirt.

Once the kindly woman caught Rose's hair up in a wide, white ribbon, she stepped back to admire the final look. "Perfect," the woman said.

Rose beamed at her reflection in the mirror. "I'll take it."

The store owner clapped her hands in delight. "You look beautiful, Miss, but we can't let your groom see you in it. I'll wrap the dress up promptly."

"That won't be necessary. We're getting married right now."

"How romantic!" the woman cried.

Rose emerged from the dress shop as if on the lightest cloud. Drago was waiting for her on the walkway. He gazed at the sight of her in her bridal dress with all the things she'd hoped to see in his eyes: admiration, affection, approval, and pure love.

Offering her his arm, he led her toward the chapel situated on the edge of East Hampton. Halfway there, Rose stopped abruptly in her tracks. "Rings! We don't have wedding rings!"

Drago patted his breast pocket. "Not to worry. I bought them while you were trying your dress on."

"You think of everything."

When she stole a look at Drago, she noticed he was perspiring profusely. "Are you nervous?"

"I suppose I am."

His energy seemed to deplete substantially as they neared the chapel. And his hands began to shake. "I don't know if I can go inside."

"You're having second thoughts?" Panic seized her.

"Not at all."

"What's wrong, then?"

"It's been a long time since I've been inside a church."

She laughed. "I'm sure lightning won't strike."

"You don't understand," Drago said, becoming unhinged.

"Are you really too nervous to go inside?"

"Yes." His limbs joined his hands in an uncontrolled tremor.

"I've always dreamed of having a church wedding," she said, "but I can compromise for you."

"You're willing to do that?"

She nodded. "It looks like there's a courtyard next to the chapel. Maybe the pastor will marry us outside."

He gripped her hand. "Would you mind asking him?"

"Of course."

Thankfully, the pastor agreed—and even brought out his wife as a witness. The warm hues of sunset showered the brief ceremony, while a crisp breeze fluttered the modest bouquet of flowers Rose held in her hands.

After they exchanged wedding vows, Drago kissed her, long and soft, and she couldn't help but think it was the happiest day she had ever spent.

Unbeknownst to her, their union marked the start of an eerie, downhill spiral.

Drago's new show was set to open in three weeks. After Rose sent a telegram to the Marconis telling them she'd married Drago, the starry-eyed newlyweds spent a relaxing week in East Hampton. Then, it was time to rush back to the city to prepare for opening night.

As Rose settled into their rehearsal schedule *and* Drago's apartment near the theater, her guilt started to weigh her down. She'd had no contact with Olivia, Elena, Lorenzo, or Anthony, which increased her shame and sense of disconnection.

In those weeks, she was left to wonder if Richard had made good on Drago's demand that he recommend her to the editor of *The Daily Gazette*. More importantly, had Richard destroyed the photo of Drago on the laundry line?

Rose was dying to know, but she didn't see how she could find out. Rather, she concentrated on performing. The Herndon Hippodrome was undoubtedly the most intimidating theater along Broadway. Large and stately, the theater emanated an aura of authority. In fact, it towered over the other auditoriums with a presence that said, "Anyone who performs here has hit the big time."

Unfortunately, Rose didn't consider herself one of those worthy people. At best, she was an amateur. Compared to Drago's polished showmanship, she was even pathetic. She'd lost count of how many props she dropped during their rehearsals—yet Drago remained patient and loving.

"Do it again, Rose," he would encourage with a hand pressed to the small of her back. Fortunately, Drago's authentic abilities left little for Rose to actually master. An experienced professional, he could astound spectators without revealing the fact that he was a real-life sorcerer.

A half hour before the show started on opening night, Rose pulled her costume out of the wardrobe and eyed it with distaste. Comprised of fishnet stockings, black elbow-length gloves, and a tiny leotard covered in sequins, the costume was daring to say the least.

She sought Drago out to complain. "Don't you think I ought to wear a skirt of some sort—to cover my legs?" she asked.

He drew her to him. "Showing your magnificent legs is the idea. Remember, distraction is the key."

Rose took a glance around to make sure they were alone in the dressing room. "But you don't need an attractive assistant to distract the audience. Your magic is real."

"You're right. I could do the show with my eyes closed," he joked, "But then I couldn't see your fabulous legs."

She laughed—and it felt good because she'd been close to tears all day.

"Now hurry and dress darling. We open in twenty minutes."

Rose's gut clenched. *Can I really do this . . . perform in front of hundreds of people?* She couldn't erase her self-doubt. As a result, her nerves soared to a faulty high. Drago seemed to sense her apprehension because he gave her an enormous hug.

Archibald McMillan entered the dressing room and grinned. "Break it up, you two lovebirds." He extended his hand to Drago. "You're about to make us some serious money. Are you ready, Starkov?"

While Drago shook McMillan's hand, Rose studied the thin manager. Pencil-necked and clean-shaven, he stood even taller than his client. McMillan reminded her of a giraffe. And while he wasn't the warmest character in the world, he was savvy to the ins-and-outs of show business.

"I'm as ready as I'll ever be," Drago replied.

"Right then. I suggest you slip into that slinky costume, Rose. Meanwhile, I'll tell the house to open the doors." McMillan strode to the door then stopped and looked back. "It's show time, folks!"

Nausea stuttered up her throat. She must have gone pale since Drago squeezed her hand. "What have I been saying all along? You can do this, darling."

She managed a smile. "If you say so . . ."

"I'll meet you in the wings in five minutes. We need to get into position."

She nodded before Drago left the dressing room in his formal finery. Trying to convince herself that they were simply holding another rehearsal without an audience, she changed into the minuscule costume and headed out the door, too.

A swelling overture swept through the theater. From the wings, Rose stole a look at the auditorium. It was filled to the brim. Judging by the expressions on the patrons' faces, some were wholly skeptical while others were wholly fanatical. The varied looks told Rose that the stakes had risen since Drago's time at the Sunshine Theater.

Pulse thrumming, she stepped onstage behind Drago. Thunderous applause greeted them and when Drago introduced her as his wife, the applause increased.

With trembling feet, Rose took a step forward. That's when she spotted Patrick and Anthony in the second row.

CHAPTER 20

The theater fell into a surreal silence around Rose. In the back of her mind, she knew people were actually talking but as she watched Drago's mouth move, she couldn't make out the words. Anxiousness crawled up her spine. Her stare flitted back to Patrick who gave her an emphatic scowl. Meanwhile, Anthony flung her one of his sour expressions.

Rose turned to Drago. He'd locked eyes with Patrick and Anthony, too. But in keeping with his professional persona, he smiled their way and went on with the show. His composure helped Rose snap out of her nervous fog. She and Drago went on to perform the "Sawing a Woman in Half" trick and the "Boxed Person with Missing Abdomen" illusion. Then Drago temporarily hypnotized a half dozen people with highly entertaining results.

The spectacular show, with its fanfare of exotic sets, birds, and dancers, couldn't have gone better.

Perspiring, Drago escaped into the wings afterward and growled instructions to Archibald. "Now that the show's over, don't let anyone backstage! Do you understand?"

"Got it," McMillan replied.

"I mean anyone." Drago said. "And you held the reporters outside, right?"

"Yup." McMillan pushed his hat back on his head. "You seem especially testy tonight, Starkov. What's wrong?"

"I'm fine. Just do as I say."

McMillan shot him a contemptuous look but left it at that.

Rose found Drago backstage and rushed into his arms. "You saw them, too? Patrick and Anthony, I mean."

"I saw them all right. Why the hell can't they leave us alone?"

"How did you remain so calm during the show?"

"Why give them the power?" He paused. "At least during the performance."

She drew back. "*During* the performance?"

"Now I'm going to teach O'Leary a lesson once and for all."

"Don't hurt him!" Rose cried.

His eyes turned dark. "Why? Do you still have feelings for him?"

"He was never anything more than a friend. But I broke his heart."

"He's a big boy, Rose."

"Let it go," she pleaded. "We're married now."

That seemed to settle Drago down. "Maybe you're right." The redness drained from his face. "I have what he wants, and nothing will change that." Struggling to compose himself, he left her in order to change.

"Rose?" Patrick's voice stopped her cold. She wheeled around and saw him coming up the side steps of the stage. A security guard barred his way. Emotions tore at Rose. Should she talk to him or send him away?

Finally, she gave the guard permission to let Patrick continue up the stairs.

"How were you allowed to stay inside the theater?" she asked.

"My cousin moonlights here as an usher." Fidgeting with his hat, he gave her a smile. Half of his face was slightly misaligned and she realized that his jaw must not have healed properly after Drago pounded his face. "Anthony is here, too. He's waiting for me in the lobby."

"I know. I saw both of you in the audience."

"You look well, Rose."

"You should go, Patrick. If my husband sees you—"

"That's right." He cut her short. "You're married to that monster now."

"Monster? How dare you!"

He stepped closer. "The police have discovered scandalous things about your husband. Furthermore, Richard Bellum is working with us to expose Dragomir Starkov as a fake."

Alarm pulsed through her. *Richard hasn't stopped his antics . . .*

"You're in a dangerous situation. I'm urging you to leave Drago," Patrick said softly.

"I won't leave him. In fact, I'll be relaying this information to him." She lifted her chin.

"I'm sure you will, but it won't matter. When Bellum gets done with Starkov, he'll be the laughingstock of the nation—and you'll sink into humiliation alongside him."

She swayed on her feet. "What do you mean?"

"This is your chance to get out, Rose."

"I'm perfectly fine where I am."

"Look at yourself." Patrick's eyes roved over her scanty costume. "Look what you've lowered yourself to."

"Thank you for the warning, Patrick, but I have no intention of abandoning my husband," she repeated. "Now leave before I fetch him myself."

With pain in his eyes, Patrick nodded. He treaded down the stairs and disappeared into the lobby. Meanwhile, Rose turned to find Drago. To her surprise, he was hidden in the shadows, fists clenched.

"I heard your conversation," he growled. "It took everything I had to stop myself from pummeling that bastard all over again."

She sucked in a breath. "I had it in hand."

"I'm proud of you," Drago ground out.

"What do you think the police have discovered about you?"

"I can only imagine."

She went to him and touched his jacket lapel. "And what are we going to do about Bellum?"

"He's a jackass who doesn't deserve to live."

"You can't kill him!" Repulsion tinged her words.

"I'm not going to kill him," Drago said. "But I am going to scare him into keeping his mouth shut."

* * *

Later that night, Drago stormed off to tinker in his workshop. Alone in their apartment, Rose lay in bed, listening to the sounds outside the window. Motorcars beeped loudly, streetcars hummed along their tracks, and pedestrians scurried to late night activities.

The noises made it impossible for her to sleep so she got out of bed and threw open the window. Shades of autumn had settled over New York, bringing with them a biting wind. As Rose breathed in the crisp air, a soft knock at the door made her spin around.

"Who is it?" she called out as she shut the window.

"It's Olivia."

She hastened to the door, thrust it open, and pulled Olivia into a hug. "It's so good to see you!"

"Oh, Rose. We've been so worried about you!"

Rose could feel Olivia's heart beat wildly. Her adoptive sister stepped inside the warm apartment and removed her coat.

"How did you find me?"

"Drago's manager gave me your address," Olivia replied.

"He did?"

"I told him who I was. After that didn't work, I flirted with him a little."

Rose smiled and invited her to sit on the sofa.

"I came because Anthony saw the magic show tonight," Olivia admitted.

"I know. He was there with Patrick."

Surprise lit Olivia's eyes. "Did you speak to them?"

"I spoke to Patrick." She paused. "Unfortunately, he didn't have very nice things to say to me."

"We've been so concerned about you. Mama and Papa are beside themselves."

"It all happened so fast," Rose explained as she joined Olivia on the sofa.

"What happened so fast? Drago sweeping you off your feet?"

"Yes."

Olivia took in a breath. "It hurts that you haven't contacted me."

"I sent a telegram telling you and your family that I got married."

Olivia shot her a forlorn look. "I was talking about *after* you came back to New York." She paused. "Are you sure you know what you're doing, Rose?"

"I've never been happier." She sighed. "Now I have someone to belong to."

Puzzlement washed over Olivia's face. "You've always belonged to our family."

"Not really," Rose murmured. "You have no idea what it's like to be adopted."

Olivia squared her shoulders. "Drago isn't the answer to all your problems. Don't you wonder about what the police and the press have uncovered about him?"

"I think Patrick just said that to scare me."

"No, it's true. Anthony claims that everyone is banding together to discredit Drago."

Rose wrung her hands. "Then I wish I knew what Richard and Patrick know. I'd be able to if I could polish my parents' gift of clairvoyance."

"You wish you could see the future at will?"

"Yes. I only see snatches—and there are long intervals between visions."

Olivia shook her head. "No, thank you. Knowing what's going to happen would be a terrible gift."

"I think it would solve a lot of things."

The dark-haired girl crossed her arms in protest as Rose went on. "Although I can't tell what will happen, I know someone who can."

Olivia clutched her handbag tightly. "Who?"

"My mother."

"No. Mama said your parents want no contact with you until after your twenty-first birthday. Until they know it's safe for you to seek them out."

"You don't understand! Drago has telepathic abilities and he senses that Morvina is close to me *now*."

"And you say you're happy?" Olivia quipped.

"Okay, maybe I'm a little concerned."

"You have every right to be."

Rose considered Olivia's words. Finally, she wrung her hands. "I guess I should give up on telling the future."

Olivia studied her disappointment. Then she let out a resigned huff. "Maybe you can find out where your parents are from clues in the photo album Mama showed you."

"That's a great idea!" Rose said. "Would you be a dear and bring it to me?"

"Why don't you pay Mama and Papa a visit yourself?"

"They're bent on keeping me away from Drago."

Olivia's lips quirked. "I don't know if I should . . ."

"Please? And before the weather gets too brutal, I'd love to have my favorite winter coat."

Objection shadowed Olivia's face. "It's a lot to ask."

"What are sisters for?" Rose smiled.

"All right. I'll be back in an hour."

As promised, Olivia returned, but her face was awash with concern. She handed Rose the photo album and said, "I looked for the coat."

"And?" Rose asked.

"It's been cut up."

"Cut up?"

Olivia gulped and nodded. "I found shreds of it at the bottom of your closet."

"My God," Rose muttered. *Has Morvina been inside the Marconi home?*

Trying to stomp down her sense of alarm, she sucked in a breath. Then she sat on the sofa and flipped through the photo album Olivia handed her. Several minutes later, she came across a faded article about the séance room the Hayes set up on the Upper East Side. "This is it! A lot of mediums live next door to their séance rooms. My parents might still reside there!"

"I hope you're right," Olivia said ruefully.

"I'm going to make an appointment for a tarot card reading under a false name," Rose informed her.

"Are you going to tell Drago?"

"Of course," she replied. "I want my parents to meet my husband."

*   *   *

"It's a bad idea," Drago protested when Rose spoke to him about it the next night.

"Why?" she asked, as they lay in bed.

"You may get your feelings hurt."

"How?"

"Your parents might deny that they're really your parents."

"Why would they do that? I'm sure that they want to be reunited as much as I do."

Drago shifted toward her. A lock of his chestnut hair fell over one of his eyes. "What if your mother tells you things about your future you don't want to know?"

"You're not considering this the right way," she protested. "Maybe my mother can tell me who Morvina is disguised as."

"It's a bad idea anyway you look at it, Rose."

Tears sprang to her eyes. "Why? Are you afraid a tarot reading will reveal more secrets from your past?"

He didn't answer her.

"I'm sorry I said that." Rose looked down at her hands. "But I want to go and I want you to come with me. I've waited a lifetime to meet my real parents. Now that I know they're only blocks away I don't want to wait any longer."

He reached for her hand. "You must understand, darling. I think your parents instructed the Marconis to keep you hidden for a reason."

Rose titled her head as she listened. "I know. For my safety."

"You have to remember what your mother saw in her vision."

"She saw me plummeting to my death."

"And she was scared enough about it to want your identity to remain a mystery. In other words, keeping you hidden from Morvina remains the safest thing to do."

"Maybe you're right," Rose softened her tone. Olivia had said the same thing.

"Of course I'm right. You see, we're able to calm each other down. That's the sign of a good marriage."

Rose wasn't sure if their marriage was good—or even normal. But Drago did have the ability to talk sense into her. She squeezed his hand and snuggled close. "I've waited twenty years to meet my real parents. I guess I can wait a few more months."

He sighed. "That's the spirit."

That was close, Morvina thought as she used every source of witchcraft available to sense the conversation between Rose and Drago. Rose had nearly sought her birth parents out to ask for their help. The idea sent unease rattling through Morvina like a roller-coaster at Coney Island.

The last thing she needed was Rose and Drago finding out who she was disguising herself as. Then she'd have to assume a different identity. *I'm glad you talked her out of it, Drago. You always had a selfish streak. And I bet you were worried what Florence Hayes would have seen about you during the reading.*

Anxious that Rose might insist on seeing her real parents again, Morvina grabbed her jacket and marched outside. Colorful fall leaves spun in airy circles around the male dress shoes she wore. Drifting snowflakes landed on her head. She knew exactly where the Hayes' townhouse was located. Although it may take some time to set up the "accident", she decided that the place needed to go up in flames.

CHAPTER 21

Drago's urgent voice shook Rose awake. "Read the morning paper."

Groggy-eyed, she sat up in bed and accepted the newspaper from him. When she read the headline of the article he was pointing to, she gasped.

Dragomir Starkov Proved a Cheap Fake.

Drago watched her intensely as she scanned the rest of the exposé written by Richard Bellum. It revealed Drago's association with Felix Huxtable, the biggest con artist around. It also claimed that Drago had attended Harry Houdini's shows to take notes and to steal his catchphrase: *I have one secret that explains everything I do. I challenge you to discover it.*

The damaging article also included an interview with Drago's former assistant, Katherine. Because of her bitterness toward him, she lied by swearing his illusions were falsified gimmicks. Gimmicks that could be explained step-by-step. She damaged Drago's reputation further by claiming that anyone who participated in his shows was in on the act.

Then there were the photos. While Bellum hadn't printed the one of Drago disappearing on the laundry line, he claimed he saw a mirror on the top floor of the tenement opposite Drago's . . . a mirror the magician used to perform his vanishing act. And the photo Bellum did include had been tampered with. It displayed a wire that was seemingly pulling down the clothesline—as if to suggest that the laundry line was bearing a person's weight.

Bellum even had the audacity to print a photo of himself—as Drago slammed him against the wall in the Bowery. Apparently, it'd been taken in secret that dark night by someone Bellum hired.

But the icing on the cake came when Richard suggested Drago had married Rose so that he could have someone to manipulate.

Where Starkov's wife, Rose, is concerned, Bellum wrote, *perhaps Drago actually performed a valid feat of hypnotism. He bestowed an ancient Egyptian talisman upon her. The amulet is said to bring death, suicide, and destruction to its wearer. It's my belief that this talisman gives Starkov cruel control over innocent Rose.*

Bellum concluded the article with the following summation: *If Dragomir the Magnificent is a charlatan bent on fooling the public, he's a man low enough to seduce a woman into doing what he wants, when he wants.*

"I thought Richard was determined to expose you as a dark wizard. Not a fake," Rose cried.

"People come to my shows in the hopes that I'm different. That I can do the impossible. It's what makes them flock to my performances."

"Bellum knew this kind of story would hurt your career more," Rose said miserably.

Mortified, she put a hand to her mouth and shook her head. She finally added, "I guess you didn't scare Richard into keeping his mouth shut."

Drago took the newspaper from her and crumpled it up. "He is one clever bastard."

Rose got out of bed only to sink into a nearby chair. Running her hands through her rumpled hair, she fought off tears. "Maybe this is a good thing. I hate to think what would happen if people believed you're a warlock, Drago."

"We'd cross that bridge when we came to it." He paced in front of the bed. "But we have this to contend with right now."

"I'm sorry your reputation has been affected."

He scowled back at her. "Affected? My reputation has just been thrown in the toilet."

She eyed the newspaper on the bed with disdain.

Drago punched the wall and didn't even shake his hand from the pain. "I wish I could ring that vulture's neck!"

"It won't undo the damage the article has already done," she said sadly.

"That's what a civilized person would say." Drago stalked with his fists pumped. "But I'm not always civilized, Rose. In fact, as soon as I read Bellum's article, I went to *The Gotham Times* and asked to see that lowlife. Lucky for him he's out of town—but I'm sure he planned it that way."

Rose couldn't stand the anguish in Drago's face. "Only time will tell the long-term effects of what Bellum wrote. Maybe it won't be as bad as all that."

Time did tell. Eventually Drago started playing to a half-empty house, then a sparse house, and then an empty house. Worse yet, spectators wanted refunds for tickets they had purchased in advance. The fiasco turned into ruination—which led to McMillan terminating his contract with the Starkovs.

As if the gods knew she couldn't take anymore, Rose received more bad news.

"There's been an accident." Drago's words roused her from a deep sleep one night. "It's your parents, Rose. Malcolm and Florence Hayes are dead . . ."

Rose disintegrated into a ball of tears and sorrow, useless to anyone for many days.

In the weeks that followed, she couldn't understand how the fire started. The firemen attributed it to faulty wiring in the Hayes' townhouse. The police, on the other hand, suspected arson. Further investigation proved that the fire started when a spark ignited a bottle of kerosene which had been left in the midst of a gas leak.

What was a bottle of kerosene doing in my parents' home?

Rose didn't have the answer. And that made her absence from her parents' funeral all the more painful.

Her skipping the funeral had been Elena Marconi's idea. Elena had sent word to Rose immediately following Florence and Malcolm Hayes's demise. She'd asked to see her in light of the tragic news.

Teary-eyed, Rose's adoptive mother met her in the park on a Saturday afternoon. Rose managed to keep the appointment secret by telling Drago she was going shopping. Elena approached her, then enfolded her in a hug to break the ice. They sat and talked for hours. In the end, they came to the conclusion that the fire was Morvina's handiwork.

"It's best that you stay away from your parents' funeral," Elena said before she left. "If that witch spies you at the ceremony, she'll have located you. Then, heaven help you."

Rose felt as if her heart was being ripped from her chest, but she reluctantly agreed. Her parents were people she would never know now. The cold, hard fact killed a piece of her spirit.

"Will you report back to me about the funeral?" she asked Elena.

"Of course. And I'm glad we're talking again."

"So am I."

Elena rested a hand on Rose's arm. "I'm sorry that I cannot accept Drago as your husband. At least for the time being."

"Do you still think he is the creature that will destroy me?" Rose asked.

"According to what your mother saw in her vision, I have no reason to believe otherwise."

"I wish I could convince you that Drago loves me more than life itself."

"I hope to God that's true," Elena said before they parted.

It turned out that New York's most prominent people attended Malcolm and Florence Hayes's funeral in upstate New York. The mayor. Film stars and aristocrats. Even Harry Houdini, whose appearance made for a startling photograph that ended up in the morning paper. Apparently the famous magician had forged a close connection with the famous mediums before they died.

Rose steadied herself on Drago's arm as she made her way to a church on Twentieth Street. Drago remained outside while she slipped in to light a candle for her parents. Tears spilled forth as she studied the candle's flame—a reminder that there were so many unanswered questions.

Why hadn't her parents foreseen the fire? Had Morvina been able to block the vision to protect herself? And had they wanted to reunite with her as desperately as she wanted to reunite with them?

Rose's body ached with the fact that she *would* have met her parents if Drago hadn't talked her out of it.

That week, the show at the Hippodrome closed completely. A cloud of depression hung over her and Drago as a result. Fall rolled into winter—and the dismal December weather only added to their unhappiness.

One night, she and Drago lay together on the sofa. "Let's go away," Drago said suddenly. "Far away. There's nothing left for us here."

"Nothing?" She frowned. "New York City is my home."

He locked eyes with her. "I was going to whisk you away in June, right before your twenty-first birthday. But let's go now."

"I thought you wanted to redeem yourself professionally."

Drago pulled her closer. "Success is heady stuff, but you're more important. You need to clear your head and get a fresh start. I hate seeing how depressed you are."

"I know you're just as sad as I am. For a different reason. Your show . . ."

Drago scowled. "It's not about me enjoying the limelight, Rose. I promised my father that I'd be much more than a farmer one day. We shared a love of magic, and I wanted him to be proud of me." He paused. "But all that has changed."

She managed a smile. "I'm sure your father is proud of you no matter what."

He kissed her on the forehead.

A long silence ensued in the small parlor. Finally, Rose whispered, "I'm scared, Drago. Scared of Morvina."

He sucked in a breath. "Then please agree to go away with me."

"Where should we go? Won't she find me anywhere?"

"Not if we go somewhere unexpected and remote."

"Where?"

"I never took you on a honeymoon, did I?" He was trying to lighten the mood, but Rose wasn't having it.

Drawing her to sitting position, he looked into her eyes. "Why don't we visit my château in France?"

"You have a French château?" How much money *did* he have?

He hugged her tightly as she buried her face in his chest.

"When can we leave?" she asked.

"Any time we want. In fact, I'll book us passage on the next ship."

"That sounds wonderful. A hiatus might give the public time to forget Bellum's blasted article," Rose said.

"Once you live through your twenty-first birthday, which I'm damned certain you will, maybe I can come back and resurrect my career."

Rose clung to him and listened to his steady breathing.

"Morvina will get her comeuppance," he said. "You'll see. Do you remember what Edmond Dantés carved on his prison wall in *The Count of Monte Cristo*?"

"God will give me justice."

He nodded.

"I didn't know you were religious," Rose said softly.

"I used to be."

Following an extended passage to Europe, Rose found herself gazing at the rolling French countryside. It was winter, and while the temperatures here were chilly, at least sun shone over the landscape.

Rose's first glimpse of Château de Maincy—Drago's stately home—stole her breath away. Situated fifty-five kilometers southeast of Paris, the lush estate bloomed with vibrant history. What's more, it possessed expansive gardens touched with frost, ornate domes topped in pale blue, and an actual moat.

"The house was built in 1683 for Jean-Daniel Girard, the Viscount of Maincy," Drago explained above the hum of the taxicab.

"It looks more like a palace than a château," Rose said as she held onto her hat.

"Actually, it *was* a palace in those days."

"Really?"

Drago nodded. "The Viscount of Maincy was a distant heir to the French throne."

The cab clamored over a wide stone bridge. Rose glanced at the façade of the estate. Two pavilions flanked a central *avant-corps* engraved with golden fleurs de lis. And the vaulted, two-story portico that canopied them as they drove under it overwhelmed Rose with its grandeur.

How on earth did Drago afford to buy this house? Even if he was a renowned magician in Romania?

The taxi driver helped the couple bring in their luggage. Judging from his greedy gleam and extended hand, he expected a substantial tip. Grinning, Drago slapped thirty francs into the gentleman's hand.

The driver tugged on his hat brim and told them he'd be happy to assist them further.

"Will we be alone in this house, like the one in East Hampton?" Rose asked as she perused the large foyer.

"No. I keep a full staff on. The house is too big and I don't want it to fall into ruin."

A housekeeper materialized and smiled warmly at Rose. "*Bonjour,* Madame Starkov."

Embarrassed, Rose felt her cheeks flush. "I don't speak French."

"It's no problem," the stout woman replied in perfect English.

"Oh, thank goodness." Rose put a hand over her heart. She took a minute to study the middle-aged woman. Her unlined face contrasted a full head of gray hair. Around her thick middle she wore a starched white apron trimmed with gray scallops.

It didn't take long for Rose to decide that she liked the matronly housekeeper.

"I'm Madame Pontbriand. But you may call me Madame P."

"It's lovely to meet you."

"It's wonderful to see both of you." The housekeeper continued to smile. "We received your telegraph yesterday, Monsieur Starkov. You were away too long this time."

"I agree," Drago said kindly. "I'd like to settle in before I show my wife around. Is our suite ready, Madame P?"

She nodded. "Follow me."

Rose and Drago strode hand-in hand behind the stout house-keeper. The more Rose saw of the house's astonishing interior, the more in awe of it she was. A scrolled staircase layered in silver leaf ascended to a lofty second level lined with plush carpets and brilliant frescoes of seventeenth-century France. And Rose and Drago's suite was beyond stunning. A bed draped in periwinkle blue curtains centered the huge room, which was replete with a sitting area and a balcony that stretched over a boxwood garden.

The suite combined the taste of a sophisticated woman with a young girl's fairy tale dream, and Rose loved it. She opened the French doors to a sharp breeze. The fresh air refreshed her soul—and gave her hope that she could chase away her grief.

"The air's a bit cleaner than in New York, eh?" Drago came up behind her.

"Hmm . . ." she replied.

"Do you like the house, darling?"

"I adore it! However did you leave this place for that shoddy apartment in New York?"

He laughed as he encircled her waist. "*You* were the only thing enticing enough to lure me away from here."

Madame Pontbriand cleared her throat as she stood in the doorway.

Drago peered at her over his shoulder. "Thank you, Madame P. That will be all."

"Will you and Mrs. Starkov be coming down to supper?"

"I don't think so," he replied with a sly smile.

As soon as Madame Pontbriand shut the door, Drago swiveled Rose around for a hot kiss. The feel of his mouth over hers made her sigh and moan at the same time. Like he'd done the first night they made love, Drago actually *tasted* her. She melted against him and let his hands wander over her curves. Soon, the need for him to make love to her burned a trail from her stomach up to her lips. She never could resist his touch.

Drago took her face in his hands and claimed her mouth some more. Rose made herself breathe slowly, so as not to relay the sorrow she'd hidden deep inside. More than anything, she wished he could make the past month vanish like one of his stage doves.

As if he'd read her mind, he uttered, "I'm so sorry for everything, Rose."

She clung to him, tears pricking her eyes. When he slid his tongue forward gently and intertwined it with hers, she emitted a tiny cry. Emotion sprang between them—and while he caressed her face, they fitted their bodies together with familiarity and a reignited lust.

Drago lifted Rose in his arms and laid her down on the bed. After brushing her mouth with another scintillating kiss, he explored her body through her clothes. Passion burst through her and she relaxed in his arms.

After moments of being tender, Drago showed his impatience. He yanked off her blouse and stared at her breasts through the transparent chemise. Then he tugged the straps of the chemise down over her shoulders. And after he bunched the material under her breasts, he pushed them upward.

"Look at that," he said as he swept the pads of his thumbs over her risen nipples. "Now that is truly erotic."

Swiftly, he removed every scrap of Rose's clothes. Then he unbuttoned his shirt and peeled it off. His muscular chest rose and fell in quick breaths and Rose could see his shaft straining against his trousers. He proceeded to kick off his shoes and strip off his pants, releasing his engorged sex. With his lips slightly parted, he looked at her. *Really* looked at her.

"Have I told you you're the most beautiful woman I've ever seen?" He gave her one of his infamous crooked grins before he joined her on the coverlet.

"Oh, Drago," she murmured.

Once he'd rolled on top of her, he kissed her deeply. Rose responded by running her fingertips along his bare back. For a minute, she stared at the canopy above them. Then, finding it hard to believe that she was here in these elegant surroundings, she gave a small smile. Her breasts rubbed against Drago's smooth chest and after he pushed her thighs apart, he slid his hand into her moisture.

"You're already wet," he said hoarsely.

"Yes—"

"I like that." He kissed her neck—and when he began stroking her folds with more pressure, red-hot desire flushed through Rose. Before she knew it, he'd located her cleft. With his special touch, he petted it, then vibrated it. As a wonderful friction built at the apex of her legs, her breasts grew heavy and sensitive. He seemed to sense it. Dragging her nipple into his mouth, he played over it with the tip of his tongue. All the while he went on stimulating her with two stiffened fingers.

"You feel so good," he bit out.

"God," Rose cried as he caught her erect nipple between his teeth. She closed her eyes—and let the sensations of his fingers against her petals and his hot mouth suckling her breast charge her right to a pinnacle. When the throbbing subsided, she met his stare.

"Close your eyes again," he instructed softly. "The key to magic is letting yourself *experience* something."

Lifting the bulk of her breast to his mouth again, he continued to play over her nipple with his tongue . . . groaning with pleasure as he did so.

Reveling in the feel of his mouth, she grew damp again.

"Your breasts are so sensitive," he said. "I want you to peak once more."

Drago lapped at her tender bud, teasing and sucking it into a point until an intense heat rippled through her. Nodding, he pressed his erection against the cushion of her thigh. He gave his shaft a few pumps with his hand before he rubbed its tip against her slit. She looked down at the shiny crown of his penis.

"Spread your legs for me, Rose," Drago's nostrils flared. "I'm as hard as sin."

His raw voice spawned her desire to a new high. Anxious for him to fill her, her knees fell away from one another. Her center beat in hot pulses.

"Are you ready for me?" he asked.

She nodded. He sank into her and as she grasped his muscular shoulders, he rocked his cock forward like a ship maneuvering the high seas. Rose looked up at him, astounded by his male beauty all over again. With his trim torso, sinewy waist, and hardened forearms, he seemed to be sculpted from granite. But she knew Drago was only hard on the outside. She loved him—and she wanted him to come, too.

Cupping her breasts in her own hands, she played seductively with her hardened nipples as he hovered over her. Then she shot him a seductive, doe-eyed look.

Drago glanced down at her. Lust darkened his stare before he arched his head back. "Christ, Rose. Do you know how sensual that is?"

She smiled coyly.

"If you're willing, I want you to touch yourself."

Slowly, she lowered her hand to her soft mound of hair. Drago was inside her so she was only able to rub the top half of his shaft. Next, she caressed her own flesh and the exposed column of his sex simultaneously. Nothing had ever felt so carnal.

"That's my ultimate fantasy," he murmured. "And if you touch me underneath, you'll make me climax."

Under his shaft? Rose wondered. Unsure, she slid her fingers beneath his sack.

"Fondle me."

She did. Squeezing his testicles gently prompted him to grab her hips. Thrusting more fervently, he said, "Squeeze them harder."

She was afraid she'd hurt him, but when she gripped his balls tighter, he slammed his way to an astounding climax. Perspiring and shuddering repeatedly, Drago let his weight sag on top of her.

When his breathing eventually evened, he gathered her close. "Do you know how much I love you?"

She nodded because she loved him back the very same way.

CHAPTER 22

Afternoon faded into night. Rose lay awake, listening to Drago's soft snore. Since she was facing him, she was able to study him while he slept. It proved fascinating. He drew his brows together from time to time, as if he were experiencing a nightmare. But then a hint of a smile would replace his frown—telling Rose that he'd begun dreaming of something more pleasant.

As she swept a lock of hair off his forehead, she decided that she preferred him like this. Relaxed. Hair mussed. Face unshaven.

Drago was such a complex man—and only when he was at rest did he seem peaceful. While he insisted on formality and professionalism in the public eye, Rose knew him better. He'd moved beyond his humble beginnings to reach stardom. But she assumed the journey hadn't been an easy one.

"I wish I could have known your parents—and my own," she whispered in the darkness.

Rolling onto her back, she glanced over at the night table. As moonlight filtered through the parted curtains and a sudden breeze swatted a tree branch against the window, she eyed the bracelet of Amenhotep. The Romanian lei coin sat adjacent to it on the table.

These objects never leave my possession except when I sleep. She remembered Drago's words and they flushed temptation through her veins. Should she pick up the coin?

Taking a peek into Drago's past was something Rose yearned to do, but she couldn't break his trust.

Instead of picking the coin up and prodding it for information, she lay in the shadows and listened to the gurgle of her empty stomach. She was starving. While the aroma of beef had wafted up to the suite hours ago, she and Drago had been too busy making love to go down to dinner.

Apparently, the rumbling was loud enough to wake Drago. Opening his eyes, he shot her a playful expression. "I thought I wore you out."

She smiled. Then she folded her hands and looked up at the billowing canopy. "I'm too hungry to sleep."

He sat up and scrubbed a hand over his face. "We can't have that. Let's put on our robes and raid the kitchen."

"Can we?" she asked in astonishment.

"It's our house, darling. We can do whatever we like."

Cheeks flushed, she left the bed and pulled on a dressing robe. Meanwhile, Drago yanked on a sapphire blue robe. As he tugged her out the door and down the stairs, she noticed that the house sat quiet amid shadows that seemed desperate to speak.

"After we eat, remind me to show you something," Drago whispered.

They entered a spacious kitchen and Rose eyed an old stove, a hanging pot rack, and a large servants' table. Drago extracted food from the icebox and balanced it in one hand.

While he and Rose sat by the empty stone hearth and she feasted on cold roast beef, grapes, cheese, and wine, he snuggled close to her. He even fed her a few grapes and shared the last of the delicious wine.

"That was scrumptious," she said in a whisper. "Shall we go back to bed now?"

"There's something I want to show you, remember?"

"What is it?"

Drago looked at her through the shadows. "First of all, let me inform you that this château is haunted."

"Haunted?" The thought raised her neck hair.

"Yes. The Viscount who owned this house originally, Jean-Daniel Girard, died a mysterious death. Some claim it was murder. Some say it was suicide."

"His ghost haunts these halls?"

He nodded. "Numerous people have seen it. The chambermaids, the groundskeeper. Even Madame P. had a run-in with this ghost."

"Have *you* seen it?" she asked.

"Yes."

"Is it an angry spirit?" He'd piqued her curiosity.

Drago led her into the main drawing room. After he illuminated a gas lamp, he guided her to a wall of portraits.

"Girard's apparition didn't seem angry to me," he said. "It seemed more morose than anything."

Goosebumps prickled Rose's arm as they stopped in front of an enormous painting. "The story goes that the viscount was a notorious bachelor," Drago continued, "a man who stole women's hearts without a glance back. That is, until he met *her*."

Rose was about to ask who "her" was, when Drago raised his lamp. Its beam shone upward and shed light on the massive gilded portrait before them. The figure in the painting had been created to nearly human scale, and he was dashing. In fact, the nobleman appeared so life-like that Rose half expected him to step out of the painting and converse with her. Tall and muscular, Jean-David Girard wore a white, curled wig and early eighteenth-century clothing. But beneath all the frivolous period attire, she could see his vivid aquamarine eyes and angular face.

Despite his good looks, Rose sensed that agony lived behind his physical features. "Who is the woman you mentioned? Girard's true love?" she asked.

Drago replied grimly, "She was a servant and amid a scandal of the aristocracy, she left him."

"Do you know what happened?"

"I just know that this woman was a scullery maid in his castle. *This* castle. And that their love affair was an outrage."

Rose laced her fingers around Drago's arm. "That's such a sad tale. People should be able to be together—regardless of their social standing."

He nodded solemnly.

Still looking at the portrait, she said, "Those who die under tragic circumstances manifest themselves as ghosts. In their ghostly form, they can haunt a place forever . . . without crossing over to the other side."

Drago slid her a sideways glance. "How do you know so much about specters?"

Rose snapped out of her glazed state. "I've always been interested in the supernatural."

"Well," he said lightly, "that's sufficient warning about our resident spirit. In case you spot the handsome Monsieur Jean-Daniel, you'll be prepared."

She smiled. "Thank you for the history lesson."

As they made their way upstairs, Rose caught sight of a door hanging open on the second level. "Where do those steps lead?"

"To more bedrooms," Drago replied. "Oh, and to a sewing room. It contains one of those old-fashioned spinning wheels."

"Really?" she said excitedly. "Can you show me?"

"All right." Drago led the way. The light of his gas lamp stretched around the stone walls and aided their journey up the winding steps.

"In here," he said.

Rose stepped into a tiny room. In the corner sat the spinning wheel. Moonlight shone on the tip of its spindle. In contrast to its centuries-old surroundings, the object seemed strangely alive.

"How long has this been here?" Rose queried.

"It was here when I bought the house."

"Can you believe people had to *make* yarn back then?"

"Thank God they had servants."

Rose chuckled as she ran her hand over the waist-high object.

"Be careful of the spindle," Drago warned. "It's sharp."

She stepped back.

"I just had a thought," he said. "Maybe this spinning wheel could be part of an amazing magic trick."

"What kind of trick?"

"If I hypnotized someone and commanded them to touch the spindle, they'd do it in a dreamlike state—even though *consciously* they would never put their finger on something sharp. The action would convince people that I'm a viable magician with the ability to spellbind."

"I suppose it would," she said.

"I'm always thinking of ways to redeem myself."

"Don't worry. You will."

"Never mind that." He cocked one eyebrow. "Let's go back to bed so I can ravage you once again."

The next morning, a pair of songbirds chirped outside Drago and Rose's suite. After the birds' insistent tweeting urged Rose out of bed, she dressed in an off-white skirt, Beatrix blouse, and half boots. Scurrying downstairs, she located the bright-eyed housekeeper in the foyer.

"Good morning, Madame Starkov."

"Good morning," Rose greeted.

Madame P. smiled. "It's an unseasonable warm day."

"How nice."

The housekeeper paused. "It seems we had mice in the kitchen last night. Mice large enough to pull the remnants of dinner from the icebox."

"I'm sorry if we left a mess."

"I'm only teasing." The kindly woman's smile broadened. "Are you hungry for breakfast?"

"I am. Has my husband already eaten?"

Madame P. shook her head. "He's waiting for you in the gardens."

Claiming that she could find her own way, Rose thanked the woman and meandered outside. She descended a small slope to the geometrically-designed grounds. Bordered by a fruit orchard and a vineyard that Rose was sure would be lovely in spring, the boxwood gardens were breathtaking. Filled with expertly clipped cypress trees from Italy, and beautifully carved fountains, they beckoned to Rose.

Beyond the gardens, she spotted Drago seated under a shaded pavilion. She passed a deep pond littered with water lilies in order to reach him. He stood and planted a kiss on her cheek.

As Rose sat, she gazed at the display of food covering the glass table. Mounds of muffins, plates of scrambled eggs, and platters of potatoes were waiting patiently for her to dig into.

"Is this enough food?" Drago draped a napkin across her lap.

"More than enough! I'll gain a hundred pounds and become horribly spoiled if I stay here too long." She laughed.

"I'll still love you," he joked back.

A splashing fountain broke the silence as Rose ate. Meanwhile, Drago sat back and took in the stunning view. She watched him between bites. He looked extremely tired, as if he hadn't slept at all in these tranquil surroundings.

Maybe he was still more torn up about his career plummeting than he was letting on.

Stuffed, Rose leaned back in her chair. "I want to ask you something."

He raised an eyebrow.

"I've never seen you consume one morsel of food."

Drago pulled on his starched collar, his face flushed. "It's a personal quirk of mine."

"What is?"

"Eating in solitude. I don't like anyone watching me."

"I'm not anyone. I'm your wife," she reminded him gently.

"I'll get over the idiosyncrasy, but it will take time." He reached for her hand and pressed a kiss to it. "I've been alone for a long while."

Despite the picturesque landscape, the delicious food, and the impressive house, a sense of sadness washed over Rose again. "I've lived with that feeling too. That's why I was looking forward to meeting my birth parents."

"I know." He lowered his voice. "Did you bring the photo album with you? Perhaps that will make you feel close to them."

"How can I feel close to people I never met?"

"Your parents saw you when you were a baby, Rose. They held you and loved you for whatever brief amount of time."

"But *I* don't remember."

"I was hoping you'd forget your sorrow here," Drago said forlornly.

"I haven't. Being away from New York is making me feel more disconnected from the shreds of familiarity I had."

His face flushed deeper. "You're missing your old life more than I thought."

She flung him an emotional look.

"You've been here one day, Rose. Please give this place a chance."

Because she was left with no other option, unhappiness churned inside her. She agreed to give their time in France a chance, but afterward, she fell tensely silent.

CHAPTER 23

Drago never ate anything—and it was beginning to drive Rose crazy.

How can he possibly sustain his health? It was a subject she'd broached with him the day in the garden, but now she'd come to realize that he never even excused himself to eat in private.

Doesn't he have to eat to stay alive?

When she asked Madame P. about it, the housekeeper simply shrugged her shoulders. "Monsieur Starkov will eat when he's good and ready," was her response the third time Rose brought it up.

Feeling shunned, Rose avoided raising the subject again.

Drago's sleeping habits were equally strange. He slept the majority of the day, then seemed to come to life at night. It wouldn't have been *that* odd—if Rose hadn't tried to awaken him during the day so that he could sit in the garden with her or take a turn about the estate. She likened the attempts to waking the dead. He refused to move or stir. And the few hours he spent teaching her to drive his motorcar or having an afternoon picnic, he seemed drained of energy—as if he'd been taken ill.

She knew why Drago had an aversion to mirrors, but there were his bizarre interactions with the lei coin, too. Rose had seen him talk to it when he thought she wasn't looking. From the angle and distance at which she stood, she couldn't make out the images the coin projected. She had asked him to show her, but he refused.

That made her more desperate to handle the object herself.

Weeks turned into months at Château de Maincy and Rose and Drago began to argue more and more. Eventually, leisurely days filled with sunshine and tepid breezes built an icy wall that separated them. As the wall thickened, it stopped Drago from pretending to be happy without his magic—while it fueled Rose's angst over being separated from the Marconis.

They started doing fewer and fewer things together. Gradually, Rose's curiosity over her husband's strange habits escalated into annoyance, then alarm.

One morning in May, she sat down at the vanity to brush her hair. Because of Drago's aversion to mirrors, she was forced to use a small compact from her handbag to see her reflection. Flooded with irritation, she tensed when he called out to her from the washroom.

"Darling? Would you like to have lunch in the garden?"

Rose's spine tingled. Was he actually suggesting they do something together in the daytime? "That sounds lovely," she answered blandly. *He'll probably call it off as he usually does.*

As she set her brush down, he emerged from the washroom.

"Do I sense sarcasm in your tone?"

"It's just that I'm so tired," she said.

"We slept until ten o'clock today."

She looked up at him.

He knelt before her and traced the dark shadows encircling her eyes. "You *do* look tired."

"I wouldn't know," she replied dejectedly. "I can only view small portions of my face with this compact."

He winced and she looked away.

"What's really wrong, Rose?"

"We've had this conversation before. I wish I had known a lot of things about you before I married you."

Drago's thick brows drew together. "Am I all that bad?"

Her face heated.

"I'm sorry for not telling you everything," he said. "I guess I got swept up in romancing you."

Letting out a dismal sigh, she reached for his hand.

"You're everything to me," Drago reminded her. "I didn't want to lose you when we first met."

She made no reply.

"Doesn't this place make you happy?"

"I'm sure plenty of women would find it dazzling," she replied. "But I feel out of my element."

"Out of your element?"

"We're fooling ourselves, Drago. You sensed Morvina was disguising herself in New York, but she'll find me anywhere. I want to go back home."

"*Home*? Your home is with me." He gritted his teeth. "And it's easier to protect you here."

"I don't care." She began to cry.

He hesitated. "What do you mean you don't care?"

"I don't know myself anymore." She sobbed.

"I don't understand."

"I gave up everything to be with you. I don't regret it, but I think I lost myself along the way."

Brows knitted, he studied her. Then he sat back on his haunches and let out a deep sigh. "I wanted to keep you hidden from Morvina, but if going back to New York is what you want, then we'll return."

"Really?" She stopped crying.

"I'll do my best to guard you there." He paused and shot her a dire expression. "Besides, I have a feeling you'd go back there on your own. Am I right?"

She nodded as she wiped away her tears.

"You're a handful, but I love you, Rose." He tried to lighten the mood.

"I'm sure if people knew about my curse, they'd think I'm crazy to return to where Morvina might be."

"Damn other people." He caressed her cheek with the back of his hand. "I want *you* to be happy—and I intend to keep you safe from Morvina."

"I'm sorry I've been so melancholy lately."

"And I apologize for being so distant." His eyes twinkled. "I want to see you smile more often than every two or three weeks."

Rose heaved forward and hugged him. "When can we leave?"

"In a few days . . . after I make the necessary arrangements."

"Thank you!" she cried.

They embraced for a long time. Meanwhile, relief vibrated through Rose. As she breathed in Drago's fresh scent, she decided that returning to New York would be good for both of them. He could resurrect his career and she wouldn't be stuck here alone while he slept the days away.

He gave her a tender kiss before he stood up. "Now lie down and take a nap, darling. I'm headed to the village to get some toiletries."

"Why don't you send François instead?"

"Because the last time I sent that kitchen boy, he came back with six varieties of shave cream."

"He *is* incredibly eager."

"Do you need anything?"

"A mirror, perhaps?"

Drago laughed. "I'll see you when I get back." He blew her a kiss from across the room then left.

In the silence, Rose heard a bird singing on the balcony. She passed through the opened French doors and went to the small creature.

To her surprise, the bird didn't retreat or fly away.

"You're beautiful," she said softly. The blue songbird bounced onto her outstretched fingers and tweeted out a tune.

What a fortunate animal, Rose considered. *There's no malevolent aunt in your closet ready to watch you fall to your doom.*

The bird chirped melodically, then it bowed its head in her direction. Once it swooped away, Rose gazed out at the estate's vast gardens. Suddenly, a tremendous surge of hope lifted her spirits. She stepped back inside and eyed the bed. Although she considered Drago's suggestion that she take a nap, she decided not to crawl back under the covers.

Her eyes shifted to his bedside table. That's when she spotted the Romanian coin and the bracelet of Amenhotep. Shock rifled through her and her senses came alive.

Obviously, Drago had forgotten to replace the objects in the pocket of his trousers—as was his custom every morning. Assuming their conversation had sidetracked him, Rose moved to the small table. She stood before the coin, her hand outstretched. Then she swiveled her gaze to the bedroom door.

Madame P. and Chloe, the chambermaid, never entered unless they knocked first. *I'm completely alone. And if I pick up the coin and I talk to it, no one will know.*

She stood frozen, contemplating her next move. In a surreal moment, sunlight slanted through the window and landed on the coin. Should she take that as a sign?

Her contemplation snowballed into an agonizing inner debate. Finally, her curiosity won out.

Rose picked up the large coin. Tracing its ancient design, she cleared her throat. "Show me Drago when he was a child."

She didn't know why the coin reacted—perhaps it was the aptitude for clairvoyance that ran in her family—but she tingled with excitement when the coin exploded with light. It shook with the force of a tornado ripping across the plains. Rose could barely hang on to it as it charged through projected images in furious succession. The frames flipped backward, then slowed down when they reached a certain point in time. Finally, the images stopped at the sight of Drago inside his family's farmhouse. As a boy, he sat on the floor with his three brothers and two sisters, watching their father perform his magic tricks. Drago's blue-green eyes grew as wide as saucers and when his father pulled a rabbit out of a hat, he offered a round of thunderous applause. He was adorable. All gangly limbs and waves of thick hair combed boyishly across his forehead. And the hints at his poverty didn't seem to dampen his spirits at all.

Rose smiled at the representation then sucked in a breath. "Show me how Drago gained his magical powers."

The coin streamed through more images until it came to a halt. Then it shot forth a vision of Drago stealing along the empty streets of a Romanian town. Rose watched him enter an eerie-looking sorcery shop. After he moved through a pair of black velvet curtains, he spoke to someone she couldn't see. Rose presumed an old woman sat across from him because she caught a glimpse of gnarled, female hands resting on a crystal ball.

The fortuneteller performed a tarot card reading before she asked

Drago if he'd like to possess the power to perform real magic. He replied, "Yes".

The teller informed him that his powers came with an added bonus. *"Immortality*," she said.

Immortality? Rose's head began to spin. *How can that be?*

Her heart hammered violently as she watched the fortuneteller present the lei coin to Drago. The woman explained that the coin would give him the ability to perform real magic and remain immortal, but if he accepted it, it came at a high price. Drago took the coin anyway. He studied it as he exited the sorcery shop. Meanwhile, Rose struggled to catch a glimpse of a date—any indication of the year, but there wasn't a newspaper in sight.

The coin turned dark and her nerves unraveled. Gulping down the panic that was inching its way up her throat, she croaked out another request —one she hoped would either confirm or refute his immortality. "Show me Drago seventy-five years before I met him."

The coin waved and glimmered as it charged backwards in time. Finally, it halted at an image of Drago in the early days of Queen Victoria's reign in England. Yet, to Rose's astonishment, he wasn't an infant. He stood before a crowd of regal-looking men and women dressed in clothing from that time period, astounding them with his magic.

He looks exactly the same as he does now.

Rose clamped a hand over her mouth and fought to hang on to the coin. Drago had lived much longer than he claimed . . . thanks to the old fortuneteller.

Then a dark realization struck her. Hadn't the fortuneteller told Drago he was required to do something every year to keep his powers? *The women on Coney Island were attacked on the same day every year.*

Shaking her head against the possibility that he could be the demon who'd left two of the victims comatose and had crushed the third to death, Rose whispered her final command to the coin.

"Show me Drago in New York City. Two years before I met him at his magic show."

The coin shuffled furiously, then projected a spine-tingling scene. Drago was performing at a tiny theater along Coney Island's Boardwalk. Rose peered closer. Handsome in a black tuxedo, he was trying to gain the respect of a barely-interested crowd of ruffians. Unfortunately, he failed to impress them. The spectators even had tomatoes in hand, ready to throw. But then he put a hundred dollar bill into one of five empty paper bags. Next, he set fire to the bag in which he'd inserted the money. One bag remained onstage and the other three bags were handed to people in the audience. Drago instructed a portly gentleman in the front row to open the bag he held in his hands. Miraculously, the hundred-dollar bill sat unharmed inside of it.

He received a standing ovation. And after taking a hasty bow, Drago slipped offstage and stole into the night. Hurrying, he reached the edge of the amusement park. Rose's pulse raced. She gazed into the coin and her whole world came to a standstill. Among the shadows, Drago transformed into a hideous demon. Cragged jaws burst forth, razor sharp claws protruded under his rippling cloak, and his stature grew to an unearthly height.

Eyes narrowed, he grabbed an unknowing girl as she made her way to the restroom. She cowered from him and tried to escape his grasp, but she was too weak. Even though the young woman was heartbreakingly close to her group of friends, she crumpled to the ground . . . unconscious from having most of the life squeezed out of her.

CHAPTER 24

Rose has discovered my darkest secret. Drago dropped a bottle of hair tonic on the floor of the drugstore. The bottle smashed into bits and left splashes of green liquid on his shoes. But he didn't look down.

She knows I'm a demon. I can feel it in my bones.

He gripped the counter by the cash register and tried to breathe.

"*Êtes-vous d'accord, Monsieur Starkov?*" the store's owner asked.

Drago shook himself. "I'm fine, Yves."

But he was far from fine. He groped for the coin.

Damn it! I left it back at the house.

Knowing his instincts were never wrong, he ran out of the store and sprinted back to Château de Maincy with his heart in his throat.

Rose let the coin slip from her grasp. *Drago is an immortal, soul-stealing monster. That's his real secret.*

Her limbs convulsed with repulsion and fear. She was too stunned to move. All the signs had been there of course—including her mother's premonition, but she'd refused to put two-and-two together.

It didn't matter. What mattered now was that she knew the shocking truth. *Drago might kill me next. Maybe that's why he gave me the amulet,* she thought. *I can't end his life because he's immortal, but I can certainly kill myself in accordance with the amulet's curse.*

Desperate to get away from her husband, she dove into action. Snatching the coin off the ground, she stuffed it into a satchel, along with the bracelet of Amenhotep. After she added a few pieces of clothing and a stack of cash Drago kept in a drawer, she crept out the bedroom door. Stepping into the corridor, she heard muffled voices on the ground floor. Without making a sound, she descended the staircase and began to look around for a place in which to hide the amulet and the bracelet.

Instead of protecting me, they'll probably lead to my doom.

Drago had lied about being a demon—and odds were he lied about the powers of the necklace and the bracelet, too. Maybe taking them off *could* sever their hypnotic spell.

Terrified of her husband, she wanted to make it impossible for him to use them on her again.

Padding along the marble floors, she peeked inside the enormous drawing room. A large vase, a writing desk, and several cigar boxes offered potential hiding spaces. But if she hid the articles of jewelry inside one of these objects, they would be discovered very soon.

Perhaps I should throw them in the pond.

No, she decided. The amulet and the bracelet might not be retrieved from its depths. Rose couldn't bring herself to toss away such historic objects.

That's when an idea struck her. She should hide the trinkets inside something that would never be destroyed. *The portrait of Jean-Daniel Girard.*

Her breath hitching, she tiptoed to the wall of portraits Drago had shown her. Chloe, the chambermaid, emerged from the kitchen at the end of the hall, but thankfully she rounded a corner and disappeared.

Clutching her satchel, Rose sagged against the wall with relief.

As her pulse spiked, she moved closer to the portrait. A suit of armor stood nearby. In the knight's grasp, he held a sword. Setting her bag down with trembling hands, she tried desperately to unclasp the amulet of Tousret. It proved impossible—as though she were battling an invisible force. Hot tears rolled down her cheeks as she made a third attempt to rip open the necklace's clasp. This time her fierce determination won out. She stuffed the amulet inside her satchel and took the sword from the suit of armor.

Perspiring, she glanced up and down the hall. Once she was convinced the coast was clear, she moved back to the portrait and pulled the frame's bottom corner away from the wall. The angle at which she sliced the heavy matte of the portrait with the sword was awkward, but she managed to form an opening big enough for the amulet and its matching bracelet.

Now that the objects were hidden safely inside the painting, she returned the sword to the suit of armor. Feeling free, Rose picked up her satchel, but before she stole outside she felt a presence behind her—a presence real enough to raise the hair on her arms.

Wheeling around, she caught a glimpse of a white apparition. *The ghost of Jean-Daniel Girard.*

Before it vanished, Rose could have sworn it murmured, "Don't be fooled . . ."

Lungs stinging, Drago finally reached the château. As he entered the house, he was greeted by an eerie silence. *Rose is gone.* He sensed it. He also sensed that she'd taken off the amulet of Tousret.

"Rose?" he called out desperately.

There was no answer. He searched the drawing room and the library.

Madame P. hurried out of the kitchen, smoothing her dress. "Monsieur Starkov?"

"I'm looking for my wife. Have you seen her?"

"No." Concern shadowed her face. "Maybe she's lying down . . ."

Drago bounded up the stairs two at a time and hurried into the suite. There was no sign of Rose. Nor was there any sign of the lei coin or of the bracelet of Amenhotep.

He yanked open the desk drawer and saw that the money was gone. His heart sank and he tried unsuccessfully to fight back his emotions.

Rose is headed back to New York City. He knew her plans as clearly as he knew their marriage was in dire straits.

* * *

Will Drago come after me? Rose stared out at the ocean waves as the steamer she'd booked passage on plowed toward New York.

He's smart. Smart enough to figure out where I've gone.

Pulling the lei coin from her jacket pocket, she moved to a private area on the ship's deck. In a low whisper she spoke to it again. "Show me Drago—when he returned from the town of Maincy."

The coin burst forth an image of him searching for her in their suite at the château. Then it showed him pitching to his knees in frustration. Before it went dark, the coin projected a scene of Drago booking passage back to America.

I was right. He's coming for me.

Rose couldn't be sure if the hypnotic spell cast over her might remain despite the fact that she'd taken the amulet off, but she had refused to wear the necklace another minute. Learning the truth about Drago had turned her world upside down. He'd made a deal with the devil. In return, neither of them would ever be the same.

Weeks later, Rose heaved a sigh of relief as the steamer neared the Port of New York and let out a deep bellow. In the distance loomed the Statue of Liberty—and the sight comforted her. It was good to be home, yet she didn't feel like rejoicing.

Olivia, the Marconis, Anthony, Richard, and Patrick had all been right in distrusting Drago. Obviously, they'd read him much better than Rose had—and she owed them an apology. Should she tell them that Drago was the demon who'd terrorized Coney Island? How could she not? She'd never forgive herself if her husband killed someone else.

Rose's hands shook as she glanced down at her simple wedding band. When Drago's show at the Hippodrome began to pack audiences in, he had taken her to several high-end jewelry stores to look at diamond rings. The stunning jewels had certainly impressed Rose, but she'd refused the let Drago buy one. She wanted to keep the simple band he bought her in the village of East Hampton. It would always remind her that their relationship was built on the simplest, purest form of love. *Love at first sight.*

How the tables had turned. Now Rose was trying to get far away from him—to return to the only place that was familiar.

The ship docked and Rose's spine tingled. She looked wildly about. Only she knew what Drago was capable of—and she wouldn't put it past him to appear out of thin air. That's why she'd taken the coin.

When she stepped off the ship, she stuffed the coin in her pocket. Before she'd left France, she telegraphed Patrick in a panic about her return to New York. She told him that she was about to face her wicked aunt. Worse yet, she was running away from Drago, who was a more fearsome monster than Morvina.

Once she spotted Patrick on the dock, her fear sent her racing into his safe embrace.

Drago sensed that Rose was enfolded in Patrick's arms. Rage flushed through his veins with the fury of a hurricane. *Damn it!* Things were playing out as they had in his original vision, yet he had every right to be infuriated by it. He hadn't merely seen the other remaining demon coming to America and Rose's subsequent fear of the witch's curse, he'd witnessed what happened at the end—when all the players came together in a result that was beyond dramatic.

He thought taking Rose to France would have been an effective way of avoiding Morvina and the final scene of his vision, but he was beginning to doubt that these things could be eluded. Besides, Rose had been so miserable there.

Christ! He gripped the railing of the large steamer he'd booked passage on.

Years ago, the fortuneteller Drago had visited claimed that he'd have no chance to reverse a predestined chain of events. But he sure as hell wanted to try. Although a vision was a prediction of what was about to take place, was he a lord of black magic or not?

He'd gotten the sense earlier that Rose had taken off the amulet. Did she still have it in her possession? In addition, the bracelet of Amenhotep was nowhere to be found. What had Rose done with it? Without both objects, his power to save her had lessened. Doubt that he could manipulate what happened beyond the vision hovered over him like a storm cloud. He didn't even have the lei coin.

Worse still, Rose leaving him had knocked him to his knees. In her absence, he felt as if his lungs had collapsed and his heart had broken in half. She was his entire world and he couldn't tolerate being without her. Although he longed to draw her close and feather his hands along her soft skin, Patrick might be doing those things instead.

As the steamer plowed through the ocean waters at full speed, he marched under the deck's overhang. He preferred to conserve his energy from the sunlight so that he could plan his reunion with Rose.

Why had she sought solace in O'Leary's arms? She knew her former suitor was in cahoots with Richard Bellum. Worse yet, the arrogant cop seemed bent on stealing her back.

How can I not hate him?

Drago suspected that Patrick only saw Rose as a challenge. Once he conquered that challenge, he'd throw her away when his interest waned. And Rose was especially vulnerable right now. No doubt she'd seen Drago in his demonic state—naturally, she'd be terrified out of her mind.

Drago grimaced. That was probably the reason she was seeking solace with Patrick.

He folded the collar of his jacket up against the strong Atlantic wind. It was a twenty day voyage back to New York. Rose had departed on the ship prior to his—which meant she'd have almost two days alone with O'Leary. While Drago's powers extended to transporting objects through time and space, he could only transport himself in his demonic state. It was too bad, because if Rose shared what she saw in the coin with anyone, Drago would be a sitting duck for the police in New York. Anthony Marconi and Patrick O'Leary would arrest him.

Feeling his energy drain completely, he pulled the brim of his hat lower and closed his eyes. He must come up with a plan of escape. After all, he wasn't going to be clueless enough to step off the ship at Ellis Island straight into O'Leary and Marconi's hands.

CHAPTER 25

Patrick's arms felt strong and sturdy around Rose—and it was just what she needed in the moment. He said nothing, but held her for a long time at the edge of the dock. She leaned against him. She needed him to be her rock in the terrifying days to come. And there was so much she wanted to tell him.

"Are you all right, Rose?" he asked as he gently smoothed her hair.

"No," she replied honestly.

She drew away and looked at him. He'd changed. His frame had grown more muscular and his boyish face had matured. And against the colorful background of the city, his green eyes appeared especially vibrant.

Because he looked incredibly handsome, Rose wondered why she'd never allowed him to court her.

Adjusting his boater hat, Patrick wrapped his arm around her shoulder and steered her toward the luggage desk.

"I don't have much baggage," she said. "I only purchased a few clothes and a small suitcase on board."

"You *did* leave in a hurry!" Patrick took a step back. "Be honest. Did that bastard Starkov hurt you and then drive you away?"

"No. It's not that . . ." her voice trailed off.

Patrick frowned. "Don't worry. We have all afternoon to catch up. I took the day off."

"Thank you, Patrick."

She tucked her hand through his bent elbow. Without heavy luggage weighing them down, they decided to walk. They meandered through Battery Park and strolled all the way to Chelsea Pier. Patrick asked her if she was hungry, but she shook her head.

"I think I need a drink."

Patrick gave her a look as if to say, "You've grown up".

He led her into a pub. Once they settled at a table, they ordered two lager beers. Rose took a long swig of hers, but she squished up her face in disgust and set the glass down. Patrick offered to finish it for her.

Trembling, Rose shook her head and sat back in her chair. "I need something to steady my nerves, but that tastes terrible."

"I'll order you a glass of wine instead." He smiled. After it arrived, he surveyed her nervous state. "I want to know everything that happened to you while you were away. When I saw you at the Hippodrome, I got the feeling you were miserable. That you were giving up a hell of a lot for that shady magician."

"I did," she replied penitently.

He took in a breath. "One of my fellow officer's discovered Drago has a police record. He was arrested under a different name for theft."

"Theft? When was this?"

"Years ago." He paused. "A man claimed he stole money from him."

"Maybe one his magic acts was misconstrued." *There I go defending him.*

Patrick looked nonplussed. "I still think he's shady. A fraud."

"You don't understand, Patrick. I didn't come back to New York because Drago is a fraud. I came back because he really *can* perform magic."

He raised an eyebrow. "What?"

The wine came. She drank a good deal of it, which made her tongue looser. "Richard Bellum's newspaper exposé was all wrong."

"The exposé that ruined your husband's career?" he asked with a glimmer of pleasure in his eye.

"Yes—and don't look so smug about it." She went on. "What Bellum didn't include in the story was the secret of Drago's Romanian coin."

"His *what*?"

Rose nodded. "Drago possesses a silver coin that gives him black magic powers. It also allows him to see the past and the present."

"You've lost me, Rose. You know I don't believe in hocus-pocus."

"That's a naïve mindset, Patrick." Her tone was firm.

He downed his beer. As he unbuttoned his jacket and stuffed a hand in his trouser pocket, his eyes narrowed. "Are you telling me that *all* the illusions Dragomir Starkov performed have been real?"

"Yes."

"That cad can actually make a woman float in space and bring a dead kitten back to life?"

She pursed her lips together.

"Holy hell, Rose! That's impossible!"

"I'll show you proof in a minute, but we need to go somewhere private."

Patrick threw some money on the table, then escorted Rose outside. "I'll take you to a place the police use for stake-outs. It isn't far."

They made their way to an abandoned building. After Patrick drew the curtains, he leaned against a wall. "Show me your proof."

At first, she hesitated. Here she was, back in New York one hour and she was spilling Drago's secrets. But she didn't have a choice. If Drago was capable of killing someone once, he'd surely do it again, and the police needed to know.

Sucking in a breath, she extracted the coin from her pocket and presented it to Patrick.

"It doesn't *look* magical," he remarked.

"It is," she said softly.

Commanding the coin to show her Drago at Coney Island, the object projected the tell-all vision of him transforming into a demon and compressing one of the Coney Island victims into a crumpled heap.

"Christ!" Patrick cried. "Starkov *is* the monster that attacked those women!"

"I had to tell you." Remorse stabbed at Rose.

Pushing himself off the wall, he began to pace in circles. "I . . . I don't know what to say. I've never seen anything like it."

"A long time ago, Drago made a deal with an old fortuneteller. It turned out to be more like a deal with the devil," she explained. "In exchange for his magical powers, Drago needs to suck the life out of someone on the same day every year."

From the look on his face, she knew what Patrick was thinking. *This can't be.*

After swallowing a dry lump she said, "That day happens to be my birthday."

Patrick stopped pacing and grasped her shoulders. "My God, Rose. Do you think Drago has been saving you for his ultimate victim?"

"I don't know."

"If killing you is what this fiend has in mind, we have to protect you from him!"

Her hands trembled as she scrubbed them over her face. "Now he's as terrifying to me as my Aunt Morvina."

"I hated Dragomir Starkov from the minute I laid eyes on him. Your aunt—who may be dead for all we know—seems pathetic compared to your husband, at least when he turns into a demon." Patrick blew out a breath. "But I still don't understand. *Why* does Starkov have to suck out someone's soul once a year?"

Rose looked him straight in the eye. "It makes him immortal."

Apparently, that's all Patrick needed to hear. Over the next twenty-four hours, he used his new status of detective to scramble his sources together. The police discovered that Drago would be arriving behind Rose on another steamer. That prompted them to immediately raid Drago's Tenth Avenue apartment, looking for additional proof that he was a demonic sorcerer.

Rose insisted on accompanying Patrick and the police force he'd assembled to meet the *Astoncia* when it arrived the following day. The ship docked but Drago didn't disembark.

"Where the hell is he?" Patrick scowled.

"Maybe he turned himself into a seagull and flew ashore," one of the officers said snidely.

"You just bought yourself surveillance duty, McCracken," Patrick replied harshly. "You and Greboski stay here and notify me if you see any sign of Starkov." He thrust an artist's rendering toward the wise-cracking cop.

"And *you*, O'Leary, you need to get on that ship and search for Starkov," Patrick's boss, a ruddy-faced police captain, barked.

"Yes, sir."

"Where do you think he is?" Rose asked Patrick as she hurried by his side.

"First of all, you're a lady and you need to stay here," Patrick said. "Secondly, I have no idea where Drago is, but I intend to find out."

"How?" She frowned.

"Rose. One lone magician can't outsmart the entire New York City Police Department."

Her stomach clenched violently. "You don't know Drago."

CHAPTER 26

Rose had stayed the past few nights in a hotel. Finally, Patrick convinced her to go home. When she arrived at the Marconis' brownstone, she fell into Elena's arms.

"It's all right, *cara*," Elena murmured through tears. "You're home now."

Lorenzo Marconi stood behind Rose and gently stroked her hair as she sobbed. "No worries, my dear. You'll never hear us say, 'We told you so.'"

"Lorenzo!" Elena said sharply.

Rose found extreme comfort in Elena's embrace. She didn't want to pull away, but she made herself step back eventually. "Is Olivia home?"

Elena nodded.

Just then, Olivia came rushing down the stairs. "Rose! I've missed you so much!"

They hugged one another and Rose could feel her adoptive sister's heart beating wildly. Anthony appeared and gave her arm a hardy squeeze. "Glad you're back, sis."

She smiled. He'd never called her that before.

Exhausted, she let Elena tug her into the parlor. Nothing had changed. It still smelled of lilacs, Elena's favorite flower. Rose sat on the sofa and eyed a small bouquet of the blooms on a sideboard in the corner.

"Where's Patrick?" Anthony asked.

"He dropped me off here, then went to set up a barricade around the harbor."

"Barricade?" Lorenzo asked.

At the family's prodding, Rose relayed everything. Drago's alliance with the fortuneteller. The coin the old woman gave him. And his demonic immortality.

Everyone in the room met her story with gaping mouths.

"He doesn't deserve to be roaming the streets after what he did to those women," Elena said with alarm.

Rose took in a breath. "He only killed one woman. The others were left alive." She realized how foolish her words sounded as soon as they escaped her mouth.

"*Just* killed one woman!" Elena cried. "Drago took someone's daughter away from them, forever." She made the sign of the cross.

Rose shook her head. "I wish I'd seen him for what he is."

"How could you have?" Olivia asked gently. "He hypnotized you. He's an expert at that."

Instinctively, Rose reached for the amulet—only to remember that it was back in France.

Am I still under his spell? After all, the legend of the amulet claimed that its wearer needed to don it only once . . .

Anthony paced the room. "The police will get Starkov," he said. "Have no doubt about that."

"No one can fathom how powerful he is," Rose said.

Anthony shot her a dire look. "It's possible that he's working with Morvina."

Rose's mouth went dry. *My birthday is in ten days. Will I actually fall to my death?*

"This might not be the best time to tell you this," Olivia patted Rose's hand, "but some strange things have been happening right here."

"What things?"

"I told you that your favorite coat was ruined."

"Yes."

"Well, some of your other possessions have been sabotaged as well."

"Sabotaged?"

Elena cut in. "Two months ago, there was a fire. Everything in the bedroom you used to share with Olivia went up in smoke."

Rose bit her lip.

"Your clothing, your jewelry—all the gifts Drago ever gave you, except the music box," Olivia said. "That's missing."

"Could the fire have been an accident?" she asked.

"I'm afraid not."

"Thank goodness the music box wasn't destroyed. "It was my favorite gift—" She stopped herself. Wasn't she supposed to be furious with him? Terrified out of her mind? "Were your things ruined as well?" Rose asked Olivia, to cover her words.

"Yes," Olivia said sadly.

Guilt seized her and she loathed the fact that other people were involved in this dangerous drama, too.

As the family gathered around the dining table for supper, Rose found herself lost in thought. *Whoever started the fire despises me.* The harshness of the realization stole her appetite. She excused herself and went to her old bedroom. With its fresh layer of wallpaper and new bedding, it looked fine, but once she flung herself on the bed, she breathed in traces of smoke.

The walls seemed to close in around Rose. If she thought she was depressed in France, her current mental state put those moods to shame. She had given up everything for Drago. From the moment she met him, she'd trusted him enough to explore her curiosity. Not only had she surrendered her innocence to him, she'd followed him into risky situations. She'd even married him on the thread of a whim. All because she loved him desperately.

Now all of her excitement and hope for the future had disappeared. Thanks to one look in that blasted coin.

Olivia entered the room. "Mama wanted me to check on you."

Sighing, Rose patted the mattress.

"This is like old times," Olivia smiled forlornly as she sat beside her.

Nodding, Rose sat up and pulled her knees to her chin. "Everything seems so unreal."

"I can't imagine what it was like living with a demon." Olivia scooted back against the headboard. "On a smaller scale, I've been terrified to sleep in this room."

"I don't blame you."

They sat in comfortable silence for a long time. Finally, Rose stood, shut the door, then settled in an upholstered chair near the bed. "Olivia. I know my thoughts are muddled right now—and that I'm probably not acting like myself—but I have an idea."

"What?" Olivia cocked her head.

"Before I left for France, I learned that Morvina is here in New York, disguising herself as someone. If I can find out who, maybe I can stop her from harming me on my birthday."

"Morvina is *disguising* herself as someone? That's insane, Rose!"

"As insane as Drago transforming into a demon?"

That gave Olivia pause. "Who do you think your aunt is hiding behind?"

A shudder ran through Rose. "I tried to see it in the coin, but the image is being blocked. Morvina is powerful enough to do that. But there's another way I can find out."

"What other way?"

She leaned forward. "I can try to contact my mother."

"Your mother is dead, Rose." Then Olivia seemed to comprehend what she was suggesting. "A séance?"

"Yes. A séance."

Days later, the front page of *The Gotham Times* announced that Drago would perform a death-defying illusion on June twentieth. Rose's heart drummed as she read the headline. She would turn twenty-one on that day—and Drago would be compelled to show his demon self again.

The article also claimed that Drago would reveal more details about the magical feat soon. This made Rose wonder if his performance, whatever it turned out to be, might serve as an open invitation for the police to capture him.

During the days leading up to the séance, Drago was nowhere to be found. Where could he be hiding? He continued to evade the police—and Rose was enormously conflicted about that.

Nerves prickling, she busied herself with learning about the current spiritualist world in New York City. She discovered that a prominent medium named Madame Majinska had reached celebrity status, just like Rose's parents had. This Madame Majinska held séances in her brownstone on Seventy-Second Street. Unfortunately, Majinska's impressive reputation meant that her séances were booked well in advance.

"I can't believe you got an appointment for us," Olivia said as they arrived at the medium's slim brownstone.

"It wasn't easy."

Olivia nodded.

Soon, she and Rose were greeted by Madame Majinska's faithful assistant. With trembling hands, Olivia handed the middle-aged woman her hat and gloves. Rose did the same, with steady ones.

She looked down at them with surprise.

"Did you tell Madame Majinska's assistant who your parents were?" Olivia whispered the question.

"I had to," she whispered back. "I wouldn't have secured an appointment otherwise."

The solemn assistant ushered the girls through a cozy parlor littered with white candles and books on the occult. Then she led them into a spacious but eerily darkened room. Rose took note of the single candle glowing in the center of a circular table. She also noticed the four guests who were gathered around it. The first was an elderly lady with a black, netted veil hung over her face. When the woman began to sniff tears into a handkerchief, Rose presumed she was a widow.

An attentive caregiver sat next to her, while a sour-faced man of about thirty was hunched in his seat to the caregiver's left. Rose watched him stick his index finger into his starched collar and gave a nervous tug. *Maybe he's a businessman hoping to contact someone who stole money from him.* She suppressed a smile.

Peering at the fourth guest, Rose noticed that the stocky man was leaning back in his seat. Half of his face was set in the shadows, but the features Rose was able to see included a strong forehead, wide cheekbones, straight-set mouth, and wavy hair that formed deep ridges from a center part.

It's Harry Houdini!

All of the astonishing locations the famous magician had escaped from ran through her mind. A prison. A Chinese Water Torture Cell. A beer cask. Iron-clad handcuffs, a steel safe, and a straightjacket.

Houdini was very talented, but who, Rose wondered, was he here to communicate with?

Rose sat at the table and leaned forward. Houdini glanced at her and gave her a respectful nod. *He must have seen me assist Drago at the Hippodrome.*

She reciprocated with her own nod then looked away. As the medium's assistant began to offer an explanation of what was about to happen, chills sped through her.

"Ladies and gentlemen. Welcome to Madame Majinska's humble home. Before each of you arrived tonight, you provided the name of a departed person with whom you wish Madame to make contact. As you well know, a spiritualist is an *instrument* through which souls communicate. If Madame Majinska is able to channel one of your loved ones, their spirit may show its presence by making rapping sounds, moving objects in the room, or by speaking through her. It is my duty to inform you that none of these things are guaranteed to happen. Please be advised that your talking, coughing, or restlessness will detract from Madame Majinska's concentration. Furthermore, if any of you are secretly skeptical, you will prevent the séance from being a success." She took in a breath. "It you aren't a skeptic then you've chosen your spiritualist wisely. Madame Majinska has carved out a name for herself as a rare physical manifestation medium."

The assistant backed out of the room. Rose and Olivia exchanged glances. *This has to work*, Rose thought. *It's essential that I know Morvina's covert identity.*

In the apprehensive moment, there was—how else could she describe it?—a dead silence. The room grew cold. The temperature dropped nearly to the degree of a meat locker, in fact. The hush that remained over the guests was maddening . . . until a firm voice filtered through the heavy air and broke it. "Please hold hands."

Rose and the other sitters obeyed the command. After they formed an unbroken circle, Rose looked around and tried to locate where the voice had come from. She spotted a vertical cabinet covered with curtains in the corner of the room. It seemed the only possibility.

The exasperating silence continued. *Will Madame Majinska contact a spirit tonight?*

Rose tried her best to sit still. She'd never forgive herself if her squirming stopped the medium from summoning an entity.

"The spirits are excited tonight," the same voice floated through the air. "Closing your eyes will encourage them to appear."

Rose pinched her eyes shut. Her body tingled.

"The circle of energy in this room is excellent," the voice said.

Another moment of silence ensued. Rose squeezed Olivia's hand. Then she opened one eye and stole a glance across the circular table. The elderly woman had lifted her veil, revealing a pained expression. Was the woman thinking of her departed husband?

The woman's apparent pain broke Rose's heart. It made her think of Drago. *Where is he?* She couldn't exactly pull the coin out and talk to it here, but assuming he'd arrived in New York, she was surprised that he hadn't contacted her. Did he know that his darkest secret had destroyed their love like a hammer shatters glass?

What kind of torment is he going through right now?

Rose swallowed hard. She couldn't afford to let her thoughts wander to Drago.

"In the reverent silence we've created, I can hear the dead speak to me." Madame Majinska's voice jolted Rose back to reality. She grasped Olivia's and Harry Houdini's hand so tightly that her knuckles turned white.

"Samuel?" The elderly lady looked around the room in desperation. "Is that you? Are you speaking to Madame Majinska?"

"Silence!" the voice inside the cabinet commanded.

Let it be my mother who's speaking, Rose thought.

The candle flickered and stuttered—as if someone were trying to blow it out. The room grew even darker and Rose strained to see through the shadows. Although she sat very still, she sensed Olivia shaking next to her. Then a transparent vapor materialized. It hung in the corner like a weightless cloud—and as it increased in size, it took on an ethereal form. Ghostly white and faceless, the apparition floated above the ground.

Rose stole a glance at Houdini. Scowling, he looked as if he was about to bolt out of his seat. Her eyes flickered back to the specter. To her disappointment, it vanished as quickly as it had appeared. She wanted to put her hand out in anguish, but she didn't dare break the circle.

Just then, the cabinet door creaked open. A pretty, if not somewhat overly-made up woman stepped from its depths. Garbed in scarves, bangles, and a dark, bohemian style dress, the red-headed woman walked to the table. She looked no one in the eye.

"Rose?" The medium called in a low timbre. "Is that you?"

"Yes, it's me!" Rose's blood rushed in furious streams. "Mother?"

Madame Majinska's eyes rolled back eerily. The way she clutched the edge of the table made the sitters cower—and when she began to moan in an unearthly fashion, the table lifted off the floor and began to rock back and forth.

"Jeepers!" Olivia gasped.

"I'm happy that we've been reunited, my darling Rose," the medium-cum-Florence-Hayes said in a sweet voice.

Tears welled in Rose's eyes. *Is this really happening?* The table continued to tilt and convulse, but oddly, fear evaded her. She was determined to get answers. "I've come to ask you something, Mother."

"Let me guess, my dear. You've come to ask me about your Aunt Morvina."

How could the spirit invading the medium's body know that unless this sitting was genuine? "Yes," Rose croaked out. "I want to know who Morvina is disguising herself as. Can you tell me?"

A pregnant pause ensued. Writing appeared on the adjacent wall and she gasped. In red chalk, the message spelled *Rose your father and I love you very much.*

Shock skewed her vision. She steadied herself by gripping her fellow sitters' hands even tighter.

The medium spoke again. "I know Morvina's current identity. She's disguising herself as—"

In a flash, Houdini leapt out of his seat and turned on the lights. The brightness of the room illuminated the medium's assistant, who stood at the wall. She was draped in black and grasped a piece of red chalk in her hands. The chandelier's light also revealed a fog-making device sitting in the corner . . . precisely where the apparition had appeared.

"You're a fake!" Houdini pointed a finger at Madame Majinska.

The accusation seemed to knock the medium back to her real self. "How dare you disrupt this séance!" she fired back. "You must leave at once!"

Houdini shook his head. He plunged to his knees and looked under the tablecloth. "Just as I thought. A hydraulic pump is making the table go up and down. What's more, I saw the outline of your assistant and spotted the fog making apparatus in the dark."

Turning beet-red, Madame Majinska hemmed and hawed.

The others stood up and glanced under the tabletop. Indeed, there was a mechanism in place. Disappointment sent Rose's heart plummeting.

The large man who'd been sitting next to Houdini withdrew a badge from his jacket pocket. "Jim Scarborough. With New York City Police, Department of Fraud. We've been trying to catch you in the act for a long time, Ms. Majinska," he said as he clamped handcuffs around her wrists.

"Damn you!" the woman said miserably.

Scarborough turned to Houdini. "Thanks for making my job easier."

"You're welcome." Seemingly pleased with the medium's unveiling, Houdini shook Scarborough's hand.

The detective escorted the medium out of the room. Close behind them were the elderly lady and her caregiver.

"How am I ever going to find out who Morvina is disguised as?" Rose asked Olivia. Before Olivia could answer, Houdini came to stand before them. Rose was surprised to find that in person, he was shorter than she was.

"I'm sorry none of this was real, Mrs. Starkov." Houdini extended his hand. "I'm disappointed, as well. There are several loved ones I wished to contact, too."

"It seemed real," Rose said as she shook it forlornly.

"That's because there was a good amount of 'true-believers' syndrome filling the room tonight."

Rose sucked in a breath. "But how did Madame Majinska know those things about me?"

"Fake mediums have been known to go through people's trash—and pay their clients' closest acquaintances to rat information," Harry Houdini continued on.

Anthony? Rose thought.

Olivia glowered reproachfully at the magician and threaded her arm through Rose's.

"This is my best friend, Olivia Marconi." Rose introduced them.

"I'm sorry, Miss Marconi," said Houdini. "I'm sure you and Mrs. Starkov aren't happy with me. But it stands to reason that the longer these fraudulent séances go on, the more misled and traumatized sitters will be."

"It seemed legitimate. Right up until you blew the whistle," Olivia commented.

Houdini shrugged. "Information about Florence and Malcolm Hayes is public knowledge.

And I'm certain Ms. Majinska, if that's her real name, knows that when someone books a séance, more often than not, that person is a blood relative of the departed."

"When I referred to the apparition as 'Mother', I suppose I gave 'Madame Majinska' even more ammunition." Rose grimaced.

"Unfortunately, you did."

Rose's shoulders rolled forward.

"I think of my illusions as a way to entertain people, but it's cruel to deceive the public so outwardly."

Rose's mind darted to the misleading newspaper article Richard Bellum wrote about Drago. "It's a shame when journalists do the same thing."

"You can't believe everything you read in the press." The magician shot her a knowing look. *Was he making a reference to Drago?*

"No, you can't," she agreed.

Her stomach twisted. Recently, the newspapers had interviewed

Patrick. He, in turn, had passed along Rose's words. Did Houdini believe Drago was capable of murder because of what she'd said?

Rose was about to ask the magician if he'd read the article when he turned to leave. "Give my best to your husband, Mrs. Starkov," he called over his shoulder before he vanished into the dark corridor. "I admire him greatly."

CHAPTER 27

Following the séance, Rose and Olivia exited the brownstone. A warm rain greeted them and as they strolled along the slick streets, Olivia's expression revealed her agitation over the disastrous gathering. Rose's footsteps lagged for the same reason.

"I can't believe people make a living out of deceiving others," Olivia fumed.

"It's unfathomable," Rose agreed gloomily. "But séance goers are vulnerable. I guess that makes them gullible, too."

Olivia threaded an arm through hers. "I'm sorry you didn't find out how Morvina is camouflaging herself."

"Me, too." She craned her neck back as they strolled, allowing raindrops to splatter on her face.

"What are you going to do now?" Olivia asked.

"I really don't know."

"It's three days until your birthday, Rose."

She shuddered. "Don't remind me."

They passed a clothing boutique, a bank, and a barber shop without saying a word. But as they strolled passed a newsstand, Olivia burst out, "Look, Rose. Drago has revealed another detail of his magic act in today's paper!"

Hands trembling, Rose picked up the latest edition of *The Gotham Times* and read the headline.

"Magician to Climb Summit of Woolworth Building"

The paper rattled in her grasp as she scoured the article.

> *Dragomir Starkov—a talented illusionist stripped of his reputation—has returned to New York City seeking redemption and retribution. He intends to get those very things on June twentieth. From high atop the Woolworth Building, Starkov will hypnotize his wife, the beautiful Rose Starkov, by way of an accursed amulet he bestowed on her. Following in the footsteps of everything mysterious, the ancient Egyptian necklace comes with a spell. Will Mr. Starkov's wife (a self-proclaimed victim of vertigo) wear the amulet of Tousret and join her husband as she climbs from the building's pier level to its topmost spire?*
>
> *The more important question is: If Rose Starkov succumbs to the amulet's curse, will it cause her to kill her husband before she takes her own life—just as the Egyptian prophecy predicts?*
>
> *Legend has it that only its counterpart, the bracelet of Amenhotep, can save them.*

Olivia, who'd been reading the article alongside Rose, whistled with disbelief. The air escaped Rose's lungs and she fought to breathe. "I left the amulet and the bracelet behind in France."

"Does Drago know that?"

"I'm not sure."

Rose was more worried about her mother's prediction. *You will fall to your doom from someplace high and a demon will cause it to happen.*

"Apparently, Drago has this whole thing planned out," Olivia said.

"But I don't understand why he's publicizing it so heavily. It's an open invitation for Morvina to sabotage the whole thing—and for the police to capture him."

The color seeped from Rose's face.

A luminescent moon brightened the top of the Woolworth Building in the distance. She'd learned in grammar school that the structure stood over seven hundred and ninety-two feet high and had taken over three years to construct.

She'd been in the lobby only once. And though she'd been astonished at its beautiful veined marble and vaulted mezzanine ceilings, she never dreamed she would be on *top* of the building.

She shook her head vehemently at the thought. *No. I can't possibly climb it.*

Olivia tightened her grip on Rose's arm. "It seems diabolical that Drago wants you to climb to the pinnacle of a building when he knows you have vertigo."

Sometimes Olivia wasn't very smart, but Rose loved her anyway. "That's the point. If I heed his commands, it'll tell people his hypnotic powers are genuine." *He got the idea from the spinning wheel at Château de Maincy.*

Rose remembered Drago's words that night. "If I hypnotized someone and commanded them to touch the spindle, they'd do it in a dreamlike state—because *consciously* they would never put their finger on something sharp. The action would convince people that I'm a viable magician with the ability to spellbind."

Olivia took the paper from her and threw it in a trash bin. "I hate to see Drago's face when he finds out you're not wearing the amulet anymore."

Rose fell silent. She touched the faded brass locket she wore instead. Once she opened the locket, she stared at the tiny artist's rendition of Drago she'd cut from a show program. She should be scared to death of her husband, but she still felt a certain pull toward him.

Was there more to what I saw in the coin?

Worried that she'd been rash when she notified the police, Rose took another look at Drago's image. His enigmatic eyes gave her chills and made her misgivings multiply. What if there was *another* demon stalking the city? An alternate demon that was responsible for killing the girl in Coney Island last year?

After all, Drago couldn't be the only one. But who was it?

Damn! Rose wished she'd been able to actually communicate with her mother at the séance.

"You miss Drago, don't you?" Olivia asked gently.

Rose nodded numbly. "I saw him turn into a demon, but I didn't actually see him kill anyone in the vision."

"What are you saying?" Olivia eyed her dubiously.

Rose's cheeks flamed. "Maybe someone else killed the last Coney Island victim."

"You should have thought of that before you got the entire police department involved."

"I'll give you that, but my shock made me panic."

Olivia gave her a sympathetic look. "Why don't you ask the coin who killed the girl?" she suggested.

"That's a wonderful idea!" Rose said.

As she and Olivia sat on a streetcar bench, she delved into her handbag. The coin wasn't there! Adrenaline rushed through her veins. She fished inside the handbag's lining. "It can't be!" Tipping the purse upside down, her heart sank when nothing fell out. "The coin's gone!"

"Did you lose it?" Olivia asked urgently.

"I don't know."

"When did you see it last?"

"It was in my handbag last night. I checked on it before I went to sleep—and I didn't open the bag up until now. There's no way the coin could have fallen out."

"Let's go home and look for it."

The girls did just that. They practically tore the house apart looking for the lei coin, yet it was nowhere to be found.

Exhausted, Rose lay in bed hours later. A thick cloud of uneasiness hung over her. *Who would have taken it while I slept last night?*

She replayed the evening's events in her head. The family had gathered around the dining room table for Elena's famous rigatoni, antipasto salad, and focaccia bread. Patrick had joined them. After the meal, they'd sat in the parlor, listening to Elena play the piano. Rose had excused herself and gone to bed before anyone else.

There had been five other people in the house. Who was the thief?

* * *

"Your coming out of hiding is commendable, Drago," Archibald McMillan said as he sat in his office chair. "But as your manager, I think you should have stayed in New York to defend your reputation—instead of traipsing off to France."

"I disagree," Drago replied dourly. "Leaving the city gave people time to forget that blasted newspaper article."

"*Forget?* Is that what you think they did?"

Drago cast him a deep scowl.

"You wish, Starkov. Bellum's article shot holes in your reputation like a .45. You're lucky I signed you on again!"

Drago's blood heated—as it always did when the day he was going to morph into a demon again drew near. "After this illusion, McMillan, I guarantee you'll want me as your only client."

McMillan scowled back. He took several drags from his cigarette, snuffed it out, then surged to his feet. "I don't know about that, but it's a good thing you're rich. Getting permission to use the Woolworth Building cost a pretty penny."

"I know, and my bank account knows," Drago said grimly.

"Do you also know that when your show closed, it tapped my finances out?"

Drago nodded. He studied his manager. Thin and extremely hyper, McMillan seemed to survive on nothing but coffee and cigarettes. He was a man with no wife and no children and it was said that he had only his job to keep him company.

The smallness of McMillan's life made it impossible for him to understand what Drago was going through. But it didn't matter. Drago didn't need him to understand. He just needed McMillan to promote his next illusion like it was the last glitzy spectacle on earth.

"All right," he said. "I have a lot to make up to you. Now is the chance."

Grunting, McMillan shoved his hands in his pockets and moved to the window. Over his shoulder he said, "If you disappoint me again, Starkov, I'll hunt you down like a pathetic animal."

Drago rose and stalked toward McMillan. He wasn't taller than his manager, but he was a hell of a lot more muscular, and stronger.

"I wouldn't threaten me if I were you. You're not the only game in town."

McMillan wheeled around. He lit another cigarette. "That's right. Starkov. I'm not the only game in town, but I'm the best."

The next morning, Rose stumbled to the kitchen. As the aroma of espresso pried her eyes open, she saw Elena sitting at the tiny breakfast table.

"Rose. Sit. Sit." Elena urged. "I'll pour you some coffee."

Rose murmured a "thank you". With her hair askew and her face pale and thin from fatigue, she surely looked a mess.

"Didn't you sleep, dearest?"

"No," Rose admitted. "I tossed and turned all night."

Elena handed her a cup of espresso. She took a sip. The house was quiet since Lorenzo and Anthony had gone off to work and Olivia was still sleeping. Elena peered at Rose for a moment, then shook her head. "Olivia told me about your missing coin. I can't believe it."

"No one broke in to get it," Rose said with certainty. "Someone in the house must have taken it."

Elena glanced at the pope's photo she'd hung on the wall last year and did the sign of the cross. "I trust everyone who was here last night. Don't you?"

"Yes," Rose replied between sips of espresso. She did trust everyone, including Patrick. She'd rushed into his arms when she returned from France because she desperately needed an ally.

A few moments of silence ensued. Rose finally said, "You're a deeply religious person, Elena. I know that. But what do you think of supernatural things?"

"What do you mean, exactly?"

"Do you think extraordinary things exist beyond this material world?"

Elena ran a hand through her dark curls. "Olivia told me that you girls attended a séance. Is that what you're referring to?"

Olivia. Sometimes she's too honest for her own good. "Yes," Rose replied unsteadily.

"This is what I think of ghosts and goblins." Elena sat back and folded her arms. "If we are honorable on earth, then we go to heaven. If we are disgraceful, we go to hell. There are no other options. Therefore the things that exist beyond this material world are either the work of an angel—or the devil."

Demons, Rose considered. *Are they really fallen angels?*

"Elena," she asked, "was it hard for you to be friends with my parents, their being mediums, I mean?"

"Your parents tried to help innocent people contact their loved ones. I saw nothing wrong with that."

Rose paused. "Here's another question. What if people are good on earth, but then they do one horrible thing while they're still alive?"

"Then God will punish them by making them endure a living hell in this lifetime." Elena replied firmly.

That's precisely what's happening to Drago, Rose thought. She desperately wanted to help him, but she didn't know how to reverse the deal he'd made with the fortuneteller. Nor could she make contact with her real mother. Both failures stabbed her heart.

"I wanted to summon my mother's spirit last night," she admitted to Elena.

"What would you have asked her?"

"About Morvina. I'm beginning to sense her evil energy all around me."

Elena reached across the small table and clasped Rose's hand tightly. "I hate to remind you but your birthday is tomorrow."

Icy shivers jolted Rose's body. "I wish I could go back and change everything. The fire that killed my parents. Learning Drago is a demon. Even meeting him in the first place."

"At least you found out what Drago is," Elena said darkly. "Thankfully you took off the amulet he gave you."

"How do you know I took it off?"

"Olivia told me about that, too." Elena paused. "If I were you, I'd stay far away from your husband. I'd also stay away from the Woolworth Building. Oh, yes. I read the newspapers, too."

Rose nodded in understanding.

A dog's bark and a squeaking streetcar disrupted the momentary silence, but she barely heard the noises. What was it she'd read once? That children of people with special gifts often inherited their parents' talents?

If I could hone the ability to see the future, like my parents did, I'd know exactly what was going to happen on my birthday.

Could Elena give her some essential tips? She decided to lead into the subject gently. "Elena, I'd love to know what my mother was like."

Elena set her cup of espresso down and smiled ruefully. "Lorenzo and Malcolm Hayes were childhood friends. But the more I got to know Florence, the more I thought of her as a sister." She paused. "She was witty and gentle and kind. And very pretty. Much like you, *cara.*"

Rose smiled, too. "Am I similar to her in other ways?"

"What do you mean?"

"I read once that children can inherit certain traits from their parents. Do you think I have any type of clairvoyant abilities?"

Elena drew back suddenly. "I don't know anything about that."

"What I'm saying is that I've had several premonitions. Just a few, mind you, but maybe I can make more happen, over time." Rose's limbs tingled. Unfortunately, time was something she was running out of.

"I don't remember you doing anything odd as a child, if that's what you're asking." Pale-faced, Elena stood.

"I didn't have visions?" She paused. "Did I show *any* signs of my parents' gifts when I was a little girl?"

Elena clutched the collar of her robe together. "No."

"This is no time to lie, Mama."

Rose spun around. Olivia was standing in the doorway.

"I'm not lying, Olivia." Elena's voice quivered.

Olivia entered the kitchen and went to her mother. "You've kept things from Rose to protect her, but she can use all the help she can get right now."

Elena remained silent. The sight of her lips trembling flushed alarm through Rose. *What is she so scared to tell me?*

"What has been kept from me, Olivia?" Rose begged.

"Don't, Olivia!" Elena cried. "It was horrible—and we agreed to never speak of it again!"

"Rose deserves to know, Mama. Show her the paper."

Elena's knuckles went white as she grasped her robe. "But you were terrified that night, Olivia. And Rose was so traumatized by our reaction that she blocked it out of her mind."

"Please. She needs to know."

Elena closed her eyes and fell silent for an excruciatingly long moment. Then she opened her eyes in surrender. "Very well. Follow me."

Rose held her breath as she, Elena, and Olivia traveled down to the basement. A single lightbulb hung from the low ceiling, lending the space an eerie glow. Elena stepped out of the light's circle to retrieve a box. She dragged it toward Rose's feet.

"I've been saving these things for you," Elena said. "To give you . . . someday."

Rose's pulse thrummed wildly. She started to delve in, but her adoptive mother put a hand on her arm to stop her.

"First you must know the events of that dark evening," Elena spoke carefully. "When you were about seven years old, you awoke in the middle of the night. As if you were possessed by something unearthly, you grabbed a piece of paper and began writing furiously."

"Your eyes rolled back in your head and your face went completely white," Olivia chimed in. "It scared me to death and I couldn't sleep for weeks afterward."

Elena nodded before she went on. "The word, which wasn't written in your normal penmanship, was almost illegible. *Almost.*"

"What did I write?" Rose asked excitedly.

"Take a look."

Rose's gut wrenched. As warm tears rimmed her eyes, she quickly sifted through the items inside the box. There was a photograph of her as a baby. She was being held in her mother's arms, and just as Rose had ascertained by way of the scrapbook, Florence Hayes looked a great deal like her.

Rose replaced the photograph with a smile. Next to the photo sat a baby rattle. She picked it up and ran her fingers over its indentations sentimentally. Then she returned it to the box.

Her hands brushed a folded piece of paper. With trembling hands, she picked it up and looked at Elena. Elena nodded solemnly.

Breathing unevenly, Rose unfolded the large sheet. It read, "*DRAGO.*"

"My God," she gasped. "I'm a psychic and a spirit writer."

CHAPTER 28

Rose sagged against Olivia for support.

Grasping her arm, Olivia asked, "You knew you'd meet Drago someday?"

Rose sucked in a breath and tried to gather her wits. "I guess I did."

Olivia dug her fingernails in. "How?"

"Spirit writers channel spirits through meditation," said Rose. "They record what they hear. But the messages are penned without the conscious thoughts of the writer because they come from the departed."

Elena frowned. "They come from the devil, you mean."

"These spirits, whether they are good or bad, take control of the hand of the medium."

"With no harm done to the medium, I hope?" Elena asked.

"As far as I know, the medium remains safe," Rose said.

"How do you know so much about spirit writing?" Olivia cocked a brow.

"I told you: I've always been fascinated with the supernatural."

Olivia crossed her arms. "Can this type of channeling become scary? You should have seen yourself that night, Rose."

Rose shook her head. "If it's monitored, a spirit writing session can be fascinating instead of dangerous or scary. A medium can pen sentences, even paragraphs, in languages unknown to her—and she can remain under a trance long enough to transcribe entire books."

"If that's the case"—Olivia smiled—"are you thinking what I'm thinking?"

"If you're thinking that I should try spirit writing to see whose body Morvina has invaded and to find out if Drago is innocent then . . . yes."

Footsteps sounded on the stairs. The three women spun around. Anthony emerged from the shadows into the circle of light. "Be careful, girls. I've been listening from the landing and it sounds like you're playing with fire."

"Don't worry, Anthony," Olivia said quickly. "This is exactly what Rose needs to find out about Drago. I'm sure she'll make her parents proud."

He stuffed his hands into his trouser pockets. The stance exaggerated his burly shoulders and stocky frame. "Rose, I was sorry to hear about your parents' passing."

He's doing it again, Rose thought. *Speaking without a hint of emotion.* "I just need you to support me right now, Anthony."

"You have my support," he replied. "After all, you'll celebrate your twenty-first birthday tomorrow."

She cringed. " 'Celebrate' is hardly the word."

With an ache in her gut, Rose excused herself and dragged Olivia upstairs so they could dress. A quarter of an hour later, they were hurrying to the New York Public Library. There, Rose settled in to devour all the information on spirit writing procedures Olivia brought to her.

"Do you think you're prepared enough to conduct your own writing session?" Olivia asked, once they'd emerged into the warm June afternoon.

"No, but I'm running out of time," Rose answered. The stack of notes she'd taken in the library fluttered in the breeze.

From what she'd read on the subject, Rose knew script writers received messages from disembodied spirits with whom the writer may or may not be acquainted. While the spirit who had given Rose the message when she was seven years old remained a mystery, she hoped to discover its identity soon.

She had also learned that in order to receive a message from beyond the living world, the writer must meditate heavily. At seven years old, she hadn't meditated at all. She'd simply received and penned the message—and the innocence of it meant that her powers must have great potential.

But why hadn't she been able to do spirit writing since? Rose decided that whether it was because she hadn't sat down and tried or if the spirits hadn't much to say until now, it didn't matter.

If I did it once, I can do it again. And this time I'll contact my mother.

Morvina had had enough of the foreign body she was trapped in. She wanted to look in the mirror at the beauty she'd gained prior to overtaking this male identity.

Wait one more day, she told herself. *Rose has come back to New York and that means my plan is in full swing.*

Settling into an armchair in the privacy of her parlor, Morvina flipped Drago's lei coin over in her hand. She could feel the object's extraordinary power even now.

In one of the coin's visions, she'd seen that Rose had been strong-willed enough to remove the amulet of Tousret. Unfortunately, the protection of the amulet remained over her niece. Adding to Rose's bad luck was her debilitating vertigo. Could she actually reach and touch the sharp apex of the building's spire during Drago's spectacle—as the newspaper challenged?

Dealing with her fear of heights would cause Rose tremendous anguish. Morvina, on the other hand, loved the idea that Rose would suffer.

Rose had left Drago in France. That was another foolish move. *You don't know where your husband is now. And that means you're all mine.* Morvina had doomed Rose to spiral off something high on her twenty-first birthday. And so she would.

That night, the wind howled outside Rose's bedroom window. Thunder boomed and a bolt of lightning ripped through the sky.

As a rainstorm began to beat against the windowpanes, it seemed a fitting backdrop to the spirit writing session about to take place.

Rose and Olivia huddled together. After she gathered her courage,

Rose drew the curtains, lit a candle, and locked the door. Then she gave Olivia specific instructions. Olivia was to ask the questions Rose had written down ahead of time and watch Rose record the answers. Once Rose penned something, Olivia was supposed to remove the piece of paper and place it in an organized stack.

"Are you sure you want to do this?" Olivia asked dubiously.

"I'm sure."

"But you won't know what's going on. Aren't you afraid to enter 'an unearthly trance', as you call it?"

Rose gripped her adoptive sister's arm. "I'm not afraid. Besides, conducting this session is the only way I can find out the truth." *The truth about Morvina and Drago.*

"I suppose you're right." Olivia gulped. "All right. I'm ready when you're ready."

Rose sat at her desk. Olivia dropped stiffly into an adjacent chair. Rose exhaled slowly and attempted to shut her mind off to conscious streams of thought. It wasn't easy, however. The rain at the window proved incredibly distracting—and even the sharp crackle of the candle interrupted the silence.

Eventually, Rose managed to push the noises into a quiet place.

As she slipped into a deep, meditative state, her body relaxed. Her hand hovered over the paper for a moment, the pen in it shaking ever so slightly.

"Spirit guards," Olivia said, "please come and talk to Rose."

Rose's hand started to move rapidly. She seemed unaware of what she was inscribing. Was she too busy coaxing the spirits with her mind?

As Olivia sat and watched Rose, she realized that her verbal pleas needed to be heartfelt, as opposed to mechanical.

"Please spirits," she whispered again. "Rose will keep writing until you appear."

Rose scribbled furiously. It was gibberish at first—until something commanded her to switch her pencil to her non-dominant hand. When she did, Olivia assumed a spirit had crossed over and was speaking to Rose clearly.

"Who are you, spirit?" Olivia asked.

C-o-n-e-y-I-s-l-a-n-d, Rose wrote.

Olivia saw Rose grip the pencil tighter. "Are you the girl who was murdered at Coney Island last year?" she asked.

Y-e-s

Emotion welling inside her, Olivia looked at the instructions Rose gave her. She asked the second question, "Did Dragomir Starkov murder you?"

N-o

Olivia read the word and gasped. Deep in her trance, Rose, who didn't seem to hear her, transferred the pen to her other hand and proceeded to write in different penmanship. "Are you a new spirit?" Olivia queried.

Y-e-s

"Tell Rose your name."

L-e-n-o-r-e-J-e-f-f-r-i-e-s

"Who are you, Lenore Jeffries?"

G-r-a-n-d-m-o-t-h-e-r

Olivia nodded. "You are Rose's mother's mother?"

Y-e-s

"Are you the spirit who contacted Rose when she was seven years old?"

Y-e-s

"Is Rose's mother with you?"

N-o-t-h-e-r-e

Rose's hand shook as much as Olivia's voice did. Deciding to toss the pre-arranged questions aside, Olivia demanded, "Is there something you want to say, Rose's grandmother?"

Y-e-s

Olivia felt a whisper of cold air filter over her face. Rose remained stone-faced. "Is it about Rose's husband?"

N-o

The silence that followed made Rose draw large circles on the paper. She created no readable words so finally, Olivia asked, "What do you want to tell Rose?"

M-o-r-v-i-n-a

"Can you tell Rose who Morvina is disguising herself as?"

Books started flying off the bookshelf. Clothes were flung across the room and a loud banging began to sound without an origin.

In the midst of the pandemonium, the pen flew out of Rose's hand. Then a scent drifted under Olivia's nose. She wondered if, in her heavy trance, Rose had smelled the distinct scent of cigarette smoke, too.

CHAPTER 29

The ruckus ceased. Exhausted, Rose slumped over the desk. Her trance eventually lifted.

"Did you smell it?" Olivia asked, excitedly.

"Smell what?"

"The cigarette smoke!"

Wide-eyed, Rose shook her head. "Why? What did I pen?"

"Let me show you these." Olivia handed her the papers that said "Coney Island" and "No."

"I don't understand," Rose said in a groggy voice.

"The spirit of the girl murdered at Coney Island came through you. When I asked her if Drago killed her, she said 'no'!"

Relief rifled through Rose. "You mean the girl was pointing her finger at someone else?"

"Yes. Drago's innocent," Olivia cried. "And despite the fact that we didn't find out who Morvina is disguising herself as, the cigarette smoke is a clue."

Rose frowned. "Who smokes?"

Olivia thrust her a blank expression.

Trembling, she sat back in her chair. "I can think of two men. Archibald McMillan and Richard Bellum."

"Then it has to be one of them."

"But *which* one?'

"Your guess is as good as mine," Olivia replied with a hint of dejection.

Rose's nerves were shot from the session. "At least we know Drago isn't the Coney Island Murderer," she said.

"Thank God. I guess you feel horrible about telling the police he was."

"Yes, Olivia. Thanks for rubbing it in."

"Sorry."

Rose sat in silence for a long while, her shoulders rolled forward. Then she abruptly shot out of her seat. "I just had a vision! I know where Drago is. He'll help me figure this out."

But she was weaker from the session than she thought. She swayed on her feet and reached for Olivia.

"You're in no condition to go anywhere," Olivia said firmly. "Sit back down."

"You don't understand." Rose tried to steady herself. "Drago deserves to hear my apology. He didn't kill that girl."

Feeling a little more stable, she made for the door. "I'm going to him. I'm also going to the Woolworth Building tomorrow night."

"You can't go anywhere, Rose!" Olivia cried out as she left the room. "Have you forgotten that tomorrow is your birthday? Even if Drago isn't the demon meant to destroy you, you'll have Morvina to contend with!"

Rose didn't respond. Instead, she raced downstairs, grabbed Lorenzo's car keys from their hook on the kitchen wall, and hurried to his car. *Thank God Drago taught me how to drive in France.*

The heavy downpour pounded Drago's East Hampton house.

It was nearly eleven o'clock, but he couldn't sleep. Abandoning the effort, he climbed out of bed, moved to the bedroom window and envisioned New York's serrated skyline. He'd been forced to go into hiding—disguising himself with baggy clothes and a fake beard when in public. All because Rose had alerted the police about him.

Still, he couldn't blame her. Propelled by curiosity, she'd spoken to the coin at Château de Maincy. The coin was gone and he suspected Rose had it in her possession.

What, exactly, had she seen it project? Him killing other immortals by severing their heads? After all, that was the only way they could be killed.

Whatever Rose witnessed had been horrific enough for her to set the authorities after him.

While Drago didn't blame Rose, he wished he still had the lei coin. Then he would be able to see her current state of mind.

Where is she? Is she all right?

Tomorrow night would be the most important evening of their lives. His instincts told him Rose would be there. Although she wasn't wearing the amulet anymore, the hypnotic state he'd woven over her remained. When she arrived to follow his commands, she'd be counting on him to save her from Morvina. Drago would gladly kill Rose's diabolical aunt. Then he would go on to destroy the final Immortal.

There could be only one victor. Drago knew it. He had endured centuries of self-loathing for that very title. If he persevered, he'd be rid of this despicable soul-craving. More importantly, he'd be able to live a normal life with Rose. Possibly have children with her . . . even grow old alongside her.

That in itself was priceless. Furthermore, it was only fair. There was no justice in Rose dying at twenty-one and him living forever without her.

Drago moved away from the window and fastened his hands on his hips. The police's appearance at the Woolworth Building tomorrow night was inconvenient and unavoidable. But then again, he'd told Archibald McMillan to bribe the authorities into waiting until after the show to arrest him for the Coney Island murder.

That way he'd have time to perform his illusion.

Of course, there were no guarantees that Patrick O'Leary and Anthony Marconi wouldn't try and capture him before the show was over.

Being separated from Rose again was a possibility that curled Drago's hands into fists. Adrenaline flowed through his body at an astounding rate. It was a rush like he'd never known, except, perhaps, while making love to his beautiful wife. When she'd lain beneath him, flashing those violet eyes . . . when she'd fondled him—my God! He'd come as close to heaven as a demon would ever get.

Short of breath, Drago felt his demonic urges coming on. He stalked around the bedroom, face reddening. As his mouth went dry, he tried to relax. But it was useless. After drinking several glasses of water, he decided to take a bath to calm down.

Drago ran the bathwater, undressed then slipped into the tub. Eyes closed, he soaked in silence until his thirst for a new soul dispelled temporarily.

As his mind cleared, he realized that tomorrow evening would be the final feather in his cap as a magician. His chance to go out with a bang, as the press would say. However, Drago's career didn't matter to him anymore. Instead, his last illusion was a way to whisk Rose away to safety and leave their dangerous ties to New York behind.

Drago still had his eyes closed when the doorbell rang. Glowering, he tossed his bath sponge to the side and pushed himself out of the water.

Who the hell can that be? He'd let the maids and the grounds-keeper go.

Barely bothering to dry himself off, Drago wrapped a towel around his waist and marched downstairs. Drawing the curtains aside, he looked outside. *Rose!*

His heart leapt to his throat. He opened the door. Breathless, he watched her wild gaze glide over his wet body. Then she fell into his arms, becoming as soaked as he was as she clung to him desperately.

Drago's heart pumped as he inhaled her scent. "Thank God you came to me."

She tightened her grip around his waist. "I was so stupid, Drago, and I'm sorry. For leaving you. For telling the police your darkest secret. For taking your coin and for not believing in you. For everything."

He lifted her face so that he could gaze into her eyes. "I forgive you. God, I missed you so much."

"I felt lost without you."

They embraced again. And as Drago hugged Rose tightly, he

looked over her shoulder. The unfamiliar car in his driveway caught his eye. "Did you drive here?"

She nodded as he grasped her hands. "I nearly crashed half a dozen times."

"Well, you're safe with me now."

"I need to tell you why I sought you out," she said in a winded voice.

He cupped her face and listened.

"I conducted a spirit writing session tonight."

"You can spirit write?"

"Yes. Apparently, it's an ability I've had since I was seven years old. Elena was too scared to tell me about it."

He raised an eyebrow. "What did you record?"

"That you're innocent of the Coney Island murders."

"Thank God you know." He sucked in a deep breath.

"I'm sorry for accusing you."

"Don't worry." He gave her a gentle smile. "Like I said, all is forgiven."

"When I saw you turn into that demon . . . in the lei coin—"

"I'm sure it terrified you. But now you know I've never killed a mortal." He paused. "The first two women who were attacked at Coney Island will eventually recover. It'll just take time."

Her hand trembled in his.

"What else did you learn?" he asked.

"I asked the spirits to give me the name of the person Morvina is hiding behind."

"And?"

"I didn't get a name but I got a clue. *Cigarette smoke.*"

"Cigarette smoke?" Drago took a step back. "McMillan smokes like a fiend."

Rose bit her lip before she added, "So does Richard Bellum."

Drago's face fell into a scowl. "Bellum! That bastard."

Shuddering, Rose wrapped her arms around his waist. "I don't know *who* to trust right now."

Drago stroked her hair. "We'll find out in less than twenty-four hours." As he clutched her tightly, Rose's warm fragrance spawned the lust he'd put on hold since she fled. He'd missed her undeniably and uncontrollably—and now that she had given him another chance to protect her, he wanted to make love to her.

Slipping a hand into her wet curls, he tilted her head back. Then he caught her mouth with a fierce kiss. The softness of her lips brought back flashes of their previous lovemaking and nearly drove him mad.

"Come inside," he whispered gruffly.

Taking Rose by the hand, he led her through the foyer and up one side of the central staircase. When he turned to look at her, her flushed cheeks and violet eyes made him hard.

"Were you in the middle of a bath?" she asked softly once he guided her into the warm bathroom.

"Yes. You can join me in a minute." He reached across his torso and unknotted the towel he wore at his waist. As it drifted to the ground, Rose's stare dropped from his abdomen to his protruding erection. She sucked in a breath.

"I didn't forget how handsome you are," she said, trembling in her damp state.

"And I pictured your beautiful face every day we were separated."

Blushing, she lifted her blond locks, then swiveled away from him. Drago moved behind her and silently began unfastening the line of buttons down her back. His penis brushed against her backside. The contact made it throb hotly.

Drago unclasped her blouse hastily. Rose slipped the garment off in a forward motion, then peeled her chemise down to her hips. When she turned back around, Drago inhaled sharply. Her tantalizing breasts were as stunning as he remembered—and in the sensual moment, he chose not to dwell on the fact that she wasn't wearing the amulet.

Reaching for her, he traced her lips, her neck, and then her collarbone with his thumbs. And when he dropped his touch to the outline of her breasts, he grunted with passion. How he'd missed the way the skin around her nipples puckered when she was aroused. And how he'd longed to caress her derriere, and—.

"Christ, Rose! You make me so hard." Grinning, he glanced down at his cock. It was as erect as a flagpole.

She smiled, too.

"I want to touch all of you," he rasped.

Unhooking her skirt, he yanked it to the floor. Next, he tugged off her blouse, chemise, and undergarments and slid his hands over her creamy flesh. It was as soft as a baby's. Rose knew how to spawn his lust and fuel his deepest fantasies without trying. She was the only woman he'd ever loved. *Would* ever love.

It was as simple as that.

"I want you as excited as I am." Drago stepped in and nuzzled her neck. After he skimmed his hand down her bare arm, he clutched her hand. By cupping her chin with his other hand, he was able to slant his mouth over hers and deliver a slow, hot kiss. Then, showing his impatience, he swept his tongue over her lower lip and pried her mouth open. When he glided the length of his tongue into her mouth, Rose reeled in his arms.

Squeaking out sounds of ecstasy, she melted against him like butter softening in the sun. As she grazed his chest with her fingertips, she pressed the tips of her breasts against his pectoral muscles. Drago nearly spilled his semen right then.

He kissed her again—this time tasting her pleasure until he knew he'd ignited her unbridled excitement. "I want to satisfy you before we make love."

She nodded, wide-eyed.

"Sit on the edge of the tub," he instructed.

"Oh, Drago," she murmured with a half-smile.

She did as he said and he pulled a stool over on which she placed her delicate foot. Smiling devilishly, Drago plunged to his knees. Meanwhile, Rose gripped the edge of the tub and opened her legs. He began petting her nether hair in languid circles, noticing that her curls shone a beautiful bronze color in the lamplight. Initially, he traced her outer folds. Then he used the pad of his thumb to put pressure on her cleft. The friction caused Rose to arch back in delight. Moisture started to flow from her folds—and he could smell the sweet scent of her arousal.

Yearning to taste her cream, he put his mouth to her slit and lapped at it.

Moaning, Rose balanced herself with one hand and fisted his wet hair with the other.

"Yes," she whispered sharply. "Just like that."

"Come, Rose. Come in my mouth."

She pulled his face closer. Her hips danced in time to his mouth moving. After minutes of him swirling his tongue inside her and licking her potent ambrosia, Rose nodded. Her body stiffened and she cried out.

"That felt so good," she said breathlessly.

Wiping his mouth with the back of his head, Drago stood. He yanked a large towel off a rack and spread it on the floor. Urging Rose down, he settled in between her damp thighs. Grasping his rigid shaft, he plunged himself inside. Rose moaned. Once she enveloped his waist with her long legs, she slid her hands over his hips and squeezed his buttocks.

The firm kneading made Drago even harder.

"My love," he said as he gazed down at her. Her golden locks spread across the bathroom tiles like fine strands of silk and her pert breasts bounced gently with every thrust he gave her. And the patter of rain at the window added an erotic aura to Rose's needy sounds.

"You're so hard," she said with a tiny smile.

That's because you're so tight, Drago thought. He continued to pump, and the throbbing of his cock nearly convinced him that he hadn't made love for decades.

When Rose trailed her fingertips up the curve of his back and cradled his face in both hands, his semen built from his balls upward. Drago honed in on her eyes the way he had at the Sunshine Theater— those purple eyes the shade of African violets—and his engorged sex pulsated with enormous pressure.

"Let me—" Before he could finish his sentence, Rose called out his name. That did it. Like a tidal wave rushing to shore, he ejaculated. And ejaculated.

Grunting, he finally stopped convulsing. Then, dizzy with satisfaction, he gathered her close.

Brushing kisses along her neck allowed him to breathe in her familiar iris scent. And feeling Rose's wild heartbeat against his chest made Drago consider that having magical powers would never compare to the pleasure she gave him. He still hated himself for seeking portions of foreign souls to sustain his existence, but at the very least, that existence had brought Rose to him.

Now he was willing to give up his magic and become mortal—for her.

Drago lifted her off the ground and placed her inside the bathtub. Then he stepped in and joined her.

CHAPTER 30

Rose was glad the bathwater was warm and bubbly. As Drago feathered a warm sponge across her shoulders, she closed her eyes. She lay turned away from him—and as he nestled in behind her, it felt wonderful to have him close again.

What she'd found out about him had cleared her conscience, at least the part about him not killing the girl at Coney Island. Of course, if Drago hadn't murdered her, someone else had. Rose inhaled sharply at the thought. She nearly panicked—until she reminded herself that she was cradled safely in his arms. Drago made her feel secure because he was the only one who could protect her from Morvina.

Because it's already midnight, and I've already turned twenty-one, we only need to get through today together . . .

Rose reached behind her. By grasping Drago's hip, she pulled him closer. Her breathing calmed as he stroked her long hair. Tranquilly, he allowed each wisp to flow through his fingers. The sensation comforted her. Drago's solid muscles strained against her backside and as his erection was rejuvenated beneath the water, she became aroused again, too.

Drago reached beneath Rose's arm and caressed her breasts with the sponge. Once he released a stream of bubbles between her breasts, he looked over her shoulder at the cluster of bubbles the sponge had left on her risen nipples.

In a rough voice he whispered, "You're so beautiful, Rose. In a vision, I saw you in Patrick's arms and I couldn't stand it."

"I'm sorry I went to him," she said quietly. "I didn't know what else to do."

"No man will ever have you except me." Determination coated Drago's voice. While his intensity might have made other women flee a long time ago, Rose was in too deep to ever leave him again. She loved him desperately.

Drago blew away the cluster of bubbles at her breast. Then he dropped the sponge so that he could tease her nipple with his fingertips. Rose's core stirred. She craned her neck and sought his lips for a crushing kiss. Meanwhile he delved a hand between her legs, petting her curls. Warm bathwater streamed around her as Rose wiggled. She separated her knees to let Drago explore deeper.

"You're wet, and it's not the bathwater," he murmured.

Once he slipped his hand away, he replaced it with his lengthy sex. Gingerly, he inserted the tip inside her then gave a firm thrust forward— filling her in every sense of the word. While Drago held Rose tightly around the waist and pumped in and out of her, splashes of water sloshed over the sides of the tub. Rose moaned and moved her hips against his groin. She built up friction that way—and her sex contracted and released around his stiffness. In no time, she climaxed along with Drago, in perfect synchronization. In mirrored harmony.

Breathing heavily, they lay still until the water cooled. Then Drago suggested they get out.

As he emerged from the tub, Rose turned and looked up at him. His wet body glistened like diamonds in the light while his hair hung in damp locks around his face. With his hulking frame and his flexed muscles, he looked like a hungry warrior, ready for battle. That's what he is, Rose supposed. A warrior, ready to do battle with Morvina.

Drago dried off before he wrapped the towel around his waist. Next, he brought a fluffy bathrobe to Rose. "Let's go to bed."

She got out of the tub and let him slip the garment over her shoulders. Cinching the waist, she padded to the massive bed in the other room. Drago was right behind her. They lay beneath the covers and as she rested her head on his chest, she stared at the darkness through the window. The quietness of the house and the calming effect of the bath put both of them to sleep.

Hours later, the sun peeked through the curtains. Drago shook Rose gently awake.

"I just had an idea," Drago broached the subject without wasting another minute.

"What?" she asked, rolling to face him.

He lifted her chin so that he could look into her eyes. "I don't want to guess about something this important. Maybe you can try and learn Morvina's identity for certain."

"You mean I should conduct another spirit writing session?" Her body stiffened.

"Yes."

She thought about it for a moment. "I was terrified during the first one, but it's worth a try."

"I'll set it up after we get dressed," Drago said.

They donned their clothes and Rose proceeded to give Drago a verbal list of the things she needed. She also instructed him about what he should do during the session.

Once everything was in place, they sat at a writing desk inside the bedroom. The space fell into a hush. Leaning over, Drago gave her an encouraging peck on the cheek. She eyed him for a minute. His face was flushed and his hair was tousled from their recent sleep—and when his blue-green eyes shimmered at her with hope, he took her breath away, just as he had the night they met.

More than anything, Rose wanted this day to be over. She longed to be enfolded in Drago's arms on a beach far away. Unfortunately, that dream would have to wait.

"Before we start," she said, "promise me that you'll follow my instructions to the letter."

"You have my word."

Closing her eyes, she lifted the pen. Sensing Drago's stare and hearing the merry birds outside the window prevented her from falling into a meditative trance right away. Finally, Rose descended into the dark place she'd visited before.

When Drago surmised that all conscious thought had escaped Rose, he called out, "Appear spirits. Tell my wife what we want to know."

Rose's hand moved over the paper in large circles. An instant later, she jerked her hand away abruptly.

It was obvious that something had blocked her communication.

Drago tried to summon the spirit again. "If you can hear me, Rose needs you."

A lengthy pause preceded Rose putting her pen to the paper again.

G-r-a-n-d-m-o-t-h-e-r, she recorded.

"Please," Drago said. "If you know who Morvina is disguising herself as, tell her."

Rose's pen hovered, silent and immobile for a moment. Then with incredible force, she wrote the letters, *E-v-i-l*.

"Thank you." Drago gritted his teeth. "But we need a name, Grandmother."

Rose jotted nothing for several minutes.

Drago closed his eyes as he continued. "I sense there's a dark spirit in your world who doesn't want us to know the name. But I'm begging you to tell us anyway."

He snapped his eyes open and studied Rose.

Again, she didn't write anything. Then in heavy, bold script she recorded, *B-e-l-l-u-m*.

Faintly—as if from a hundred miles away—Rose heard Drago roar, "Son of a bitch!"

Bursting out of her trance, she slumped forward. She was almost too tired to glance at what she'd written.

"Look, Rose!" Drago slipped the paper from beneath her out-spread arms. "Morvina has invaded Richard Bellum's body!"

She shook away her grogginess and read the name she'd recorded. "My aunt has been Bellum the whole time?"

"Yes. It explains all of that bastard's antics."

Her voice took on the same enraged tone as Drago's. "Like meeting me at your show? Offering me a job? Trying to bribe me to get information about you?"

"Exactly."

She didn't ordinarily swear, but Rose let out a doozy. "Wait a minute. Bellum seemed more bent on hurting you than me. Why?"

Drago's face turned crimson. He took her by the shoulders. "I have to tell you something very important. If I don't, you'll be terrified tonight."

Perspiration beaded her lip. "Tell me what?"

"I was sent here to meet you, Rose. But now I realize why. Morvina isn't just an enchantress."

"What do you mean?"

"I can't believe I didn't put it together sooner. Enchantresses aren't powerful enough to possess someone else's body. *Morvina must be a demon.*"

As if she'd received a painful, electric shock, Rose leapt out of her seat. "She is what you are?"

"Yes. It all makes sense now. She's the Immortal I'm destined to face in something called the Victory tonight."

Her hands shook. Drago stood and grasped them.

"Currently, there are two demons left in the world. Morvina and me. But there can be only one."

Rose's body convulsed with terror. "Then you have to win! I don't want to die—and I could never live without you."

"Don't worry," Drago replied. "Come hell or high water, Morvina will pay for terrorizing you since you were a baby."

"How are you going to make her pay?"

"I have this entire thing planned out in my head."

She remained silent, immersed in the whirlpool of her fears.

"I organized the feat on top of the Woolworth Building with confidence," he went on. "Confidence that the spectacle would reinstate my reputation as a talented magician. Confidence that I was powerful enough to save you from Morvina. But all that has changed. I don't have the bracelet of Amenhotep or the lei coin. I wish I'd created a different, less dangerous act, but in actuality, I couldn't have. The top of the Woolworth Building is the designated location. The location I saw in my vision. Tonight both of us will face what we fear most. And for everything to work out, you're going to have to trust me."

"I do," Rose said, more weakly than she would have liked.

"I need to know what you did with the amulet and the bracelet."

"I . . . I left them in France." She paused. "They're hidden inside the portrait of Jean-Daniel Girard."

Drago spun away from her and scrubbed his hands through his hair. "Damn it! I was hoping you had them stored somewhere in New York."

"I'm sorry. I was scared that day."

She came up behind him. When he faced her, his eyes were as dark as a stormy sea. "When we're on top of the building tonight," he said, "only one thing can help me kill Morvina. The lei coin—considering I can get my hands on it."

Face flaming, Rose shifted her eyes away.

Drago took her hands in his again. To get them to stop shaking, he squeezed them. "Listen very carefully. If we're going to survive tonight, I need that coin," he repeated, "to see what Morvina has planned. Do you have it?"

Rose's lungs constricted. "No."

Alarm lit his eyes. "What happened to it?"

"Someone stole it from my handbag the other night."

"I need it!"

"Are you powerless without it?"

He shot her a grim look. "My powers are depleted and I can't maintain my energy during the day. That's why I've been hiding out here."

"Your show won't take place until the sun goes down," she said with hope.

"It'll take every ounce of strength I have to defeat Morvina. You've never seen a battle between two demons. They get extremely ugly." He paused. "One of us will lose our head tonight."

She gave a violent shudder. *How can I possibly face all of this?*

Drago's nostrils flared. "Since I don't have the lei coin, you *really* have to trust me this evening, Rose."

"You keep saying that."

"I know you'll be terrified. More scared than you've ever been. Regardless, you must do what I tell you."

Following Drago's commands had gotten Rose into her fair share of trouble, but today she had no choice. She removed her hands from his then wrapped her arms around her waist. "Can you tell me exactly what's going to happen?"

"I can only tell you that if you don't do as I say, you won't make it through 'til morning."

More tears poured forward in hot streaks. "That's not helping."

"You had faith in me the minute we met," he said. "You put on the necklace, married me, and became my assistant—all because you trusted me."

"Yes—but this might be too much." Blinking against her tears, she searched his eyes for some empathy.

"Without the coin, the only way to stop Morvina is for you to risk your life and kill her yourself."

Rose's body froze. "I thought killing her was your job!"

"I cannot be one hundred percent sure what will happen on top of the building. I'm only sure of the fraction of it I saw in my vision."

"Describe what you saw."

"I saw one demon falling off the building without a head."

She cringed.

"It's imperative that you throw the right demon off the Woolworth Building tonight, Rose."

"The *right* demon?" Her stomach lurched.

Drago nodded. "Morvina and I will look identical in our demonic forms. Still, you must steal up underneath her and yank her off."

"I doubt I can go through with even scaling the building. You know I have horrible vertigo."

He cupped her chin with his enormous hand. "You have to."

"But how will I know which creature to pull?"

"You have special abilities. Use them."

She grimaced. She did possess psychic abilities, but they were minimal.

. "What about the curse of the amulet and the damnation spell Morvina cast over me?" she asked. "Either way, it seems I'm destined to die this evening."

"Not if you yank the correct demon off the building." He paused. "Now wait here."

Rose wrung her hands as he left the room. If there were any damned mirrors in the house, her reflection would've confirmed that her face was ashen right then.

A moment later, Drago returned. In his hands, he held what looked like replicas of the amulet of Tousret and the bracelet of Amenhotep. He also held the scanty costume Rose had worn during their show at the Hippodrome.

He passed the necklace and the costume to her with a dour expression. "Wear the amulet. I had a duplicate of the Egyptian pendant made in case you no longer had it. And I'll wear this substitute of the bracelet. People expect to see them, and they won't know the difference."

"And the costume?"

"You wouldn't want a long skirt hindering your climb up the building."

Heart hammering, Rose clasped the objects to her chest.

Drago gave her a kiss before lying down to conserve his energy. "I'll become a demon at seven thirty this evening. It's the exact time I accepted the lei coin years ago. But the spectacle leading up to that won't be about me hypnotizing you—like I want the audience to think. It will be about your survival."

CHAPTER 31

Eleven hours later, twenty thousand eager on-lookers surrounded the Woolworth Building. Spotlights crisscrossed in the black sky, vendors sold souvenirs from the street corners, and eager audience members shoved one another to find an ideal spot from which to watch the act.

All in all, the highly-publicized event was even more chaotic than Rose anticipated.

Drago grasped her hand protectively as he drove his Garford close to the building. Meanwhile, reporters clamored on the sidelines, readying their cameras and notepads.

As Drago and Rose emerged from the motorcar, they were joined by Archibald McMillan. He escorted them inside the Woolworth Building that, thankfully, had been sealed off to the public. Only Rose, Drago, McMillan, and a few police officers milled about the structure's brightly lit lobby.

Rose clutched the long shawl that covered her costume. She'd donned ballet flats instead of the heels she usually wore onstage. Would the slippers give her enough traction to climb properly?

Her legs quaked at the thought. She was about to face her worst nightmare and it was nearly impossible for her to think straight.

What had Drago said in the car? He'd explained that there were grooves along the building's exterior in which she could place her feet. Once she reached the base of the spire, there was a narrow, steel ladder she would climb to the very apex.

That's where Drago would be waiting for her.

"The crowd is calling for a speech, Starkov," McMillan said as he puffed on his cigarette.

"Speech?" Drago replied sternly.

"Yes, a speech. You've been in hiding. The public eats that stuff up. Now they want to hear you tell them where you've been."

They also want to hear you say you're not the murderer I accused you of being, Rose thought nervously.

"I hate reporters, but I'll do it." Drago drew his thick brows together. "I need to clear a few things up."

"Great," Archibald said as he steered Rose and Drago outside.

Camera bulbs exploded and Rose panicked. *The cameras will show Drago's lack of presence.* Nearly blinded by the thought and by the camera flashes, she groped for him and lost her shawl in the process.

"I love you," he murmured into her ear.

"I love you, too," she mouthed as he approached a standing microphone.

The crowd went insane. If the spectators were scared of Drago turning into a homicidal monster, they didn't show it. *In fact, that's why these people are here*, Rose presumed. *They're just as curious as I used to be.*

"Good evening," he said, his Romanian accent thundering through the speakers. "Welcome to my final magic act. I promise you it will be like nothing you've ever seen."

Loud applause punctuated the statement.

"I've been in hiding, it's true," Drago said. "But it doesn't matter where. What's important is that after tonight, I would like to retire from performing. I need time to be with my beautiful wife."

He glanced at Rose. Her cheeks bloomed.

"However," he took a breath, "I know that a leisurely retirement isn't in the cards. There have been erroneous rumors floating around about me—even newspaper articles claiming that I'm the creature who killed the girl at Coney Island. My wife asserted as much. But she has since learned that I am not guilty. Unfortunately, the police aren't convinced of the same thing. Ladies and gentleman, you'll see that the authorities are controlling this spectacle. After I'm finished, they intend to take me into custody."

Rose heard someone shout, "Come on, Starkov. Admit that you're the Coney Island Killer!"

Drago didn't reply.

Rose thought desperately, *How can he persuade them he's telling the truth?*

She flinched as another voice rose above the crowd. "Your wife was the one who blew the whistle on you, Starkov. You must be furious and she must be frightened of you. Did you coerce her into participating tonight?"

Drago fired the man a dark look. "Coerce is hardly the word. She's hypnotized by the enchanted amulet she's wearing."

All eyes zeroed in on Rose's neck. She wanted to run back to the car. It took every iota of strength she possessed to stand her ground.

"My wife has debilitating vertigo," Drago continued. "So her climb tonight will prove dangerous in and of itself. That's the reason I used the amulet to hypnotize her. She would never dare climb this building without it."

Rose wanted to cry out, "The amulet is a fake!"

"You're a monster—putting your wife through such torture!" A stout woman hissed.

"I'm wearing the bracelet of Amenhotep," Drago retorted, "so no harm will come to her." He pulled up the sleeve of his jacket and revealed the ornate band.

Murmurs spread through the crowd.

"Since my wife is already hypnotized, I intend to impress the public with another sort of trick," Drago went on. "I'm going to make her *disappear*."

Rose stumbled back. Luckily, McMillan caught her. *Disappear?*

That can't be Drago's plan, she thought. He told her she would need to pull the correct demon off the building.

What does he have up his sleeve?

Confused, she swayed on her feet. Once she gathered her wits, she tugged on Drago's arm.

Drago covered the microphone with his hand. "What are you doing?" he asked gently.

"I need to tell everyone the truth."

"The truth?"

"That what I saw in the coin wasn't you killing that girl," she whispered to him. "It was Morvina."

He gave her a rueful smile. "These people won't believe you."

"Let me try," she pleaded. "I don't want you to get arrested after this spectacle."

"You don't understand, Rose. Nothing will matter once we complete the magic act."

He's being so damned secretive. He didn't want to scare her by telling her what to expect—but the reality was, *not* knowing was scaring her more.

Drago would die if his head was severed. *What if I'm responsible for that? Will I pull him off the building instead of Morvina? Will I kill myself afterward?*

Knowing that her husband wasn't going to answer her questions in front of this massive crowd, Rose released Drago's arm and let him finish his address. While he explained that he'd scale the highest quarter of the building and then wait for Rose to climb to him at its apex, she searched the skies for Morvina.

Would she swoop down and attack at any moment?

After Drago thanked the crowd and stepped away from the microphone, a tense silence ensued. He removed his jacket and rolled up his shirt sleeves. Then he turned to Rose as the crowd fell into a profound hush.

"It's time," he said.

Her nerves vibrated to a new high.

"I'll see you at the top." He planted a gentle kiss on her cheek.

Rose wanted to scream and protest like a three-year-old. Instead, she fought for composure—and blew Drago a final kiss as he disappeared into the Woolworth Building.

Suddenly, a hand grasped her arm. Assuming it was McMillan, she let the gentleman lead her inside behind Drago. But when she turned to look at her escort, she realized it wasn't Archibald. It was Patrick.

"What are you doing here?" she asked breathlessly.

"I'm running this circus, but more importantly, Olivia came to me in a hysterical state. She's beside herself because you've reunited with Drago."

Olivia had witnessed the spirit writing session. She knew Drago wasn't a murderer. "That doesn't make sense," she said.

"I'm worried about you, too."

Rose scowled. "Please let go of my arm. You're hurting me."

"You need to come with me."

"Where?" she asked in a panic.

"I'm authorized to take you up to the level below the roof—the level from which you'll start climbing."

She struggled to free herself of his grasp. "I want someone else to take me."

"Rose—" irritation shadowed Patrick's face—"you raced back into my arms when you returned from Europe. Now you've reconciled with Drago. *A monster.* Do you think that was a smart move?"

"Drago is not a monster," she protested as he pushed her inside the elevator. "I was wrong about him and Olivia knows it. I think you're lying."

"Think what you want."

"Give me a chance to explain," she said quickly. "Morvina is the one who killed the girl in Coney Island. She has the power to transform herself into a demon. You need to be looking out for her in a disguised form so you can arrest her."

There was nowhere for Rose to run inside the elevator so Patrick released her arm. She was about to tell him who to search for when he said, "I know Morvina is coming."

"What did you say?"

"Morvina sought me out and I agreed to help her," Patrick said. "As a result, she promised to do away with Drago—so that you and I can be together."

Terror pulsed through Rose's veins. She backed into the corner. "*You* helped her? *You* stole the lei coin from me?"

"Exactly." Patrick placed his hands on the walls and leaned over her. "Thanks for showing me you had it."

Rose realized she'd made a lot of mistakes, but confiding in Patrick was probably the worst one. "This isn't happening!"

Patrick tried to kiss her but she shoved him away. "I married Drago," she said breathlessly. "I love him, not you."

"Soon, there'll be no Dragomir Starkov. Morvina promised me that."

"I still won't be with you!" she shouted.

He started to grope her. Then he yanked her face in his direction and kissed her hotly. To defend herself, she slashed her fingernails across his face.

Patrick cried out. He touched his face, then studied the blood. The sight flamed his cheeks. "First Starkov broke my jaw, now you've probably scarred my face!"

"I'm sorry, Patrick." She wasn't really, but she was extremely frightened.

"If you won't be with me, Rose, I'll let Morvina kill your savage husband *and* you!" The elevator door opened and he dragged her out. "Now get up on the ledge and climb! Oh, and try not to think about Morvina squeezing you to death before you reach Drago."

"I hate you!" Tears stung Rose's eyes. *How did I miss how evil he is?*

Blinded by her tears, she turned toward the ledge. The hot summer wind whipped her hair about—and her knees wobbled.

When she looked all the way up, she could see nothing but the side of the building angling up and away from her.

Is Drago in place at the spire's topmost point, waiting for me?

The way the ornate stones were stacked provided Rose with spaces to place her feet—just as Drago promised. Still, she doubted she could scale them.

"For Christ's sake!" Patrick screeched. "Get up on the ledge. Morvina doesn't have all night."

Mouth parched, she shook her head.

Seething, Patrick lifted her onto the ledge by her waist. She gave a teeter and tried to balance herself. Patrick laughed as he stepped back inside the elevator.

"Don't bother calling for the elevator again," he said. "I'm going to disable it once I reach the lobby."

Rose's heart sank. She told herself not to look down, but she couldn't help it. The street was more than seven hundred feet below her—and the commotion lining it waved in and out of focus. She came close to inching across the ledge. Then a debilitating fear gripped her. Vertigo was precisely that. A paralyzing phobia of heights that made a person's limbs freeze and their pulse stutter wildly.

She was about to give up and slide down when she heard Drago's voice. "Come and get me, Morvina!" he boomed.

Rose licked her dry lips. Hands shaking, she tilted the small clock-pin fastened to her costume and stared at the time. Seventy thirty on the dot.

Drago had turned into a demon.

CHAPTER 32

Stretching her arms out in order to balance herself on the ledge, Rose summoned all of her courage. Once she reached the point where she could start climbing, she placed her foot on the closest stone and stepped up.

"Morvina!" Drago's voice was octaves lower than normal and coated with a preternatural rasp. It was barely recognizable to Rose, but still, it brought her back to what he'd said at his East Hampton house. *"Tonight both of us will face what we fear most. And for everything to work out, you're going to have to trust me."*

Stifling the fright that swept through her—at least for a moment—Rose picked up her pace. With every centimeter she conquered, she tried to brace herself for seeing Drago in his grotesque form.

He's still my husband, she reminded herself. *And if I don't look down, I might overcome my vertigo.*

"Is Rose alive?" She heard Drago boom to Morvina.

"She's on her way up," came the voice of evil. "I want her to suffer before I put her out of her misery. Her vertigo is seeing to that. That's why I'm going to kill you first, Drago."

Heart racing, Rose continued to scale the incline. Each inch was painful, excruciating, terrifying. Thus, she wasn't moving nearly as fast as she wanted to.

How can mountain climbers do this for a hobby?

"I have the lei coin," Morvina crowed, "so don't deny it. You know that I was Richard Bellum."

"Yes. That's what makes me want to kill you even more," Drago growled.

"You don't stand a chance."

"I'm stronger than any person you could possess," he challenged.

"I wouldn't be too confident, Drago," Morvina fumed. "You don't have the lei coin. I do. Plus, I have another secret."

"What secret?" Drago scoffed.

"When I was a child, I was disfigured by arthritis. My mother was a beautiful fortuneteller who dabbled in the occult. In a horrible accident, I fell off a horse and lay dying. My mother gave me an enchanted coin to save me." She paused. "Not only did it save me, *it gave me the ability to live forever.*"

"My God!" Drago bellowed. "You're the fortuneteller who doomed me!"

Rose sucked in a sharp breath.

"Yes!" Morvina hissed. "When you came to me, I looked into my crystal ball and learned you'd be my opponent in the Victory. All I had to do was get you to accept the coin. And you did."

"You bitch!"

Morvina tsked mockingly. "It was your choice to become immortal."

Horrified but unseen, Rose clung to the side of the building. *Keep talking, Morvina. It'll give me time to reach you.*

"Forget me, Morvina," Drago said. "Why did you curse Rose?"

"Long ago, I asked my crystal ball to show me the most beautiful woman in the world. The ball wouldn't tell me. I asked the cards. They wouldn't tell me. Then I knew. The woman hadn't been born yet. I decided to draw on my mother's spirit. During a spirit writing session, I penned the name 'Rose Hayes'."

Bile edged up Rose's throat. Her foot missed a groove and she floundered to maintain her hand grip.

"So I settled into the body of Rose's aunt—before I became Richard Bellum. When I was Morvina, I cursed Rose to die on her twenty-first birthday—which happens to be the anniversary of your turning, Drago. I figured Rose's beauty would peak in her twenty-first year. Now I can kill both of you on the same night. How deliciously convenient!"

"Rose has hardly begun to live," Drago said. "You're a she-devil!"

"No one deserves to be that beautiful—especially when there are hideous children in the world." Morvina paused. "Everyone thought my cursing Rose had to do with an argument I had with her mother. But that was all nonsense and drivel. I just want her youth and beauty."

Hearing Morvina's admission nearly knocked Rose free of the tight contact she had with the building. Hanging on for dear life, she remained frozen for a moment. Then she lifted her shaking hand to the next brick. She commanded her feet to follow the action of her hands—although the ballet slippers she was wearing were just that. Slippery.

Reaching down, she yanked the heel of one of her shoes off her foot. In doing so, she caught a glimpse of the spectators' blurred faces. It made her vision disjointed and she nearly whirled off the building.

Closing her eyes to the dizzying sensation, she peeled off the rest of her slipper by feel and let it fall. Transferring her grip to her alternate hand, she managed to remove the other shoe.

Once she flung it free, she was left in nothing but her stockings. She ripped at the material until the soles of her feet were exposed. Able to grip the bricks better now, Rose continued to climb. She gulped against the gigantic lump in her throat because she heard nothing now. No voices. No car horns. Nothing but the wind whistling around the pyramid-like structure.

Were Morvina and Drago staring each other down? Or is my vertigo wreaking havoc on my mental capacities?

Ten more bricks until she'd be able to witness the Victory take place.

Before Rose reached the midway point of the pyramid, she heard Drago shout, "It's time for you to die, Morvina!" Then punches were thrown. Clothes were torn. And no doubt blood was being shed.

Who will lose their head?

Beyond anxious, Rose climbed until the demons came into view. Drago, who was garbed in remnants of his white dress shirt and dark trousers, looked exactly like Morvina. With scaled gridelin skin, scalloped wings, hideous faces that resembled gargoyles, and sharp fangs that glimmered in the moonlight, the demons clinging to the narrow spire chilled Rose's blood.

She forced her eyes to remain on the horrific scene. One creature had the other in a chokehold—and the one in the chokehold was stammering for breath. Rose's debilitating fear returned. She wanted to come to Drago's aid by clawing at Morvina but she couldn't distinguish between them. Worse, she couldn't make herself climb the slim ladder in front of her.

Struggling to tap down her phobia, Rose shut her eyes for a moment. As she groped for courage, the world calmed around her.

"Think, Rose," she murmured under her breath. "Your name was kept out of the papers when you were born. No one knew Malcolm and Florence Hayes had a baby except the people who came to your private christening. Your birth certificate was destroyed. There is no record of you living anywhere at all—just like Drago."

Rose squeezed her eyes tighter and concentrated again.

"You're destined to be with him in another time and place. Go. See what Drago has planned for you."

To her surprise, a clear vision materialized in her mind. She was back at her spirit writing session when she was seven. And she remembered the vision she'd managed to conjure that night. She saw herself falling off a building when she grew up and turned twenty-one. Now the source of her vertigo was clear! As a child, the premonition of her falling had been horrifying enough to spawn the phobia.

Also in the vision, she saw herself obeying Drago's plan and fulfilling his instructions so that they could be together.

I know which demon is Morvina now.

Rose opened her eyes. Gone was her fright. Inhaling, she began to ascend the narrow ladder. Because she was able to climb the rungs quickly and with more confidence, she managed to steal silently underneath Morvina. The demonic witch had her hands around Drago's throat.

"Say your goodbyes!" raged Morvina.

The sorceress was about to twist Drago's head off when Rose fisted the tops of Morvina's boots and gave the strongest yank of her life. The heave knocked Morvina off balance. The witch reached for the ladder rung. Meanwhile, Drago pulled a knife from his trouser pocket. In a flash, he clamped Rose's hand around the handle and both of them severed Morvina's head.

It tumbled out of sight as did her body.

Cringing, Rose climbed two more steps into Drago's arms.

"Thank God," he murmured in a ragged voice.

She clung to him and to the ladder with equal ferocity. When she looked up at him, he still wore a dire expression.

"It's time for you to do as I tell you," he said firmly.

Horror raced through Rose anew. "I already know what you want me to do."

"How?"

"I relived the premonition I had when I was seven." Her voice was shaky.

Taking her hand, he pressed it to his lips. Rose tried not to think about the fact that they were teetering seven hundred feet in the air.

"It's time," Drago said. "If I don't make you disappear, the police will hunt us down. And they won't stop until they find us."

"Where will I go?" Rose asked urgently.

"Someplace wonderful."

"What's going to happen to you?"

"I'll join you at that wonderful place eventually."

She took in a breath. Then she buried her head against him and shook her head. "I don't want to leave you."

"You trusted me from the minute we met." His voice grew emphatic. "Now you need to trust me one last time."

"Promise me we'll see each other again," Rose whispered.

"I promise."

She locked eyes with him. Drago's gruesome face hovered inches above hers but in her mind she could picture him in his normal, handsome state. Tenderly, he put a hand to her face. Even though her grasp on the sharp edge of the spire was making her fingers bleed, she refused to let go. They dangled there until a voice from the street reached them through a bull horn. "Let your wife go, you monster!"

"They may start shooting at me," Drago said as a tear slipped down his scaled nose.

A tiny voice inside Rose reminded her that she belonged to another time and place.

She exhaled. It was time for Rose Hayes Carlisle to die.

"Goodbye for now," Drago whispered.

She lifted her mouth to his lips and despite how frightening he was, kissed him deeply. Then she pulled him off the ladder. On a hushed prayer, both of them fell freely. Hurtling downward through space, a prolonged silence greeted her. The seconds ticked by. Drago tumbled out of sight. Wind sped past her.

Then Rose became unaware of everything as her world went black.

PART 2

PART 2

CHAPTER 33

One hundred years later

Drago ended his phone call and leaned back in his office chair. Sighing, he swiveled it around and gazed out the window at London's twinkling skyline. Situated in the city's banking district, Drago's sleek office had become his second home over the years. However, on tranquil evenings like this one, he let his thoughts drift back to the parting kiss Rose gave him on the ladder of the Woolworth Building. He put a hand to his heart. Their separation caused him severe pain even now. He didn't have his beloved wife anymore. Since then, he'd prevented any woman from bringing him joy.

Drago's nostrils flared as he recalled the details of that fateful night. After he and Rose plummeted off the building, he made her vanish in mid-air. Then he'd commanded her to travel to a secret location.

Teleporting. Isn't that what magicians called it today? An act subpar illusionists faked but could never accomplish.

True teleporting involved a body dematerializing from one location and rematerializing in a different spot in an instant. That's what he had done in 1913. He'd relocated Rose from the skies of New York City to someplace safe. In that confidential location, Rose lay in a dream state. Resting like a beauty in bloom... fully protected by Drago's magical handiwork.

After the Woolworth Building spectacle, the public had deemed Dragomir Starkov one of the creatures who'd attacked the girls in Coney Island. Onlookers were stunned when they saw Rose fall without hitting the pavement below.

Had Dragomir the Magnificent dragged his wife to a secretive place in order to kill her, too? The papers wrote.

Drago grimaced at the outlandish accusation. Little did the public know that he'd sent Rose away to allow one hundred years to pass. That way no one would know who she and Drago were in modern society.

In order to do that, Drago had been forced to escape many things: reporters, the fact that he didn't show up in photographs, the police, and the Marconis. He'd seen his plan through by obtaining a new identity following Rose's disappearance. In Europe, he'd chosen a stranger with whom he'd switched bodies. The last Immortal to have the coin gained that rare power.

The unknowing male ended up with Drago's original body and no memory of the spell. Thankfully, the police never discovered the switch—or the stranger with Drago's face.

Unfortunately, becoming a new person had been a huge adjustment for Drago. Throughout his 579-year existence, he had never altered his physical appearance except for this one time. In the past, he'd simply taken enough energy from someone to maintain his own.

Drago glanced at the name plate on his desk. *Julian Sloane.* That's the man he had become.

Julian/Drago heard his cell phone ring in his trouser pocket. Instead of withdrawing it, he ignored the intense vibration and pulled out the lei coin. He was lucky enough to have snatched it from Morvina while she was trying to strangle him. Over the years, the coin had allowed him to continue his necromantic abilities. It also let him check in on Rose at her secret location.

Sighing again, he returned the coin to his pocket and gazed out at the main floor of the investment firm. The other bond traders were leaving for the night. He unlocked the top drawer of his desk and withdrew a journal. He'd always kept a diary. Recording things kept his mind clear.

Lips set in a straight line, he ran his fingertips over the green leather cover. He'd started this particular journal after he departed Château de Maincy. When Rose fled the estate in such a hurry, he had raced off too—leaving his original diary behind.

Opening the journal, he flipped through the pages and located the entry he'd written following the spectacle at the Woolworth Building. Once he became Julian Sloane, he'd traveled to the secret location to confirm that Rose had been teleported safely.

The night he penned the entry, the air had been unsettlingly still . . .

June 20, 1913

Thank God Rose is safe in this sequestered castle.

Its dark furniture and eerie architecture feel familiar to me, yet it seems colder and more ominous than ever here. I'm alone without Rose's brilliant smile to keep me company and I'm starting to perspire. Maybe it's because I'm so torn about what I have to do.

Feeling nervous before an illusion is foreign to me. Magic is something I've performed for others all my life, but now I must use it for my own purpose. I thought making Rose vanish in front of the spectators at the Woolworth Building was my greatest illusion, but it wasn't. **This** *will be my most important trick—but there isn't a servant or even a lowly rat in this place to witness it.*

I'm all alone. If my magic fails, no one can help me. Or save Rose.

I'm looking at her image inside my pocket-watch. The black-and-white photograph taken for publicity purposes doesn't do her justice. Even now I can envision her luminous peach skin, violet eyes, and raspberry lips.

I long to embrace her and make love to her, but that will have to wait. She's fallen into a deep sleep, one that needs to hold fast until it's safe for her to wake again.

> *Since the police will try and track Rose, I plan to throw the watch into the fire to erase any trace of her. Then I'll say goodbye to this castle and perform my illusion.*
>
> *Hopefully, nothing will stop me from returning here in a hundred years.*

Drago slammed the journal shut. It *was* a hundred years later and he missed Rose more than ever. He missed talking to her, confiding in her, and feeling her firm curves beneath him. From where she was, she had no idea what he'd been up to. She didn't know that he'd lived for years as a recluse inside a home he had purchased in Switzerland. That he'd eventually sold Château de Maincy without ever returning to it. That he had moved to the sunny shores of Australia in 1949.

In Australia, he'd settled into an inexpensive house ten steps from the ocean. For weeks, days, and years, he had lain about like a bum, lost his Romanian accent, got a tan, and watched history pass him by. After a startling new invention called television hit the market, he witnessed the invasion of the Beatles, the Vietnam War, Woodstock, Watergate, the rise and fall of disco, and the tragic death of Lady Diana.

Growing tired of being unproductive, Drago moved to London in 2000 to become a bond trader. The profession suited him perfectly. It challenged him. It used his mind. And he figured that if it brought him astronomical amounts of money, then so be it.

That's exactly what happened.

Shaking himself, he surveyed his posh office. It was beautiful and state-of-the-art, but today it looked odd because it had been cleaned out.

"Georgina?" he called for his administrative assistant.

"Coming, Mr. Sloane!" came Georgina's sing-song voice.

As he waited for her to appear, Drago considered that this was the last time he'd be sitting in this chair. Yet he was far from sad.

"Yes, Mr. Sloane?" Charmingly pudgy Georgina stuck her head in.

"Is everything in order for my trip?"

"Of course." She smiled. "Your British Airways flight leaves from Heathrow at ten p.m."

"Please have my driver pick me up at home in a half hour."

"Will do."

"Thank you." Heaving another sigh, Drago pushed his chair away from the desk.

Georgina lingered by the doorframe. "You must be excited to be taking such a long hiatus."

"Yes," Drago replied gently. He rose and put on his Zegna jacket.

"Ah"—Georgina cleared her throat—"since you'll be gone for a while . . ."

He smiled again.

"Would you mind terribly if Lana said goodbye to you? You know how much she admires you. She's at my desk."

Drago suppressed a groan. Georgina's twenty-two-year-old daughter was gorgeous—by any man's standards. But she was irritatingly un-intelligent, not to mention the fact that he'd sworn off women. His heart still belonged to his long-lost Rose.

Still, Georgina had been nothing but wonderful to him. In fact, he had to laugh because they'd practically mastered their computer skills together. That's why he'd chosen her to be his assistant. For her humility and for the fact that she was unattractive. He had zero interest in forming a relationship.

Confident that he could resist Georgina's sensual daughter, he nodded. "Very well. Lana may come in."

The long-legged, high-breasted woman entered his office in no time. Wearing a low-cut blouse and an exceedingly short skirt, she sauntered forward. Mouth curved in a seductive smile, she murmured, "Hello, Mr. Sloane."

Drago's glance flitted over her stunning facial features, shining brown hair streaked with honey-colored strands, and glossy mouth. He felt a stirring in his groin. He was still a man, for Christ's sake. But as soon as Rose's face flashed in his mind, he was able to dispel his lust.

"Hello, Lana," he returned the greeting.

She sat on top of his desk and crossed her tanned legs. *What women wore these days! Rather, what women didn't wear.* Drago may have been old-fashioned—but in his defense he was over five hundred years old. He preferred the days when females didn't flaunt their skin. It was much sexier.

He gave a little cough. He definitely wasn't made for this century.

"Mum tells me you'll be gone for a long time," Lana said.

"That's right." He gathered his wallet and car keys then moved toward the door. "I've sold my apartment and I don't know when I'll return."

Lana extracted her smart phone from her purse. She joined him at the doorway. "I thought we could Skype while you're away."

This time instead of suppressing a groan, Drago suppressed a laugh. "I don't think they have Wi-Fi where I'm going."

Lana frowned. "Will they have the Internet?"

"Wi-Fi *is* the Internet, Lana."

"Then they have Internet everywhere!" She giggled. "Except maybe at a medieval castle."

He swallowed hard. "I'm going on a trip to unplug."

"Oh." Rejection passed over her pretty face. "I was hoping we could stay in touch."

To Drago's surprise, she trailed her hands up the front of his jacket. Then she grasped his lapels and pulled herself closer. "I have a thing for older men, Mr. Sloane. Especially ones who stay in amazing shape. Like you."

Drago still couldn't see his reflection. Therefore, he needed to go by what people said as to how he looked.

"Lana, I'm *a lot* older than you." He responded.

"You don't look it. What's your secret?"

You don't want to know. "I'm going away, remember?"

She made a face.

"Have no fear," he added. "You'll find your true love someday."

She laughed. "You talk like you're from a different century, Mr. Sloane."

There's a spark of intelligence in there somewhere. He smiled ruefully. "That's what a lot of people say."

"Anyway, what do you know of true love?" Lana raised an etched eyebrow.

"The woman I fell in love with is long gone, but my heart still belongs to her."

"Mum says you talk about her a lot. Rhonda. Was that her name?"

"It's Rose." Drago removed Lana's hands from his jacket. "I need to go."

Lana turned cold. "Okay. I can take a hint."

"Don't be angry. I see romance in your future, you know."

"Really?" Her hazel eyes lit up.

"Yes. Predicting the future is a little hobby of mine." *It's actually an ability I gained from killing Morvina.*

"Oh?"

"When I touched your hand right now, I saw something. A man. Tall, good-looking. A colleague of yours, maybe."

She thought for a moment. "At the insurance agency?"

"If that's where you work, then yes."

"Alistair James," she said, but promptly dropped her smile. "He's married. Are you pulling my leg, Mr. Sloane? Just to get me out of your hair?"

"Certainly not." He paused. "Someday you'll see that I've predicted correctly. Mr. James's wife will cheat on him. Then he'll fall in love with you."

Drago left Lana in the hallway with her mouth agape. After he bid Georgina a long and heartfelt goodbye, he climbed into his Maserati Quattroporte and sped home. Located in affluent Notting Hill, his apartment had been a steal at several million pounds. While it boasted enameled lava countertops, an Archeo copper bathtub, and a Ruijssenaars magnetic floating bed, Drago took little notice of its incredible possessions. He'd hired a designer to furnish the apartment—just as he kept a stylist on the payroll to pick out his clothes because he had no interest in such things.

Truth be told, he wanted nothing more than to be back in his tiny New York apartment with Rose.

Luckily, he'd packed earlier that morning. Now there was nothing to do but wait for his driver to arrive. Drago was thrilled that his reunion with Rose was quickly approaching. In fact, his entire body tingled with anticipation. Although he possessed the power to transport himself instantly to her, the last thing he wanted was to draw media attention. He'd spent years implementing this plan and if it failed, he would never forgive himself.

CHAPTER 34

Drago was one of the first passengers to get off the plane in Bucharest. It felt incredibly good to be back in his native country. Romania was a place he'd once lived in as an innocent mortal—before he gained his daunting powers. Before black magic tainted his life.

Although the daylight fatigued him, he stood at the airport window and smiled at the familiar city shimmering in the early morning sun.

After he claimed his luggage, he went straight to a cab stand. His nerves had started to build during the flight and now they were buzzing at an all-time high.

Rose. My face is different, but will she remember my voice?

The question made him was as anxious as an eleven-year-old boy about to get his first kiss.

As the taxi transported him through the lively streets of Bucharest, he noticed they'd grown more glamorous over the years. Yet, he was glad the city had maintained a certain degree of old "Romanian" ambience—enough to keep the tourists pouring in anyway.

The cab eventually took him to an exclusive car dealership. Using cash, he bought a black BMW sedan. Once he packed his luggage inside the car and zoomed off, he made a stop in town. Then he drove the high-performance vehicle to the outskirts of Bucharest. The car hummed beautifully along the mountain roads and soon the vibrant city disappeared behind him.

As he found himself in the Carpathian Mountains, the sun had begun to set. And despite the fact that it was June, a chill seized the air. Through the tall fir trees, Drago could see the mountain top that housed his castle. He smiled. The massive thicket of thorns he'd commanded to grow around it was still intact.

If someone didn't know the castle was there, they'd never find it.

Drago parked the car at the base of the brambles. Getting out, he glanced around. This road had always been abandoned—and the fact that it was still unpaved proved few people had been here for a hundred years.

Assured that he was alone, he walked to the edge of the mountain ravine, withdrew the lei coin, and tossed it into its cragged depths.

No one will ever find it there.

He walked back to the base of the brambles. Taking a wide stance, he massaged the air in front of him with his hands. As he concentrated, the brambles vanished. He grinned again. The torture he'd endured with Morvina had left him with some damn good powers.

Drago got back in his car and sped up the rest of the mountain-top road. After he parked the BMW and emerged from it once again, he inhaled sharply. It was time he readied himself for more magic.

This time, he closed his eyes. Nose flaring, he conjured up the sight of the castle. The medieval structure—which had been invisible to the naked eye for a century—waved like the surface of the ocean before it became material again.

Acknowledging the success of the illusion for only a moment, Drago withdrew an ornate key from his jacket pocket. Once he opened the massive entry gate, he marched up the stone-paved steps and unlocked the front doors.

Even if he were blindfolded, he could maneuver his way inside the castle. Hurrying through the foyer, he stopped at the drawing room and breathed in the familiar air. It was musty, stale—but he'd expected nothing less.

Rolling up his shirtsleeves, he strode to the fireplace. Using the poker that stood nearby, he sifted through the ashes and spotted the remnants of his pocket watch. It was melted to practically nothing, showing no trace of the photo of Rose he'd placed inside.

Pulse speeding, Drago pulled a torch from its holder, lit it, then ascended the back staircase. His dress shoes clicked along the hard stone and his breathing grew ragged with anticipation.

With his heart in his throat, he traveled to the castle's topmost tower. It was so strange to be back here. As the torch illuminated a circular room, he could swear he'd been jolted by electricity.

For a moment, he considered the torturous atrocities enacted here during the reign of Baron Vali, the castle's previous owner. Vali had been a sadist who had imprisoned countless citizens in the confines of this very tower—citizens who'd been foolish enough to disagree with his unorthodox style of government.

One dark night in 1874, Drago could have sworn he'd heard the prisoners' mournful screams. He'd traced the ghostly sounds to this spot, only to discover a secret room within the tower.

It was to that room he headed now. Moving to one wall in particular, he depressed the appropriate stone and made the wall shift enough to allow him entry. He set the torch in a holder then turned around. There Rose was. She was as beautiful as she'd been the last time he saw her.

Fast asleep, she reclined on a bed of velvet. Her long, golden hair flowed over her creamy shoulders like ribbons of sunshine and her cheeks glowed a magnificent shade of pink.

Drago knelt, but he couldn't stop his legs from shaking. Reaching out, he laid a single rose beside the music box he had given her on her twentieth birthday.

When he took Rose's hand, her skin felt like smooth satin.

If she doesn't remember me when she awakens, I don't know what I'll do. Drago had never been so scared in his life.

Standing, he brushed his hair out of his face. Then he bent over and touched his lips to hers. Her eyes fluttered open—still more stunning than the deepest amethyst.

"Who are you?" she whispered, shrinking back a little.

"It's me, *draga.* Don't be frightened. I have a new face now."

At the sound of his voice, recognition sparked in her eyes. "It *is* you, Drago," she said groggily. "I like this face better than your demonic one."

He chuckled. "Happy birthday, my rosebud."

While tears welled in his eyes, he bundled her in his arms. He could feel the wild beating of her heart. It matched his leaping pulse. Cradling the back of Rose's head, he lowered it slightly so that he could kiss her again. It was a lengthy, passion-filled kiss that conveyed everything he was experiencing now . . . as well as the countless years of loneliness and angst he'd suffered without her.

Breathless, he drew back and stared into her astonishing face.

"Where am I?" she asked as she tried to sit up.

"You're in Romania."

"How long have I been asleep?"

He smiled gently. "A long time."

"I'm stunned by the change in you," she said.

"It's taken me a while to get used to it, too."

"All I remember is letting go of the ladder." She shivered.

"And you pulled me with you," he said.

She nodded.

"Is that your last memory?"

Rose took his hand and pressed it to her petal-soft cheek. "My last thought before everything went black was the promise you made to me. That we would see each other again."

He closed his eyes to absorb the happy moment.

"Did you catch me?" she asked.

"You could say that."

"How did I get here?"

"It's a long story, Rose. I'll tell you all about it soon enough."

She smiled. "You made me travel through time, didn't you? That's why you're wearing those strange clothes."

He couldn't help but return her smile.

"I'm just glad we're together."

"So am I." He kissed her again, long and hard. Then he helped her to her feet. "I want to show you something."

They moved to a hanging mirror. In its reflection, they clung to each other, side-by-side.

Drago took in a breath. His hair was dark blond now and cut in shaggy layers. His eyes were brown and had a more rounded shape than his previous ones. Overall, he was a decent-looking man in his thirties.

"You look different," Rose said, "but you're still handsome."

"I haven't seen my reflection for centuries," he murmured with astonishment. While he preferred his original face, he didn't look half-bad for being over five hundred years old. "As soon as I woke you, Rose, I became mortal. I gave up all of my powers—and now we can grow old together."

She gasped. "Was that the prize of the Victory?"

"Yes, it was one of the prizes and the best one."

They faced one another.

"I still don't understand how we avoided the curse of the amulet," she said.

"When you pulled me off the building and everyone saw me plummeting as a demon, I was destined to die . . . as everyone knew me, anyway. That's when I flew away and sought a new identity."

Confusion clouded Rose's face. "But I was supposed to kill myself after I killed you."

Drago reached for her hands. "By pulling me off the building, you caused my 'death'. Afterward you died, too."

"What do you mean?"

"Rose Hayes no longer existed in 1913. The moment we went tumbling into space, you gave up your life as you knew it."

She ran her fingertips along his jawbone. "Do you really want to sacrifice everything you had to become mortal?"

His grin stretched from ear to ear. "You're worth it."

"Living a normal life together is all I ever wanted!" She leaned against him.

"Our house will be filled with mirrors—and wonderful food that I can finally eat," he joked. Before Drago informed Rose that the lei coin had helped him put her to sleep for a hundred years so that everyone else was left behind, he wanted to reveal some good news.

"Your real parents are alive, Rose. I saved them from the fire Morvina set."

"You did?" Relief exploded in her voice. "I can't believe it!"

"It's true."

"I never thought I'd see them again." Her lips trembled with emotion.

"I kept an eye on your parents' apartment," Drago said. "When it caught fire, I used my magic to take corpses from the morgue and substitute them for your mother and father. I wish I could have told you, but I didn't want to risk anyone finding out."

"You saved my parents." Rose choked out the words. "That means the world to me. Where are they? I can't wait to see them!"

Drago grinned again. "Your parents are asleep in another part of the castle." He nuzzled her alabaster neck and purred, "Before we wake them up, I want to give you your birthday present. I'm not a magician anymore, but I can still give you something amazing."

He encircled her waist as she laughed. "Is it the kind of gift you can wrap?"

"No," he replied in a hungry timbre, "but it'll be the best present I've given you yet."

Winding up the music box, he bore her back on the velvet bed then looked down at her with a ravenous grin.

As Rose's favorite Mozart melody floated through the air, he traced her collarbone and then the rise of her cleavage. Enthusiastically, she wrapped her arms around his neck and drew him into kiss.

"Oh, Drago," she said against his lips. "Your touch will always be magical to me."

AUTHOR'S NOTE

To be awakened after a hundred years by the man who wouldn't let you die . . . How utterly romantic!

Some scholars believe Charles Perrault wrote the original version of *Sleeping Beauty*, while others believe it was Brothers Grimm. Thankfully, the premises of these dreamy fairy tale versions are identical. A princess born into privilege is cursed to die before she has a chance to grow up. Unfortunately, her own curiosity sets her curse into action.

Will a prince come to her rescue? Or, as in the case of *Sleeping Beauty and the Demon*, can magic overturn her spell?

I loved *Sleeping Beauty* as a child. Since I had long blond hair (and an overactive imagination), Aurora was the princess I identified with most. Ha! Wouldn't we all love to look like Sleeping Beauty?

When I grew up and became a writer, I watched illusionists such as David Copperfield, Criss Angel, and David Blaine perform, and their smoldering personas gave me the idea to base a romance hero on a sexy magician.

Turns out that when I actually sat down to create Dragomir Starkov's character, I ended up basing him on a more classic illusionist—Harry Houdini. Not only was Houdini one of the most alluring figures in history, it was hard *not* to believe he had a genuine connection with the paranormal. Mysterious and hauntingly intense, he was a consummate performer—and when I wrote this story, I thought it would be fun to showcase a hero who embodied those very qualities.

Dear readers, if you enjoyed *Sleeping Beauty and the Demon*, please look for *Cinderella and the Ghost* (The Cursed Princes # 4), coming in February of 2015.

Until then, you can catch up on all of the Cursed Princes stories . . .

Beauty and the Wolf

A UNION OF CURSES

Isabella Farrington's marriage was hasty. For all her new husband's riches, Lord Draven Winthrop is whispered about, avoided, and feared. Yet Isabella is drawn to Draven's dark good looks, his strength, and the charm he can turn on as easily as she can blink. The impoverished daughter of an Egyptologist, she knows there are rumors about her, too, and the amulet she wears. Nothing more than superstitious babble . . .

But when Isabella returns to Draven's remote coastal manor, she senses there is something more at work in the grim gardens of Thorncliff Towers than superstition. Draven is passionate and seductive, but he has a brutal, uncontrolled side too, and a history of secrets. To live in peace she must discover the reasons behind a gypsy curse and a mother's scorn. Especially when she learns Draven believes his sweet young bride is doomed to a fate even darker than his own . . .

"Dynamic and sensual, paranormal readers will gobble up this sexy read."
—Donna Grant, *New York Times* bestselling author of *Midnight's Warrior*

"*Beauty and the Wolf* is a deliciously dark retelling of the classic tale that will make you fall in love all over again."
—Erin Quinn, author of *The Five Deaths of Roxanne Love*

THE CURSED PRINCES
HUNGER AND DESIRE CAN TWINE INTO MADNESS...
Beauty and the WOLF
MARINA MYLES

Snow White and the Vampire

FOG AND FASCINATION

Alba Spencer thought her past in Romania and the dark magic
that haunted it was behind her forever. She is one of the first
female barristers now, safe in London. But London has its dark
side, too. A man called the Ripper stalks the midnight streets.
There are rumors that her hated stepmother has found her again,
suggestions that the nightmares of her childhood are returning.
And with them appears the cursed Gypsy boy she once loved,
grown into a man more seductive and more terrifying than
she ever could have dreamed . . .

Dimitri Grigorescu has become a surgeon, a gentleman—and a
vampire. The lusts that drive his body are scarcely under control,
and even he does not truly know what he is capable of. To fight
evil and confusion, Alba must rely only on her wits—and a
desire that overwhelms her doubts . . .

"A story to remember. LOVED EVERY THRILLING MOMENT
OF IT!"
—Addict of Romance Blogspot

"Definitely a series worth watching!"
—Bodice Rippers, Femme Fatales, and Fantasy

WHICH IS STRONGER:
FATE OR DESIRE?

Snow White
and the
VAMPIRE

MARINA MYLES

A Warlock's Dance

A Cursed Princes Novella

Encore, Please

Giselle Swenov is a radiant opera star whose beauty is second only to her voice. That is, until a jealous enchantress strips away her talent and looks, transforms her into a mute and haggard old woman, and forces her to leave the man of her dreams at the altar on their wedding day. Now there's only one person able to reverse the spell: Giselle's warlock ex-fiancé, Lucian Ivanu.

But three years have passed, and the ever-dashing Lucian seems to have moved on—he's inherited a vast fortune, forsaken his scandalous powers, and is even set to marry again. Will he recognize his former flame when she shows up at his engagement party and begs for help? Can she recover the powerful magic ring needed to break the curse before it's too late? Giselle's plight has a darker twist as she discovers just how far the enchantress's grasp reaches . . .

". . . a sweet, sweet read. Like a fairy tale for grown-ups!"
—BookBeauty's Reviews

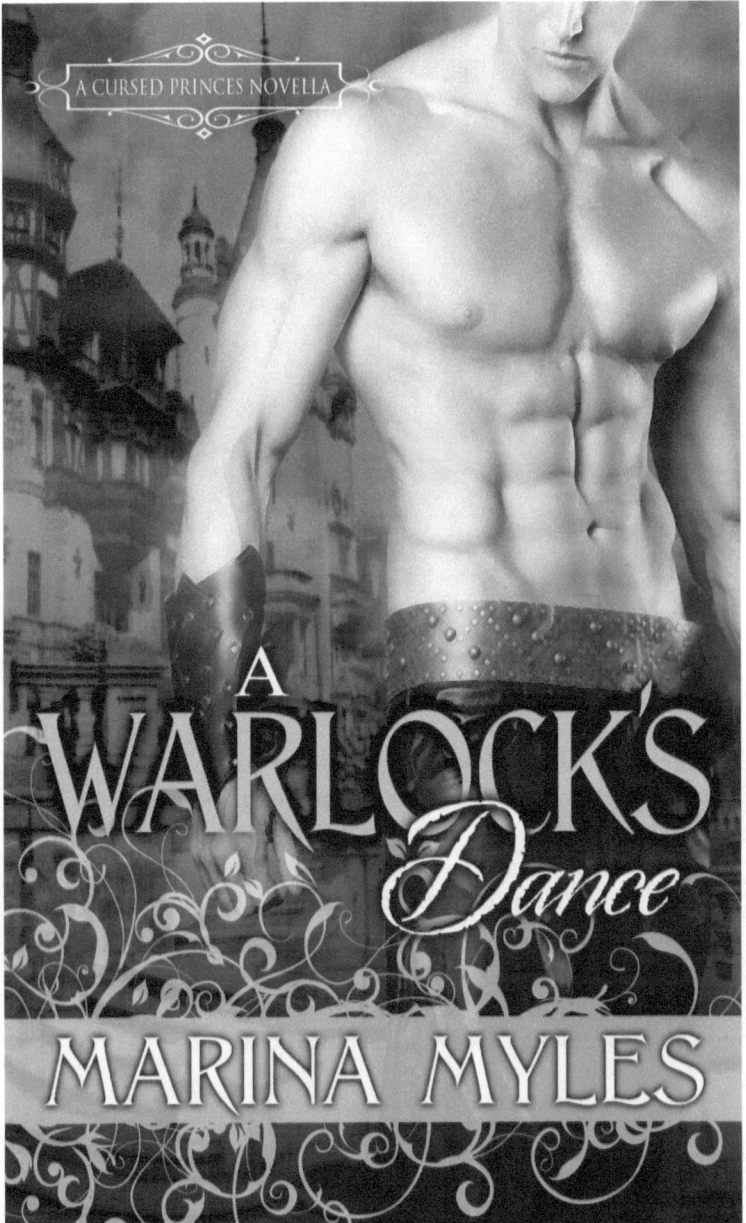

A CURSED PRINCES NOVELLA

A WARLOCK'S Dance

MARINA MYLES

About the Author

Although Marina Myles lives under the sunny skies of Arizona, she would reside in a historic manor house in foggy England if she had her way. Her love of books began as soon as she read her first fairy tale and eventually led to a degree in English Literature. Now, with her loyal Maltese close by, she relishes the hours she gets to escape into worlds filled with fiery—but not easily attained—love affairs. She's busy being a wife, a mother, and a member of Romance Writers of America, but she is never too busy to hear from her amazing readers. Visit her at www.marinamyles.com.